Ten Things My Cat Hates About You

Lottie Lucas

One More Chapter a division of
HarperCollins*Publishers*
The News Building
1 London Bridge Street
London SE1 9GF

www.harpercollins.co.uk

This paperback edition 2019

First published in Great Britain in ebook format by
HarperCollins*Publishers* 2019

A catalogue record for this book
is available from the British Library

ISBN: 9780008353636

Set in Birka by Palimpsest Book Production Ltd, Falkirk
Stirlingshire

Printed and bound in Great Britain by
CPI Group (UK) Ltd, Croydon CR0 4YY

To my husband Greg—beloved by cats everywhere.

To my husband Greg—beloved by cats everywhere.

Chapter 1

"Well, that's that then," I say flatly as the door slams shut with such vigour that it rattles in its frame. "He's gone. I hope you're pleased with yourself."

Outside on the street, I can hear the sound of a car engine starting. Within the kitchen, however, all is silent. I receive no response.

"I don't see what was so wrong with him." I shake my head, beginning to pace as I warm to my theme. Unfortunately, the available floor space could be politely described as 'bijou', and only allows for about four steps before I have to turn and walk back again. "He was polite, educated, creative. No wives in the attic, as far as I could tell, *and* he always offered to pay for dinner. What more could you want?"

I leave an expectant pause after that question. Green eyes stare back at me dispassionately.

"I mean, one has to have standards, of course," I acknowledge, resuming my truncated path across the room. "And I do, believe me. But that's just the problem. It's hard enough for a man to meet *my* standards, let alone having to contend with yours as well. It's simply impossible. No one's going to be up to it." I stop in the middle of the room, throwing my hands up in exasperation. "Something's going to have to change. And, by rights, I really think it should be ..."

I trail off as I turn to find the recipient of my lecture licking his paw.

I put my hands on my hips and glare down at him. "Are you even listening to me?"

He blinks up at me for a moment, before returning to his task with renewed dedication.

I sigh deeply, kicking off my berry-coloured patent heels. I won't be needing those any more tonight. The man they were intended to impress is probably halfway across Cambridge by now. Getting as far away as fast as possible, no doubt.

You know, I really thought it might be different this time. I met James at a pop-up photography exhibition. He was thoughtful, attractive in a winsome, boy-next-door kind of way, perhaps not the kind of guy I'd usually have noticed, but he'd jostled into me by accident and knocked my clutch bag out of my hand, then apologised and asked me out in the same sentence. Immediately, that made my pulse fizz in anticipation; I absolutely love a serendipitous meeting. *So* romantic, don't you think? I always imagine what a great story it'll make, further down the line.

Anyway, things seemed to be going well between us and, after four successful dates, I judged that it was time to initiate the final test of bringing him home to meet Casper.

Alas, Casper thought differently. Casper *always* thinks differently. He's found something to dislike in every single man I've brought home in the past two years. And when

Casper doesn't like someone, he shows it. I mean, *really* shows it. He doesn't hold back.

Little did I realise, that night two years ago, that the bedraggled cat I found on the doorstep in the middle of a violent storm would have the potential to turn my entire life upside down. Nothing has been the same since. Sometimes, I'll admit, for the better.

Sometimes decidedly for the worse.

The truth is, Casper is a singular sort of cat. I like to think of him as endearingly idiosyncratic, but others might less charitably call him something more along the lines of ... Well, I suppose they *might* call him a bit wild. Headstrong, perhaps. Maybe the more melodramatic sorts might even accuse him of being out of control.

All right, so I guess there's no point lying about it, is there? You'll find out soon enough. The truth is that he's been called *all* of those things, and more, usually in the form of a parting shot delivered by someone in the process of beating a swift retreat.

I look down again at my beloved feline. He's moved on to washing his ears, looking like butter wouldn't melt. There's no trace whatsoever of the crazed animal who chased a perfectly nice man out of the door not five minutes ago.

In moments such as these, I have to remind myself that he's just being protective. And that it's sweet, really, that he's prepared to go into battle on behalf of my honour. It would just be nice if he picked the *right* battles, that's all. And if just once I could get as far as opening the bottle of wine before he sinks his claws into their leg, or puts a decapitated mouse in their shoe.

With a sinking sense of déjà vu, I fill the kettle and put it on to boil, reaching for my favourite heart-patterned mug. Ten o'clock at night, all dressed up, and yet again my only company is a large, bad-tempered ginger cat. Not quite the evening I'd planned.

"You're back."

A figure looms in the doorway and I jump, scattering tea bags all over the counter.

Ah, yes, except Freddie. I keep forgetting about Freddie. I'm still unused to having someone else in the house, you see.

Apparently, fate has a predilection towards burly males turning up on my doorstep without warning, because three days ago Freddie did just that, clutching only a hastily packed bag and no explanation, save that he's planning to stay for 'a while'. Whatever that means.

At least, I'm assuming the bag was hastily packed, but then again, he's twenty-one years old. His whole *life* looks like that. As for the explanation ... Well, my brother's always been somewhat tricky to pin down. He's notoriously evasive. One look at his face and I realised I wasn't going to get any reasonable answers, for the time being at least. So I'm adopting the well-worn tactics of an experienced elder sister, and not asking any questions.

Patience is key in these matters. I'll find out soon enough.

Freddie scoops up Casper, who begins to purr in ecstasy. Some men he's more than happy to tolerate. Just so long as they pose no romantic risk, it seems.

"Where's your date? Did it not go well?"

I lean back against the counter, folding my arms across my

chest. "It was going absolutely fine, until Casper caught sight of him. Then it all went to hell in a handcart. As usual," I'm unable to resist adding, with a dark look at Casper, who pointedly ignores me.

Freddie's dark blond eyebrows shoot up, almost disappearing into his unruly hairline. "What did he do this time?"

"Let's just say I owe James a new pair of trousers and leave it at that." I begin stuffing tea bags back into the box.

Freddie lets out a yelp of laughter, before catching my eye and promptly smothering it. "Sorry. That's not funny. *Casper*—" he directs a stern look at the cat still purring contentedly in his arms "—that was incredibly ill-mannered of you."

Casper gazes up at him adoringly.

"Not exactly the look of contrition I was hoping for," Freddie remarks drily.

"There's no point in telling him off. He doesn't care." I begin to pull the pins out of my hair, letting it tumble around my shoulders in a caramel-coloured mass. I have to say, it's a relief; it was really beginning to pinch, and if I'd left it up all evening I would probably have ended up with a headache.

One point in Casper's favour at least, I concede grudgingly. He's saved my scalp, even if he has ruined my love life.

Freddie gently deposits Casper on the floor, brushing orange fur off the front of his jumper. "I wouldn't worry about it, sis. He obviously just wasn't the one."

"How would I know?" I say bitterly, watching as Freddie picks up the kettle. "I never got the chance to find out."

Freddie dumps a spoonful of sugar into his cup and stirs

it vigorously. "You know, Clara, maybe Casper just thinks he knows better than you. Have you ever thought of that?"

I roll my eyes. "Very amusing."

"I know, I'm a brilliant mind." He tosses the teaspoon in the sink with a modest smile. I try not to wince as it makes a horrible clattering sound. At least he got his aim right.

"Were you planning to make one of those for me too?" I ask mildly.

He looks blankly down at the mug in his hand. "Oh, yeah. Sorry."

"So, what have you been up to today?" I try to keep my voice casual as he turns and begins the tea-making process all over again. It's a well-known fact that men can really only concentrate on one thing at a time. To be honest, sometimes Freddie even struggles with that. If I'm going to winkle even the slightest bit of information out of him, the ideal time is when he's distracted.

He shrugs. "You know, this and that."

Softly, Clara, softly, I chant to myself.

"Is work still okay with you taking time off to be here?"

"Yeah, they're not bothered. So long as they've got cover."

Well, that I can believe, at least. Freddie works in a bar up in Manchester and, while they're not exactly the most diligent of employers, the casual nature of it suits his purposes while he's saving up to go travelling with his girlfriend, Jess.

They have all of these grand plans, to trek across Australia, camp under the stars in New Zealand. A part of me doesn't really want him to go, but I know that he has to. If these past few years have taught us both anything, it's that life is too short to fritter away.

Besides, Jess will look after him. She's been doing a sterling job of it for the last three years; I won't worry about him half as much knowing that she's there.

"Here." He thrusts a cup of tea at me, almost sloshing it over the rim in the process. "As requested."

"So graciously served," I mutter, peering into its milky depths. I'd forgotten what terrible tea Freddie makes.

He stretches lazily, drawing his already tall frame to a ridiculous height. I like to think I'm reasonably tall for a woman, but Freddie definitely got our dad's rangy genes. In fact, he seems to look more and more like Dad every time I see him these days.

The thought makes a lump rise in my throat and I cough, turning away to take a sip of my tea. Freddie doesn't seem to notice, retrieving his own mug from where he left it on the side and making towards the door. But not before stopping to pat me on the head. I scowl, not that it will do me much good. He already knows I hate it when he does that.

"I'm going back to my podcast. See you in the morning."

"Night," I murmur at his retreating back.

Casper's head pops up but, to my surprise, he doesn't follow Freddie upstairs. Instead, he watches me with curious eyes.

"I mean it this time," I tell him firmly, tipping the rest of my revolting cup of tea down the sink. "We can't go on like this. Much as I love you, I've no desire to end up a mad old cat lady. I'd like a man in my life who *isn't* covered in fur." I kneel down in front of him. "Can you get on board with that? Maybe help me out just a little?"

He tilts his head to one side, his eyes two unblinking green orbs, luminous in his face. I reach over to scratch his head and he nuzzles my hand lovingly. I sigh, already feeling my heart softening. I can never fight with him for long.

"Do you really think you can do better than me?" I whisper. "Do you know something I don't?"

He puts his paws on my knees and I pull him into my arms, holding him close, as I have so many times. He doesn't reply, of course. He's just a cat.

But I can't help but wonder all the same.

Chapter 2

"So hang on ..." Heather holds up a hand, disbelief written across her face. "Give me a moment to get my head around this. Freddie actually suggested that *Casper* might be a better judge of character than you are?"

I busy myself picking coriander leaves out of my salad. "That's about right, yes. And then he made me a terrible cup of tea."

"And all of this after Casper had chased James out of the house with a chunk missing out of his trousers?"

We're sitting in one of our favourite cafés on King's Parade, right in the heart of town. Heather even managed to get here early and grab the last table in the window, so we can watch the world go by. Even in the middle of the day the streets outside are packed. I'm pretty used to the bustle of Cambridge these days, but sometimes even I find myself surprised by the sheer crush that the centre turns into in the summer months. By now, in early October, the tourists have alleviated somewhat, and the students are back, giving the whole place a different feel. Less febrile, more focused. One of them hurries past the window now, laptop bag clutched in his arms, chin tucked into a red checked scarf. Probably late for a seminar, I think vaguely. Goodness knows, I've been there myself plenty of times.

"Well—" Heather sits back in her chair, her lunch still untouched on her plate "—something of an eventful evening, then." She says it with a straight face, but I can see the corners of her lips twitching.

"Don't you *dare* laugh," I say warningly, but my voice trembles traitorously as I do so, somewhat ruining the effect. "It's not funny."

She shakes her head gravely. "Of course not. Nothing humorous about it whatsoever."

Outside, the student with the scarf has joined a gaggle standing outside King's College, listening to their professor wax lyrical about the architecture. He's gesturing enthusiastically up at the building, and for a moment I'm so busy watching that I almost miss Heather's next words altogether.

"You know, I wonder if Freddie might be right. In part, at least."

I almost choke on my watermelon iced tea. She waits primly while I recover my equilibrium.

"Excuse me?" I finally manage to rasp.

It's not often that my measured, ultra-practical best friend can surprise me. But when she does it's always in style. Like the time she whipped her bra off at the tarts and vicars theme night in our second year at university. I think I might still be getting over that now.

She nods sagely, unrolling her cutlery from the napkin. "I think it makes a lot of sense. In fact, I can't believe you didn't think of it before. Could you pass the pepper, by the way?"

I hand it over in a daze. "You really think I have terrible judgement when it comes to men?"

She sprinkles a fine dusting of pepper onto her plate. "No, but I do think that you move too fast sometimes."

"Too fast?" I echo disbelievingly, putting my knife and fork down with a clatter. "This coming from the person who had a baby at twenty-two!"

"That's different and you know it." She leans forward, pushing a strand of hair behind her ear. "Look, be honest. How much did you really know about James?"

"Well ..." I hedge, before one look at her face tells me not to bother lying. She knows me far too well. "Not a lot, I suppose. We'd only been out a few times."

"Exactly!" She looks triumphant. "And yet here you are, talking as though it's a major breakup. So he was a nice, interesting man—so what? There are plenty more of those out there."

If we weren't in public, I'd put my head on the table.

This is the thing about talking to Heather; much as she might try, she just doesn't understand what a minefield modern dating is. She met her husband during freshers' week at university. She's never had to navigate the rocky waters of dating apps, or exclusivity, or the commitment-phobia which seems to be rife amongst anyone under the age of thirty. If I asked her about ghosting, she'd probably guess it was something to do with Halloween.

In her world it's easy to walk into a bar or a party, start talking to a nice man and, the next thing you know, you're buying crockery together and putting down a deposit on a marquee. Sometimes, I wonder if I should break it to her that it's not the nineties any more.

"You've always been the dreamer of the two of us," she's saying now. "You've always wanted ..." she waves her fork in the air, as though to whisk up the ideal word "... magic. Romance. And there's no reason why you shouldn't have it, but the way you just leap into things, with your heart on your sleeve ..." She breaks off with a frown, pointing the fork at me. "*Don't* pull that face. I'm allowed to worry about you, you know."

I look into her anxious blue eyes and immediately feel guilty. In her smart black turtleneck, her glossy dark hair pulled back from her face, she looks impossibly put together. But I can see the tense lines around her mouth, the too-tight set of her shoulders. She's always been like that, from the very first day we met in university halls. What was supposed to be a carefree, spontaneous time— that always proved a challenge for Heather. She could never quite let go, never relax. I suppose that's why we were drawn to one another. We both needed something the other could give, me a little of her level-headedness, her serenity, and her my sense of wonder, my open-minded optimism.

"Of course you do," I reply gently. "But I'm fine, Heather. I'm a grown woman; I can deal with my own disasters. You have plenty of other things to worry about. Oscar, for starters."

"He certainly gives me plenty to worry about." She begins to daintily cut her avocado wrap into small pieces, presumably so she doesn't have to pick it up. Heather doesn't really do finger food. I've seen her eat nachos with a knife and fork. "I have absolutely no idea where he gets it from. I was the most shy, retiring child in the playground for my entire school career. And Dominic wasn't exactly a bad boy himself."

"No," I say, trying not to smile as memories of Dominic in a choirboy's cassock and ruff spring to my mind. Heather showed me that old album when we were both a bit tipsy on raspberry vodka, and I swore I'd never mention it again.

"Neither of us have ever broken a single bone," Heather continues, sawing into her wrap with increased force. "Oscar's barely three, and he's already broken his arm twice. Thank God the second time it happened at nursery; if it had been at home again, I probably would have had social services banging down the door."

I stifle my mirth with a well-timed cough.

"You might well laugh," she says accusingly. "But this is supposed to be one of your duties, you know, as his godmother. To care and protect his sapling young mind, steer him in a more respectable direction. Make sure he doesn't grow up into a total hellion."

"That's if you *die*, Heather. Which, hopefully, you're not planning on doing any time soon. Until then, *I* get to be the fun adult figure in his life. The one he comes to for advice, or contraband ice cream milkshakes."

She groans. "Yes, because that's just what he needs. More fun in his life. He has such a dreary time of it. Nothing nice ever happens to him ... or so he'd have everyone believe. That child is a master manipulator."

"Your mother would probably say that he's been sent to challenge you."

'She says exactly that. Just about every time I see her, in fact. But whenever I ask, "What if I don't particularly *want* to be challenged?" she never seems inclined to answer.'

This time I do laugh. "You have a wonderful child, Heather. Slightly boisterous, maybe, but wonderful."

Oscar was something of a ... Well, let's say he was a glorious surprise. I still remember sitting with Heather on the sofa after she'd found out. It wasn't a particularly nice sofa, I have to admit. We were still in our last student house, on the outskirts of Cambridge. We were all ready to move out, onwards and upwards into a future which was unknown yet we were certain would be bright. The sofa was pretty much the last thing left in the barren sitting room.

We'd promised each other that nothing would change, that last summer. That adult life, and proper work, could never put an end to nights spent drinking Bellinis in the basement bars around the city, or long, lazy afternoons watching romantic comedies in our pyjamas. Even when Heather got engaged to Dominic, in an uncharacteristically spontaneous fashion, still she'd vowed that nothing would change.

Then it happened. She was just staring into space, not saying anything. For the first time in our friendship, I couldn't work out what she was thinking. Until suddenly, she'd stood, smoothing down the hem of her cobalt blue summer top.

"Well, then," she'd said, and I remember that her voice had sounded strange, and yet at the same time not strange at all. It was completely neutral. "I'd better get an appointment at the doctor's. And I suppose my parents ought to know sooner rather than later."

And that had been that. It was as though she resigned herself, in that moment, to the fact that life was about to completely, inescapably transform. She just got on with it, no looking back.

Since that day, of course, nothing has been the same. She's still my closest friend, and we make plenty of time for one another, but our lives have gone in wildly different directions. And sometimes, I look at her, with her husband and her adorable son, and her impeccable nineteen-thirties villa in a quiet, leafy suburb on the edge of town, and I find myself thinking ...

Well, look, never mind what I think. It's not important.

"You're right. I do," she's agreeing now and, although she's trying not to, I can see a radiant smile tugging at the corners of her lips. "And *you* have an equally wonderful, equally boisterous cat." She sends me a sly look from beneath her lashes. "Who apparently knows better than you do what makes a good boyfriend."

I raise my eyes to the ceiling. "Are we *still* talking about this?"

"Yes, we are." Heather picks up her own watermelon iced tea and takes a tentative sip before pulling a face. "I need to stop letting you bring me to these bohemian cafés. Or, rather, I need to stop following your lead when I order. At least it's not as bad as the beetroot latte."

"I *like* beetroot lattes," I say defensively. "And anyway, it's good for you to try something different every now and again."

She makes a dismissive motion with her hand. "If you can't get it in Waitrose, then there's a good reason for it."

"It's only a matter of time," I say ominously. "Beetroot *will* take over the world. You'll see."

She fixes me with a severe look. "We're digressing here. Don't think you can distract me with winter vegetables. We were talking about you, remember?"

I shake my head fervently. "I don't think we were."

"We most *definitely* were. Stop avoiding the subject." She pushes the glass of iced tea away with a tastefully manicured hand. There's a small pause in the conversation as a waiter swoops in upon our empty plates before she continues. "Look, Clara, be honest with yourself. Out of all of those men Casper chased away, was there anyone you could actually see a future with? Anyone you really got to know, who understood you inside out?"

"No," I confess in a small voice.

"So perhaps, in his own way, he was doing you a favour?"

I raise an eyebrow at her. "Really? You're going to pretend that you believe that?"

"Whether I do or don't is irrelevant. But, ultimately, I think it wouldn't do you any harm to guard yourself a bit more. What's the hurry, anyway? You have all the time in the world; you're only twenty-five."

"So are you!"

"Yes, but the difference is that I don't feel it," she says simply. "And, believe me, one day, before you even know it, you'll be feeling just as old and haggard as I do now, so enjoy this phase while it lasts." She raises her glass in mock toast. "Tell you what, here's a challenge. Find someone who can actually win round that cat of yours; now, that really *will* be someone worth having. If they can do that, I'll deem them worthy of your affections."

"You're right; of course you are." To my horror, I can feel heat pricking at the back of my eyes, and I blink hard. "It's just ... well, it's been ..."

"A difficult few years," Heather finishes quietly, placing a hand over mine. "I know."

We lapse into silence. I fiddle with the straw in my drink. It's paper, like they all are nowadays, decorated with a pink candy stripe. I'm staring at it so determinedly that the colours start to blur into one another. I'm pretty sure it's making my eyes cross, so I look out of the window instead. The students are listening raptly for the most part, their heads bent over notebooks or, in the case of a few more techno-logical types, tablets. I notice there are a couple at the back, however, who aren't quite so swept away by their professor's passionate lecture. They're prodding at their phones, looking bored.

"Can we talk about something else?" I mumble at last.

She exhales slowly. "Yes, of course." I can tell she feels bad because she pulls her watermelon iced tea back towards her and starts to drink from it stoically. It's not much, but I know her well enough to recognise an olive branch. "What's new at work?"

"Heather, I work in a *museum*. New isn't exactly our speciality."

I know I'm being flippant, that I'm shutting her out. But I can't help it. I know what she'll ask next, and I just can't cope with anything else right now. I can't cope with her fussing around me, trying to fix my life.

She emits a gusty sigh, plucking the laminated menu from the centre of the table to peruse the back. "I can tell I'm not going to get anything even remotely sensible out of you today. You're in one of those moods. Do you have time for pudding?"

Now *that's* a topic which is always amenable to me. It's with no small sense of relief that I take the menu from her outstretched hand. This feels like much safer ground. Pudding, I can deal with.

"I *always* have time for pudding. What are we having?"

Chapter 3

By the time I turn onto my street that evening, the sky has deepened to an inky purple, the air tinged with the promise of frost. The first star is just cresting the horizon, a pinprick of light against an otherwise blank sheet of darkness. There's no moon, I notice. I always pay attention to the moon: where it is in the sky, how full it is. I track it through its stages, watching it wax and wane, brighten and dim, the craters emerging from and then melding back into the shadows. The steady rhythm of it, ever changing and yet unchanged, is more reassuring to me than any amount of therapy.

Despite the darkness, I have no trouble finding my house. It's blazing like a beacon, lights shining from every window like a cottage on a Christmas card. One of the joys, I'm fast learning, of living with an ex-student who doesn't have to pay the bills. I'd be willing to bet anything that the heating will be cranked up to maximum too.

My theory is confirmed soon enough as I open the front door, only to be blasted by a wall of heat as dense and dry as a Saharan wind.

"I'm back," I announce, rapidly beginning to divest myself of all outerwear before I break out into a sweat. Seriously, *how* does this not bother him? Feeling the cold is a woman's prerogative; everyone knows that. Men are usually just supposed to tut and turn the thermostat down when we're not looking, or look on in disbelief as we pull on fluffy socks and dressing gowns, hot-water bottles clutched to our chests.

"We're in here." Freddie's voice floats through into the hallway.

Still alive, then. I'm amazed he hasn't boiled in his own skin.

I head into the living room, about to make a comment to that effect, but the words die on my lips. Freddie is lounging on the sofa in his favourite hoodie, a half drunk cup of tea on the coffee table in front of him, flipping through a film magazine. The TV burbles away gently in the background, the screen providing a soothing blur of flickering colour. Casper is lolling blissfully on his chair—or, I should say, the chair which he has long since commandeered as his own. It's just too exhausting to keep hoovering the cat hair off it every day. When he sees me he rolls onto his back, exposing his furry tummy expectantly.

"Honestly, you're like a dog," I murmur, leaning over to give the requisite scratch. "Cats shouldn't enjoy this."

He just purrs even more loudly.

"Good day?" Freddie asks vaguely, still absorbed in the article he's reading.

I look down at my brother's scruffy head with an inward sigh. It's hard to be annoyed with him, even if he *is* racking up the kind of electricity bill which I'd thought only existed in my worst nightmares.

Because ... you know, it's actually kind of nice to have someone to come home to, save a disgruntled-looking Casper or the odd dead rat. It's nice that the house isn't cold and dark, and that I don't have to sit around with my coat on for half an hour while the place warms up. It's *nice* that Casper has someone with him during the day. He hates being left on his own. He gets bored, I think, which is probably why he goes out of his way to cause so much mischief.

The truth is, I never planned to live alone. I've never been one of those people who dream of their own space, of no one bothering them. I *like* being bothered. I *like* having company. If I'm being totally honest, I never planned to be alone full stop. I'd always imagined that I'd be one of those people who falls in love young, then stays with that person for ever. I used to listen to my parents recounting how they met; my dad actually proposed the very first night he saw Mum, but she prudently suggested that they went on a date or two first. Obviously, he won her round, though, because they were engaged within a week.

I used to dream of something like that happening to me. It sounded beyond perfect.

Except, somehow, it's just never quite happened.

All right, so it's never even come remotely *close* to happening. My so-called love life has always been conspicuously devoid of that all-important sentiment. Relationships have started then fizzled out. Even before Casper came on the scene, none of my romantic attachments have ever lasted long.

I mean, look, it's not like I'm desperate or anything. I don't want you to get that idea. I'm well aware that I don't need anyone in my life. I get by just fine, albeit in a singular, chaotic sort of fashion.

But, then again, life's not about just getting by, is it? And just because I *can* do everything on my own doesn't necessarily mean that I want to. The last few years have given me quite enough experience of that. It could easily have knocked all the romance out of me, but instead it's actually had the opposite effect. These days, the thought of someone sweeping me off into an escapist whirlwind of breakfasts in bed and roses and spontaneous trips to Paris sounds more heavenly than ever.

And while Casper is, of course, a wonderful companion in his way, he's not much good for any of those things. His idea of breakfast in bed is leaving a desiccated squirrel on the pillow next to me, and the only spontaneous trips we make together are to the vet's.

I bring my attention back to the present, just in time to see Freddie toss a chocolate high up in the air and catch it in his mouth.

"Freddie!" I admonish. "Those were the chocolates which James brought over."

He looks up at me, all innocence. "I know; that's why I'm eating them. Wouldn't want to leave any unpleasant reminders about the place, would we?" He raises his eyebrows. "Unless you were planning to keep them as a sordid memento of your failed romance."

Sometimes, I wish I didn't get these insights into how my

little brother sees me. Images of myself as some sort of latter day—if decidedly more youthful and less cobwebby—Miss Havisham, with a specimen cupboard full of old chocolate boxes and used tissues stolen from past dates is *not* something I particularly want to entertain.

"It's touching that you think so highly of me." I flop down beside him on the sofa, reaching for the box. "Here, let me have one. It's been a hard day." I pick a chocolate at random, not even bothering to look at the descriptions. I'm too tired to care. When I'm in this state, chocolate is just chocolate. Any will do.

Freddie stares at me. "Wow, chocolate roulette. It must have been bad."

"I finally made a start on those grant applications I've been putting off for weeks. They're an absolute nightmare. No wonder Jeremy landed me with them." I bite into the chocolate, delighted to discover that it has a caramel centre. I was beginning to worry that it might turn out to be the weird fruit one that always gets left in the box. "What's for dinner?"

For a moment he looks totally perplexed, then he holds up the chocolate box sheepishly. "Er ... these?"

"Freddie!" My legs are curled up beneath me and I give him a sharp kick. "You were supposed to pick something up!"

"Sorry, I forgot." He whips out his phone and opens up an app. "How do you feel about pizza?"

Another side-effect of living with a twenty-one-year-old. I'm officially returning to a student diet.

"Fine," I say begrudgingly. "But get a side salad, won't you? I'm not eighteen any more. I need to eat some vegetables."

"I'll get a four seasons pizza. It has olives on it."

"I don't think olives count."

"Mushrooms do, though. There must be two portions on that pizza, surely."

I shake my head despairingly. "I can't believe that Jess hasn't managed to teach you about this."

There's a beat of silence. Immediately, I know I've said something wrong, although I'm not sure what. Maybe they've had a fight.

Freddie stares fixedly at his phone, scrolling so fast that I'm certain he's not really looking at it. Eventually, he clears his throat. "I'll order a mixed salad as well, then."

"I'd, er ... better feed Casper," I say abruptly, rising to my feet.

Mostly, I say it just to break the strange tension which has settled on the room, although, to be fair, it *is* actually Casper's dinner time. In fact, come to think of it, I'm surprised he hasn't already been hassling me. Usually if I'm so much as a minute behind, he lets me know all about it. But it's already twenty past six and I haven't heard a peep out of him.

It's only when I look over at his chair that I discover why. He's not there. He must have crept out while Freddie and I were talking. I frown, wondering what he's up to. It's very unlike him to disappear when food's on offer.

I don't think I heard the cat flap go, so I make my way upstairs. Sometimes he likes to burrow under the duvet on my bed. He's not there though, so I go into the spare room, where Freddie has set up camp. If I didn't know better, I would swear that his overnight bag has exploded. There's stuff everywhere, and he's only been here a few days.

I'm just pondering over how, exactly, a sock has ended up on the window ledge, when something outside makes my breath stop.

There, under the glow of a streetlamp, is Casper. And he's slinking across the road.

Damn that cat. No wonder he's looking furtive. He *knows* I don't like him going out there. Granted, I live on a quiet residential street, far too hemmed in by cars parked on either side for anyone to drive too fast down, but still. That's not the point. I fling open the window.

"Casper!"

At the sound of his name he stops, turning his head to look up. Just as a cyclist suddenly appears from behind the cars, whizzing towards him.

"Stop!" I yell, but it's already too late. The cyclist swerves violently, tyres screeching against the tarmac. I can only look on in horror as they overbalance, finishing upside down in a nearby bush, the wheels of the bike spinning uselessly.

For a split second I'm stunned into immobility. Then I'm running, bursting down the stairs and out into the street.

"Are you all right?" I gasp, snatching Casper into my arms. Mercifully, he seems more put out than anything, glaring at the bicycle as though it did him a personal injury. Out of the corner of my eye, I notice a flash of white tail disappearing into the bushes and immediately the object of his evening wanderings becomes clear. I should have known there'd be a lady involved. There's not a lot else which he would prioritise over dinner.

It's a sad fact when your cat has a better love life than you do, I think glumly. Maybe Heather was right, after all. Maybe I really *do* need to take some time to just be by myself for a bit. Stop chasing rainbows which don't exist. After all, it's not as if suitable men just pop up out of ...

I look at the bike, skewered into the bush, and out of nowhere something begins to fizz beneath my skin, a prickle of excitement.

Surely not ... I mean, it can't be. That would just be crazy.

"Oh, don't worry about *me*, I'm fine," a voice supplies from the depths of the foliage. "It's the cat we should be concerned about."

Despite its somewhat muffled tone, the sarcasm is unmistakable and I feel myself flushing, startled out of my reverie.

"Of course, I'm so sorry. Are you all right?"

The cyclist struggles out of the bush, helmet askew across his face, and, despite myself, my breath catches in anticipation. Now he's standing upright, I see that he's tall, towering over me by almost half a foot. I've always liked tall men.

I'm doing exactly what I promised I wouldn't; I'm getting carried away again. I know it. But that doesn't mean that I can *help* it. I mean, come *on*. I'm only human. And it doesn't get much more romantic than this, does it? It's like a meet cute in a movie. Any moment now, he'll push up his helmet and our eyes will meet. Electricity will spark between us. And he'll say something like ... Oh, I don't know, maybe something like ...

"Just about, no thanks to that bloody animal. What the *hell* was it doing in the middle of the road, anyway?"

I jolt backwards as though I've been slapped, his acerbic

tone acting like a sledgehammer on the lovely rose-tinted vision I'd created.

Okay, definitely *not* something like that.

"It was my fault," I say quickly as Casper bristles in my arms with a growl, obviously aware of the slight. "I called him and he turned to look. It was perfectly natural behaviour on his part."

"Yes, well ..." He straightens his helmet and I can see the outline of his face in the slanting light from the streetlamp. I can make out a strong aquiline nose, a sculpted jaw and a pair of dark eyes. Despite myself, I find myself wondering what colour they are and I mentally slap myself down. Stop it, Clara. You've already embarrassed yourself enough. Just thank every higher entity that he can't read your thoughts.

I'm cringing inside just thinking about it.

Mercifully, he doesn't seem to notice me staring. In fact, he's not looking at me at all. So much for my fantasy that our eyes would lock; he hasn't even so much as glanced at me once throughout our whole exchange. Instead, his attention is fixed upon the ground around our feet. "That's all very well for you to say. But just look at what you've done!"

I follow his gaze, and for the first time I notice that there are papers scattered all over the road. A battered folder lies in the midst of it all, its mouth gaping open, more papers spilling out from within. They're looking decidedly worse for wear, having landed on the rain-dampened tarmac. Most of them are splattered with mud, and one or two even have bicycle tracks across them.

I know I should be feeling guilty about that. But something

about his abrasiveness sets my teeth on edge. Perhaps it's the dull sense of disappointment I still feel which makes my own response somewhat sharper than I'd intended. This man is definitely no romantic hero.

"What *I've* done? Look, I've said I'm sorry. But this was clearly an accident."

I'm not sure if he's even listening to me. He's scrabbling around after the papers, gathering them into a haphazard pile.

"This is priceless research!" he snaps, although I half wonder if it might be directed more at himself than me. "Utterly irreplaceable."

Casper obviously takes exception to it anyway, because he lurches forward with a protracted hiss, compelling me to tighten my grip on him.

The man half glances upwards and, although I can't see his face in the dark, incredulity colours his voice. "Did he really just hiss at me?"

I jut out my chin defensively. "You *did* almost run him over."

"*He* got in *my* way, I think you'll find. He's bloody lucky I managed to swerve in time."

"Clara?" Freddie's standing in the open doorway, his arms folded across his body against the cold. "Are you okay? What's going on?"

Always the last one to the party, my brother. I almost want to laugh. But I have a feeling that wouldn't go down so well with the indignant man in front of me.

"It's fine. I'll be back in a minute," I call softly, relieved when Freddie disappears back inside the house. The last thing we need is to attract even more attention. I can practically feel the curtains twitching as it is. I turn back around, determined to do the decent thing. After all, despite what I said, I am indebted to this ill-mannered cyclist. I dread to think what would have happened if he hadn't flung himself to the side of the road. And that bush looked pretty spiky. I'm sure we've got a first aid box inside somewhere. Or some plasters, at the very least. I can offer to ...

My thoughts trail off as I observe that my charge is already pulling his bike out of the bush and climbing on. One of the wheels is bent out of shape, the spokes twisted at an unnatural angle.

"You're not going to try and ride that home, are you?" I exclaim. "Let me call you a taxi. It's the least I can do."

"No, I'm fine," he says tersely. Then, "Thank you," he adds in a voice which, if not exactly gracious, is noticeably gentler. He gives an awkward cough. "That's very kind. But there's no need." He tries to push off. The bike wobbles precariously, almost ending up in the bush all over again. Instinctively, I rush forward, although what I'm hoping to do with Casper still in my arms is questionable.

"Really, if you'll just let me ..." He holds up a hand, his eyes closing briefly as though in pain. Then he tries again, and this time it works. After a fashion. I watch as he cycles away from me, the bike lurching alarmingly to one side and then the other, muttering darkly to himself in a language which, for a few seconds, I can't understand. Then, out of the deep recesses of my brain, something begins to stir.

"Is that ..." Freddie has appeared at my shoulder, his voice dripping with incredulity "... *Latin*?"

"Yes," I say weakly. "I think it is."

I don't even think I've heard anyone speak it out loud since school. That's kind of the point of Latin these days. It's a dead language. You use it for scholarly research, and the odd plant name or family motto, but that's about it. No one actually *speaks* it.

For a few moments we simply stand, staring after the bike as it makes its drunken way over the brow of the hill.

"You know, sis, I've said it before, and I'll probably have cause to say it again," Freddie says at last, with a shake of his head. "But you really *do* get some strange people in Cambridge."

Chapter 4

I wind my scarf loosely around my neck as I step out onto the bright, sunlit street. It's one of those utterly perfect October mornings, all crisp blue skies and leaves swirling through the air in shades of amber, honey and gold. It's the kind of day which can't fail to put me in a good mood. Even the residual sense of embarrassment hanging over from last night seems to fizzle into nothing in the dazzling light of a new day. Better still, I'm actually running on time for work for once. Perhaps the gods really are smiling down on me after all.

The streets begin to narrow the closer I get to the centre of town, becoming labyrinthine passageways barely large enough for a single car to squeeze through. I stop briefly to allow a cyclist to pass and he holds up a hand in thanks, his coat billowing out behind him.

Cambridge looks more romantic than ever on a day like this, the sun warming the stone to its richest hue, gleaming like molten bronze in the narrow mullioned windows. Somewhere, amongst the cluster of turrets and spires, bells are ringing, a melodic, undulating rhythm which is as familiar to me now as breathing. Bells are *always* ringing somewhere in Cambridge; most of the time, I hardly even notice them any more. But today their sound seems to be everywhere, filling the air around me in cascading layers.

Sidling around a cluster of tourists peering at the grasshopper clock, I check the time on my phone, automatically beginning to pick up the pace. It's easy to dawdle in a city like this, to wander around dreamily at half speed without even realising you're doing it. Familiarity never seems to dull its beauty, its ancient magic. If I had to pin it down, I'd say that's ultimately what made me choose to stay here, rather than letting myself be drawn away to the bright lights of London, as so many of my classmates were.

I'd like to think that it was a wise choice, to an extent. My life might not exactly be flawless but, as I look around me now, I know without a doubt that there's nowhere I'd rather be. And, at the end of the day, how many people can honestly say that?

My thoughts are interrupted as the imposing facade of the Montague Museum comes into view. My glittery lilac ankle boots make a hollow tapping sound on the smooth stone steps as I ascend between the soaring Corinthian columns. One of a row of stately Georgian townhouses, it's quite an impressive-looking place of work; I still get a thrill of anticipation every time I walk up to it.

Even so, it's the inside where it really takes your breath away.

The cold air is still tingling on my cheeks as I push through the revolving door into the opulent marble foyer.

Just bear in mind, if you will, that when I say marble, I don't just mean a few niches or a bit of panelling here and there. Oh, no. *That*, someone clearly decided, would be far too pedestrian.

Instead, the entire space, from floor to ceiling, is lined in the purest white marble. It's quite dazzling to the eye if you're unused to it. Ancient Greek statues flank the sweeping staircase and priceless Chinese porcelain is scattered across every available surface.

In short, it's a health and safety nightmare. Not to mention a conservationist's one. But that's how Lord Montague, the slightly mad Victorian collector who bequeathed the house, wanted it. He actually stipulated the fact when he left the place in trust to be run as a private museum. What began as a cabinet of curiosities soon overtook his entire home, and he was adamant that it should remain that way.

It isn't a big museum, not at all, but it holds some breathtaking pieces of art. I haven't even begun to talk about the paintings – that's really my area of expertise although, in a little place like this, the role of assistant curator covers all departments, as well as some other jobs which a curator would never dream of undertaking in a larger establishment. I help out with everything: hanging pictures, showing visitors around, doing further research into some of the pieces ... Just last year, we discovered that one of the more nondescript sketches which had hung in the corridor by the ladies' toilets was in fact a previously unknown Renoir.

That's what this job's like – from the sublime to the ridiculous. I've discovered it's best not to dwell upon the sheer responsibility of it all. It only induces mild panic. Which, in turn, can only be alleviated by several biscuits and a mocha made in the largest mug in the staffroom cupboard.

That's chocolate biscuits, obviously. I mean, what else?

"You're here!" Ruby bears down upon me in a kaleidoscope of colour. "Thank God, we've been absolutely *desperate* to talk to you."

Immediately, I feel a shiver of alarm and my hands stop halfway down the velvet-covered buttons of my coat.

"What's the matter? It's not one of the paintings, is it?"

I have this recurring nightmare that I'm standing in the main picture gallery, and someone's drawn all over one of the Gainsboroughs with permanent marker. I'm trying desperately to rub it off, but the paint itself begins to dissolve, running down the wall in rivulets. Then, if I don't wake up at that point, it only gets worse, because someone *else* trips over Casper, who's mysteriously appeared, and I can only watch in mounting horror as they pitch head first into a William Etty, before ...

"We can't wait to hear all about your date," Eve, who's been following behind at a more stately pace, ventures excitedly. She claps her hands together, making the stacks of rings she wears jingle against one another.

The sound of her voice catapults me back into the present, visions of irreplaceable artworks biting the dust receding mercifully into the abyss. My relief is short-lived, however, as my heart sinks all over again, this time for an entirely different reason.

Why did I have to tell them about my date? I should know

better by now, what with Casper's track record in that department.

To be honest, after the disastrous events of last night, I'd sort of begun to forget about my equally disastrous date with James. One disaster rather eclipsed the other, if you will. But now it comes rushing back to me, with an attendant sense of acute humiliation. I really can't face talking about this now. I look down, hoping I can hedge my way around it.

"Oh, it was ... uh, fine. You know, nice. Ish. Kind of."

They're looking hopelessly confused, not unreasonably. I focus my attention on unbuttoning the rest of my coat, not meeting their eyes. "I don't think we'll be seeing each other again, though."

"Oh," they chorus, faces falling in mutual disappointment. There's a brief awkward pause, during which I brace myself for the inevitable barrage of questions. But, to my immense gratitude, they hurriedly start chattering about museum matters, Ruby recounting a story about someone who brought an illicit sandwich into the Egyptian gallery and refused to give it up, resulting in an undignified tussle with one of the room attendants. Eve chimes in every now and again, filling the gaps with amusing observations, and not for the first time, I find myself sending up a little prayer of thanks for my wonderful volunteers.

No one would ever imagine that these two would have become such fast friends. A candyfloss-pink-haired art student barely out of her teens and an elegant, cashmere-clad grandmother of four wouldn't usually even mix, let alone find so much in common. But they adore one another. They're usually to be found together, laughing over something or other in a corner. They're not exactly the most productive of volunteers; they're far too busy having a good time for that. But they're easily my favourites. The museum just wouldn't be the same without them.

Not, of course, that I'd ever tell them that. It wouldn't do for them to get too complacent.

I have a sneaking suspicion that they know anyway, though.

"But we ought not to detain you, dear," Eve is saying now. She leans towards me with a meaningful look. "You might want to get straight up to your office, if you catch my meaning. *You know who* has been looking for you."

Over her shoulder, Ruby is nodding conspiratorially, her flamingo-shaped earrings dancing against her neck.

I don't need telling twice. I head for the stairs, mouthing a thank you as I go.

It's not often that I view my poky little office as a haven. The walls are a depressing sort of magnolia colour which has greyed with age, and the tiny window looks out onto the car park. My desk is wedged into the corner at such an angle that I have to climb into my chair from the side because I can't pull it back properly. On the whole, I endeavour to spend as little time holed up in here as possible, but today, as I close the door behind me, it presents a welcoming refuge.

In here, I'm safe. No one can get to me.

Even so, it's with a lurch that my gaze falls upon the ominous-looking pile of grant applications still looming large on the edge of my desk. I really can't put those off any longer.

The odd offhand query as to their state of completion began to be flavoured faintly with vexation a couple of weeks ago. Last Wednesday, it morphed into something more closely resembling a demand. I simply can't admit to Jeremy that they're still not finished.

And I can't carry on avoiding him for much longer either, I concede reluctantly. I'm running out of pillars to jump behind and garbled excuses as to why I can't stop for a discussion. Sooner or later, the game's going to be up.

It's simple enough. I'll just stay in here all morning, finish these forms, and then I'll have nothing to worry about. He never needs to know that I hadn't even started them until yesterday.

Technically, Jeremy and I are supposed to *share* the paperwork, but somehow that never quite seems to happen. He always finds a reason to foist it all off onto me.

I spend a few enjoyable moments imagining what would happen if I pointed that out to him. He'd probably spontaneously combust.

I shake my head, feeling myself deflate. Alas, whilst that would be undoubtedly a spectacle, I don't think it's something I want to instigate just now. There'd be a lot of explaining to do.

Not to mention even *more* paperwork to fill out.

Pulling the stack of papers towards me, I select the uppermost one and stare at it earnestly. And then I carry on staring at it. To my credit, I stare at it for a full three minutes before slamming it back down on the pile with a sigh.

This is *so* boring. What kind of malevolent entity invented spreadsheets, anyway?

Sometimes, I wonder about the poor people on the other side of the process. Do they find visitor number projections and diagrams on marketing outreach as tedious as I do? Or are they the kind who love nothing better than a good graph and get a thrill at the prospect of five pages of statistics?

The next thing I know, I'm scrolling through Instagram and when I next look up it's half an hour later.

Oops. That ... wasn't the plan.

I'm aware that I might not be showing myself in the best light here. I feel I ought to interject and point out in my defence that I'm normally *excellent* at my job.

Okay, so maybe that's a bit of a stretch. Pretty good is probably a better description. But, either way, I'm not a slacker. I work hard. I don't habitually lounge around my office looking at how to do a plum-coloured smoky eye, or watching videos of high-fiving cats.

On the whole, I love what I do. It's hugely rewarding to walk in here every day and be surrounded by incomparable pieces of art. I know I'm insanely lucky to be able to say that there's very little about my job which I don't enjoy.

Paperwork, however, is about the one exception. When I first took this position, I had no idea just how much of it there would be; I was filled with romantic notions about educating people on art history. Of conserving important artefacts. Of promoting culture.

And it's not that I *don't* do all of those things. To an extent. But the sad fact is that by far the biggest preoccupation of a small museum such as this is securing funding. Grant applications are a major part of that; we wouldn't last a year without them. They're basically our lifeline.

They are also an assault course of graphs, data, and all the things I most hate in life.

It is soul-destroying. Scratch that, it's soul-*obliterating*.

What more do I need to say? I'm just really not a paperwork person. I'm a creative. I do big ideas, not tiny printed figures.

Plus, you know. *High-fiving cats*. I mean, come on. How can anyone say that's not important?

Struggling out from behind my desk, I poke my head cautiously round the door, scanning the corridor for signs of life.

All quiet. Excellent. I'm absolutely desperate for a cup of tea. I think this qualifies as a two sugars kind of situation.

I should introduce you to my sugar scale. I developed it whilst at university, and it's served me well ever since. It goes like this: two sugars for a real emergency, one for mild shock (or particularly malignant period cramps), and none for days when all's reasonably well and I can't find any excuse to justify it.

Technically, that *should* mean that I have no sugar in my tea most of the time. But somehow it doesn't quite seem to work out like that.

Collecting my cup from the top drawer of my desk where it habitually lives, safe from the clutches of office mug thieves, I slip quietly out. I'm not about to take any chances, although the absurdity of creeping around my own place of work is not lost on me.

I can see the doorway to the cramped staff kitchen area,

light gleaming around the edges. I'm only about four paces away when a deep voice rings out behind me, making me stop dead.

"Ah, there you are. I've been looking for you all morning."

Chapter 5

I whirl on my glitter-covered heel to discover Jeremy standing there, hands on hips. He doesn't look pleased, I note. But then, he rarely does.

Surreptitiously, I scan the corridor behind him, trying to work out where he emerged from. Not that it matters much now, in any event. He's here. And glaring at me as though somehow it's entirely my fault that he hasn't been able to track me down sooner.

Which it kind of is. I mean, I *have* spent the morning hiding from him. But he doesn't know that, does he?

"Are you on your way downstairs?" he asks briskly. Then, without waiting for an answer, "Good. Me too. We can walk together."

Mutely, I look at the mug in my hand. Blatantly, I wasn't on my way downstairs. But either he doesn't notice or doesn't care, because he inclines his head towards the staircase impatiently.

"Come along, then. We haven't got all day."

Resigned to my fate, I scuttle after him, amazed to find

myself struggling to keep up with his pace. For someone who gives every impression of being about ninety years old, he can certainly move fast when he wants to.

As you might have gathered by now, Jeremy is the head curator of the museum, which, regrettably for us both, means that he's my immediate boss. We're not exactly what you'd call compatible; he's run the place since ... Well, since about the dawn of time, as far as I can ascertain. I've seen old pictures of him and, believe me, he looks *exactly* the same. I'm not convinced that he's ever even *been* young. I honestly wouldn't be all that surprised if one day I caught him emerging from the fabric of the building itself.

In any case, temporal being or not, he certainly has his own, very ingrained way of doing things. He worships the status quo, his unerring vision of what a museum of this standing should embody.

I am not a part of that vision. He's made that quite clear. If it were up to him, I wouldn't even *be* here, but apparently the board of trustees decreed that what the museum needed was someone young, fresh and innovative.

All of which, apparently, I am.

Which is ... *nice*, I suppose. I'm not quite sure that I live up to that towering epithet on a daily basis, but still. It's great that someone has faith in me.

As for Jeremy ... Well, what can I say? Jobs in this field are notoriously limited. I'd struggle to get another position this good, even if it does come with certain drawbacks.

Besides, this has never been just a job to me. This place kept me sane when I thought I might drown in grief. The normalcy of it all: the unchanging paintings on the walls, Ruby and Eve's patter when I came into work each morning, even Jeremy's pompous lectures ... Somehow they made everything seem okay, even though nothing really was. I'll always be grateful for that.

So, you see, how can I really complain about a few little annoyances here and there? He might not be the easiest of bosses, but I do my best to humour him, even if it's challenging at times.

And, believe me, it is *very* challenging at times.

"I've been thinking about next summer's exhibition," Jeremy says as we power through a room filled with Dutch flower paintings.

I'm aware of a creeping trepidation, mixed with a bubbling sense of excitement. "Yes?" I venture cautiously.

I tell myself that it's unwise to get my hopes up. After all, we've been here before, and it inevitably ends in disappointment. But still, I can't help it, I'm an eternal optimist. A part of me will always hold out hope that things can turn around at any moment.

Maybe this is it. Maybe, at last, I might get my chance.

Annoyingly, he chooses this moment to fall silent, pausing on the stairs to admire a statue of Venus.

"Your ideas were ... *interesting*," he says at last, still inspecting the marble figure.

He utters that word like it carries the bubonic plague, and I feel a plummeting swoop of despondency.

He's still talking, his hands clasped behind his back as though he's about to give a lecture. To be honest, I'm only half listening by this point. I know how this next part goes; I could pretty much recite it in my sleep.

"But this is a serious institution, Miss Swift. You must understand that by now. We have a standard to uphold. People have expectations of us, *scholarly* expectations, which we wouldn't wish to disappoint. To stray too far from our blueprint, to *change* ..." He raises a fluttering hand to his forehead, his signet ring glinting under the overhead lights.

"Woe betide that anything should ever change," I mutter bitterly. "How would the world cope?"

He scowls. "What was that?"

"Hmm?" I widen my eyes at him innocently.

His lips form into a thin line. "Could only spell disaster," he finishes. Or, at least, I sincerely hope he's finished. Once he starts on a soliloquy, nothing can stop him. The whole building could fall down and he'd probably still be pontificating away amongst the rubble, blithely oblivious.

"Quite ... of course." My voice is overly bright, almost brittle. I'm already backing away, looking for an exit. I'm trying really hard to do what I normally do. I'm reminding myself how lucky I am to be here, how grateful I am. How I shouldn't feel resentful, shouldn't expect too much. But, for some reason, today it's just not working. My throat's beginning to feel tight, burning with repressed emotion. "Very ... er ... astute reasoning."

This is what happens. *Every* time. I should have known better than to try.

"I'm so glad you agree." He looks insufferably pleased with himself. "I knew that once I'd explained it to you in simple terms, you would come to appreciate the logic of it." He sighs solemnly, his gaze travelling up towards the glass ceiling above us. "As the great philosopher Aristotle once said ..."

Oh, lord. Not Aristotle. I really can't handle that particular soliloquy right now. I know from experience that it lasts for a good twenty minutes.

"That's wonderful," I say with more than a touch of desperation. "If that's all, then ..."

"Just a minute, if you will." His brows draw downwards, his tone becoming several degrees colder. "That wasn't all. We haven't yet discussed those applications."

I realise with a quiet sense of doom that I've flung myself straight out of the frying pan and into the fire. The Aristotle monologue is beginning to look really good right about now.

"Ah, yes," I manage, stretching out each word very slowly in an attempt to buy my brain some more time. "The applications."

I leave a knowing sort of pause. Unfortunately, the desired flash of inspiration fails to materialise, and it lengthens awkwardly before trailing off into more of a dead silence.

"Well?" Jeremy demands, irritation lacing his voice. "Have you completed them? Because if we miss that deadline ... rest assured, Miss Swift, I won't hesitate to lay the blame where it's due."

I draw backwards, eyes widening in shock. Was that a *threat*?

Surely he can't actually be threatening me? I mean, I know he has his faults, but ...

I look into his steely grey eyes and my conviction wavers.

"Of course they're finished," I hear myself responding coolly.

Brilliant, now I've just told a bald-faced lie. Great work, Clara. Very professional.

"I'm pleased to hear it," Jeremy says blandly. "We'll have a look at them now, then, shall we?"

The true extent of the hole I've just dug for myself hits me with a nasty jolt. My heart begins to patter in my chest. I cast a glance at his face, but it isn't giving anything away. Does he know the truth? Is he just trying to catch me out? Because, if so, I've walked right into it.

In a quiet frenzy, I cast around for a suitable excuse for a hasty departure. Through the archway, I have a clear view into the classical antiquities gallery. My mind whirs, turning over possibilities. Perhaps I could pretend that I need to check on something in there? Would he believe that?

"Absolutely," I blurt out. "I'd be glad to. It's just that ..."

He's looking at me expectantly, one bushy eyebrow raised, and to my dismay, I realise that I have absolutely no idea where I'm going with this.

"I've just spotted someone I urgently need to speak with," I say, wondering what on earth I'm saying. "I've been trying to catch him for ages. In fact, it's really quite urgent. I'll just go and ..."

"And who, exactly, would this be?"

I blink at the abrupt question. I didn't expect him to ask that.

"Er ... him." I point randomly to a man standing over by a stone sarcophagus, his head bent over a book.

Jeremy arches an eyebrow. "Really? You know him, do you?"

Heat begins to prickle across the back of my neck. What is this, the Spanish Inquisition? Why can't he just accept my lie and leave it at that? It's what anyone *else* would do.

"Yes, I do," I say staunchly. "Very well, in fact. We're ... er ... old acquaintances."

Just in case I thought this couldn't get any worse. Now I'm *embellishing* the lie. Am I crazy? Next I'll be inventing an entire history with a man I've never seen before in my life.

"Indeed?" Jeremy's voice drips with scepticism. "*You're* an old acquaintance of Professor Warwick's?"

For a brief moment, I wonder who the hell he's talking about. Then my heart plummets.

He knows, doesn't he? He *knows* that I'm making all of this up.

"Yes, indeed," I stutter. I couldn't sound less convincing if I tried. "Now, if you'll excuse me ..."

I brush past him and I'm halfway across the floor of the gallery before my sense of triumph gives way to the first creeping misgivings. Why do I just come out with these things? It was all very well and good in the heat of the moment, but now the prospect of accosting a total stranger seems beyond daunting. Hopefully ... I sidle a glance back over my shoulder, but no luck. Jeremy's still standing there, watching me suspiciously.

Oh, God. There's nothing for it. I'm going to have to do it, aren't I?

When this is all over, I am going to give myself a *serious* talking-to about the perils of fabrication and getting myself into these ridiculous situations.

I square my shoulders and walk right up to my quarry.

"I'm *so* glad I've caught you," I say loudly.

Or at least I think I've said it fairly loudly. But the museum's not exactly living up to its reputation as a tranquil, studious place of enquiry today. A school trip has taken over the far end of the gallery, the children fidgeting and chattering as their beleaguered teacher hands out activity papers. My voice is completely drowned out by the hubbub.

He doesn't even look up. His dark head is still bowed over what I can now identify as a leather-bound notebook, in which he's scribbling at a furious pace, apparently totally oblivious to everything around him.

I hover uselessly, wondering if I should try again, when one of the children barges past my legs, pitching me forwards. On reflex, I fling my arms out in front of me and, the next thing I know, I'm hanging off the unfortunate man in a strange approximation of a hug.

But that's not the worst part. Oh, no.

That would be our lips, which have somehow ended up ... Well, they're not *quite* on one another. I mean, if we're being technical about it ...

Oh, who am I kidding? They're on one another. It's a kiss. An *accidental* kiss, but a kiss nonetheless.

The next few seconds are the strangest I've ever experienced. Time seems to grind to a halt. He's gone as rigid as corrugated iron. I'm pretty much frozen to the spot myself, my brain struggling to compute what's happening.

Then, just as suddenly, clarity comes rushing back.

Oh, God. What am I *doing*? I'm kissing him. I'm kissing a total stranger.

Because now it really *is* a kiss. I mean, neither of us has pulled away.

Something tells me the museum board won't take a particularly indulgent view of this. I wrench my lips from his, closing my eyes in mortification.

"Er ... do we know each other?" he asks faintly. His lips are close to my ear, and something about his voice sends a shiver of awareness through me.

He thinks I flung myself at him. And why shouldn't he? That's what it must have looked like.

Now people are watching us, openly curious. I can feel heat creeping across my cheeks and I already know they're turning a vibrant pink. Not for the first time in my life, I have cause to curse my fair complexion.

"Sorry," I mutter frantically. My head feels like it's about to explode. *I'm* about to explode. Surely, no one can deal with as much embarrassment in one sitting without it being fatal? Even someone as seasoned as me. "Just ... sorry. Look, I'll explain in a moment."

Without thinking, I grab his hand and tug him across to the nearest window seat. It's covered in papers, but I'm too shaken to care. I just collapse right on top of them.

"My papers," he says in a strangled voice.

"Sorry, sorry." Why can't I seem to stop saying that? I pull a wad of them out from under me, intending to smooth them out on my lap. But I never get that far. Instead, as I look down at them, I'm gripped by a cold sensation.

There's something very familiar about these papers. They're crumpled and stained with dirt, like they've been on the ground.

Surely ... I mean, it's got to be a coincidence, right? There's no way it could actually be ...

I turn another one over, and there's a bicycle tyre track running diagonally across it.

Oh, no. *No way*.

Slowly, I drag my eyes up to look at the man sitting next to me.

So much for thinking the worst of it was over. By the looks of things, it hasn't even started.

Chapter 6

For an age I'm paralysed. I just sit there, staring at him. How can this be happening?

I am a good person, you know. Not perfect, but pretty damn good. I pay my taxes. I remember birthdays. I'm even an attentive listener, and that's not a widespread trait these days.

So why, oh, *why*, is the man from last night now sitting next to me in my place of work?

And why, by all that is good and holy, have I just kissed him?

Why did it have to be him?

I don't deserve this. Really I don't. I'll be having words with the Universe later.

"Are you all right?" he's asking now, peering at me with something approaching alarm. "You've gone rather puce."

Puce, indeed. Like that's going to make me feel better.

"I'm fine," I croak.

I suppose that, now I'm looking at him properly, and with the benefit of proof in the form of those cursed papers, it's obvious that it's the same man. The mid-morning sun slanting through the window illuminates those sharp features I only caught a glimpse of beneath his helmet last night, picking out hints of bronze in his black hair. And his voice ... Reluctantly, I have to admit that I thought it was familiar, although, to be fair, it has a completely different tone to it today. Last night it was angry, sarcastic; today, it sounds very different. It's almost ... nice, with a deep, cultured thread to it.

I pull myself up sharply at that last thought. *Nice? What are you doing, Clara? Now's not the time to get carried away with how nice his voice sounds.*

He's regarding me thoughtfully. "Are you sure we don't know one another? I feel like I've seen you somewhere."

Hang on ... *what*? Surely he can't mean ...

The realisation, somewhat belated as it is, hits me in a flash.

He doesn't know who I am.

How can that be the case? I mean, all right, so it was dark. More to the point, he was standing under the streetlamp, whilst I was in the shadows. And he never really looked at me properly throughout our entire ill-fated meeting. So I suppose ...

Actually, I'm not sure if I should be affronted or not. Did I *really* leave so little an impression upon his lofty mind?

Apparently so. For some reason, that piques me.

I'm about to confess everything. Really, I am. But then, when I open my mouth, what I intended to say somehow isn't there. It's like someone's mixed up the words, and instead I can only listen on in horror as what I *actually* say is ...

"What? No! Definitely not. I mean ..." I rummage in the pocket of my cardigan, brandishing my lanyard. Really, I'm supposed to be wearing it, but it's such an outfit killer I can't bring myself to. I didn't spend twenty minutes staring blankly into my wardrobe this morning trying to select a cute ensemble only to loop an unflattering black cord around my neck. "Probably around the museum. I work here, you see."

Well, that's that then. I've officially lied right to his face. That's ... that's just *fantastic*. My second monstrous fabrication of the day, and it's not even ten-thirty yet. As if it weren't enough to dig myself one grave in the course of a morning, I have to go and excavate myself a second.

Perhaps this is what Heather means when she says I'm my own worst enemy.

His cobalt blue eyes scan the card for several seconds, and I hold my breath. He doesn't look entirely convinced. At last, though, he shrugs.

"That must be it, then. So tell me," he begins casually, crossing one leg over the other, "is it museum policy to kiss unsuspecting members of the public?"

My head snaps up. Did he *really* just say that?

"I did *not* kiss you," I say haughtily. "It was an accident. One of those kids pushed me!"

He nods knowingly. "All right, well, we'll have to take your word for that, I suppose, considering the lack of any firm evidence."

"It's *true*," I say hotly.

"So you say."

I look into his dark eyes, trying to work out if he's playing with me or not. But there's nothing there to give him away. His expression is totally inscrutable. We could just as easily be discussing the weather.

Annoyed at my own confusion, I turn away, craning my neck to squint around the window casement, which screens us from both sides. To my intense aggravation, Jeremy's still there, lurking behind a stone pillar in what he clearly imagines to be an unobtrusive manner. Honestly, does he not have something else he could be doing? Since when did spying on me become a legitimate part of his job description? The only small bright spot in the whole thing is the expression on his face. It's priceless. If everything else weren't so awful right at this moment, I'd probably be enjoying myself immensely.

"And who, exactly, are we hiding from?" murmurs my new companion.

"No one."

He raises an eyebrow. "Really? No one? You're habitually this furtive, then?"

"No, I ..." I flush guiltily. "Look, you don't understand ..."

I see him sidle a dubious glance at the mug still in my hand. It has a picture of Casper on it, surrounded by clouds and rainbows. Hastily, I move my hand so it's covering the image. The last thing I need is for him to recognise the cat which dented his bike and ruined his precious research papers. That's a can of worms I really can't face opening just now.

In fact, I can't do any of this. I can't sit here, making pleasant conversation with this man. Well, semi-pleasant, at least. I stand, not caring if Jeremy's still there. "I'd better go."

He looks faintly disappointed. "So soon? Are you sure you

don't want to kiss me once more before you do?"

He *is* laughing at me. I can see it in the depths of his eyes. Who'd have thought he had a sense of humour? Unfortunately, I'm not in the mood to share it right now.

"No, thank you," I say, with as much dignity as I can muster. "I don't think you enjoyed it all that much the first time. I wouldn't wish to put you through it again."

For a moment, he looks as though he might be about to say something else, but then he simply inclines his head. It's an old-fashioned gesture, oddly formal, but it seems to suit him, somehow.

"Well, then, until next time, Miss Swift."

Good God, I think, as I scuttle away as fast as my pride and poise will allow, I hope not. If the insufferable Professor Warwick never crossed my path again, it wouldn't be a moment too soon.

***

"I'm going to hell," I moan, flinging myself across the sofa. "It's official. My fate is sealed."

"You're so melodramatic," Heather tuts, although I notice that she puts down the kettle and reaches into the wine rack instead. "It can't be that bad. Although why you didn't just tell the truth, I don't know."

"Because that would have been sensible. That's the sort of thing you would have done. *I'm* not like you. *I* panicked."

"And made an idiot of yourself, as usual," Heather remarks calmly.

I sit bolt upright. "That's not very supportive!"

She shrugs, pouring pale pink wine into two expensive-looking glasses. "Sometimes I'm here to be supportive, sometimes just to tell you the truth. And the truth is, you're an idiot. In this case, at least."

"You're right," I admit mournfully as she settles onto the sofa next to me. I hug my knees to my chest and take a fortifying sip of my wine. Almost immediately, its warming effect helps me to relax, and I sink back into the cushions. Heather has lots of cushions. And they're always perfectly plumped too. I don't know how she keeps it up, not with a rambunctious three-year-old charging around the house all day.

"Better?" she asks with a knowing look.

"Yes," I say in a small voice.

It's always nice coming to Heather's. Like visiting your mum's. Everything's wonderfully ordered, with a soothingly tasteful colour scheme. You always get offered a drink of some description from their sumptuous new kitchen, with its Carrara marble island unit and built-in wine rack. And when the drink comes, it's unfailingly from an ever-ready supply of sparklingly clean glasses in the glossy-fronted cupboard. You'll never find Heather scrabbling around for a halfway decent receptacle before eventually serving up warm wine in a chipped Moomins mug she's had since she was eight.

In fact, much as I like coming to Heather's, it always makes me feel a little ... I don't know, *flat*. Because it just highlights the ever-growing chasm between her life and mine. Heather's a grown-up, a fully fledged adult member of society with the tasteful arrangement of beeswax pillar candles to prove it. And I'm ...

Well, today was a case in point.

I look at those candles now, blazing away on the glazed fire surround. Then, slowly, I look at Heather, in a powder-blue cashmere jumper, her favourite diamond studs glinting in her ears.

"Oh, sorry. Have I interrupted a romantic evening?" Now I feel really guilty. Why didn't she *say* something?

She looks nonplussed. "Not at all. Dominic's just putting Oscar to bed, then he's got a squash match."

"You mean, this is your staying at home outfit?" I'm only half teasing.

"One has to make an effort, even if only for oneself." She cradles her wineglass against her lips, looking mischievous. "So, what I really want to know about is this man. A professor, you say?"

"Heather!" If we were at my house, where the soft furnishings aren't quite so precious, I would gladly throw a cushion at her. "Don't even think about it. Believe me, he is definitely *not* a candidate for romantic interest."

She quirks an eyebrow. "Isn't that what people always say to begin with? I wasn't exactly keen on Dominic when I first met him."

"Yes, but you slept with him anyway," I point out drily. It's about the most reckless thing Heather's ever done. And just like her luck that it should actually turn out well in the end.

I mean, don't get me wrong—I'm happy that it did, really I am. But at the same time it is the *tiniest* bit vexing when you consider that she never wanted any of this in the first place. Her sights were firmly set on becoming a top psychologist; she already had her place secured on the MA course—she hadn't even had to apply; they'd *offered* it to her. She wasn't interested in anything which could even be loosely defined as a serious relationship, let alone a husband, and children ... not on her radar at all. She'd always maintained that watching her parents thrash their way through an acrimonious divorce had been enough to put her off all of that for life.

No, it was always me who wanted those things, not Heather. And yet ... look at us.

"Quite, and thank you for announcing that so loudly," she says in an arch voice. "But what I mean is, feelings often come later. In real life, instant attraction is a very rare thing. In fact, I'm not so certain it exists at all."

"Speak for yourself," a voice behind us says. "Although it's good to know how you really felt about me back then. Don't spare my feelings, will you?"

Heather twists around to roll her eyes at her husband. "All right, so instant *mutual* attraction doesn't exist. And you already knew how I felt about you back then. I made no secret of it."

"Hello, Dominic," I chime in.

"Hello, Clara." He smiles thinly at me, dropping his squash bag onto the floor and heading towards the fridge. "And what brings you here this evening? Something to do with men, I should imagine, from the look on my wife's face."

I have a sinking suspicion that Dominic thinks I'm some

sort of man-eater. God only knows what Heather tells him. Either way, I don't think it helps endear me to him.

Dominic and I have an odd, uneasy sort of understanding. We're pleasant enough to one another but, on the whole, we try to keep our contact time to a minimum. We've never really got on, not since those early days at university. I know that he thinks I'm immature, that I create unnecessary drama. And he ...

Well, sometimes he looks at me and I'm convinced that he knows. He *knows* what I thought about him all those years ago, how I tried to persuade Heather to break up with him. How I said that he'd only hold her back.

Obviously, I was wrong. I mean, if they hadn't stayed together, they would never have had Oscar. And now here they are and ... well, clearly, it was the right choice. It should all be water under the bridge. But still, I can't help but feel that Dominic resents me for it somehow.

"She has a new admirer," Heather pipes up, eyes shining.

"He is *not* an admirer!" I sit up so hastily that I only narrowly avoid sloshing wine all over my lap. "Believe me, there's nothing even remotely ..."

"She kissed him!" Heather squeals. "And then he *bowed* to her!"

"That is totally out of context," I splutter, snatching her empty wineglass from her hand. "How much have you had to drink today?"

"I don't know what you mean," she says defiantly. "I haven't been anywhere. Except to the half-term lunch, but that doesn't count."

Ah, so that explains it. You'd think that a midday gathering with fellow school gate mothers would be a refined affair. Not a bit of it. By the sounds of things, they'd put most illicit teenage house parties to shame in terms of alcohol consumption.

Dominic frowns faintly at her before turning his attention to me. "He actually bowed to you, did he? How ... courtly of him."

The last sentence is uttered with a barely repressed smirk, and I resist the impulse to narrow my eyes at him.

"Haven't you got a squash game to get to?" I say sweetly.

It has the desired effect because he jumps to attention, grabbing an iced bottle of water from the fridge and slinging his sports bag over his shoulder.

"Oh, damn. Yes, and I'm already late." He swoops down to drop a perfunctory kiss on the top of Heather's head. "I'll see you later. Oscar's fast asleep; he went straight off. I doubt you'll hear more out of him tonight."

Heather just flaps a hand in a vague sort of farewell.

"Now we've got rid of him," she says as the sound of the front door closing echoes through the house, "do you want some dinner? Only something simple, I'm afraid, as I thought it was just going to be me."

"I'd probably better get back to Freddie," I say reluctantly, getting up and taking our wineglasses over to the dishwasher. "Lord only knows what he and Casper will have got up to in the time I've been away. They're both as bad as each other."

"If you're sure," she begins, pulling items out of the fridge. Fresh pasta. A tub of pesto. Parmesan wrapped in paper from the Italian deli down the street. "Could you look in that cupboard for pine nuts? I think I bought some last week."

I can only stare, mesmerised, as the ingredients stack up on the island in front of me. Proper food. I think of the congealed cold pizza waiting at home in the fridge and my stomach makes the decision for me.

"On second thoughts, maybe I will stay," I say casually. I can't let on to Heather how long it's been since I last had anything that wasn't reheated. She'd probably fall into a dead faint. "They can cope for an evening on their own. After all, Freddie's a grown man.

Supposedly. And Casper ..." Here, I find myself tailing off. What do I say about Casper?

Heather's busily toasting pine nuts in a frying pan, but she turns to me with an amused look. "Is a grown cat? Supposedly?"

"Has had his fair share of trouble for one week," I say firmly. "Believe me, he won't go looking for any more. He was quiet this morning. I think last night shook him a little. He's realised that he's not as invincible as he thought he was." A hopeful thought strikes me. "Perhaps he'll turn over a new leaf."

"Hmm ..." Heather prods the pine nuts with a wooden spoon, not looking wholly convinced by my logic "... I'll believe *that* when I see it."

Chapter 7

I wake with a start, jerking into an upright position in bed. Darkness envelops the room, broken only by a pale lilac light creeping beneath the curtains.

Momentarily disorientated, I fumble for the bedside lamp, relieved when its warm glow chases away the shadows, revealing the familiar outline of my bedroom. Everything looks as it should be, at least. Yesterday's dress thrown over the back of the pink velvet chair, the cream painted wardrobe hulking in the corner, the door slightly ajar as always. I bought it at an antiques centre several years ago, and it's never closed properly. My dressing table is littered with various paraphernalia: bottles of nail polish, lipsticks, a piece of amethyst given to me by my mother, its faceted crystals gleaming in the lamplight.

I sit there for a moment, the duvet drawn up under my chin for warmth, wondering what might have woken me. Normally I sleep fairly soundly. Unless I'm having a nightmare, and usually, if I've had one of those, I know all about it. I wake up cold, shaking, the remnants of the dream still clinging to the edges of my mind like cobwebs.

No, I'm pretty certain that I was sleeping quite peacefully. So what ...?

And then I hear it. A deafening, screeching sound fills the air, followed by yowling. It sounds like it hails from the bowels of the earth itself, but I know better than that.

Fully awake now, I throw the covers aside, heart already in my mouth. As I clatter down the stairs, knotting my kimono at my waist, I keep telling myself that I'm overreacting. That of *course* it's not Casper. That I'll open the kitchen door and he'll be safely there, all curled up in his ...

All right, so he's not in his basket. He's not on the windowsill either. Or on the chair. He's nowhere to be seen.

Really, who was I trying to kid? If there's a fight going on, he's *bound* to be involved. I've never known him to miss one yet.

The hideous screaming sound has stopped and I waver in the middle of the room, trying to decide what to do next. Then, with a huff of resignation, I pull on my flowery wellington boots, which now live permanently next to the back door. This isn't the first time I've had to take a nightly sojourn into the garden in pursuit of my errant pet. Far from it. But I know I'll never get back to sleep until I've reassured myself that he's all right.

"Casper?" I call softly, even as I do so wondering why I'm bothering. As if that cacophony hasn't woken the whole street anyway. He certainly has a way of making me unpopular with the neighbours.

Tentatively, I venture out onto the lawn, my boots sinking into the damp grass. The first light of dawn is bleeding into the sky, washing the garden in an ethereal pink glow. Dewdrops have transformed the lawn into a shimmering carpet and the air is bitingly cold, invigorating in its sharpness. It would be stunningly beautiful, I suppose, if I weren't too preoccupied with worry to pay it much attention.

I check half-heartedly under a few bushes, already knowing that he won't be there. He'll turn up when he's good and ready, and not a moment sooner. I don't come across his assailant either. Or – and I have to allow for this possibility – his victim. I'm not so blinded by love that I don't know what he's like. He's just as likely to start a fight as he is to get drawn into one.

Giving up the search, I trudge back into the kitchen to find a tousled-looking Freddie standing there, yawning extravagantly.

"What's going on? I got up for a glass of water and saw that the lights were on downstairs."

And yet, somehow, the screeching and caterwauling completely passed him by. My brother would make a fascinating case for medical science. His tendency towards complete obliviousness never fails to astonish me. I swear he could sleep through the apocalypse with no trouble at all.

"I can't find Casper," I explain, stamping my boots on the mat to knock the excess mud off them. "He's not in the garden."

Freddie stares at me like I'm utterly insane. "Clara, he's a *cat*. What do you expect? That he's going to just stay in one place?"

"I know, but ..." How can I explain it to him? How can I tell him how much Casper means to me? Of course, to him, it seems ridiculous. Even to my own ears it sounds it.

At that moment the cat flap rattles and Casper slinks into the kitchen, drawing up short to look askance at us both. For a cat, he has a surprisingly expressive face, and I can tell that he's wondering what the humans are doing up at this hour.

"*There* you are." Instinctively, I move towards him, the relief in my voice audible.

Certainly, he's been in a tussle of sorts; his fur is all standing on end, his eyes bright and feverish. But he looks okay, at least. To be honest, I feel a bit foolish now, having got into such a state about it all.

"See, he's fine." Freddie's already halfway through the doorway, stifling another gargantuan yawn. "Nothing to worry about. *Now* can we go back to bed?"

"Freddie ..." I've drawn my hand away from Casper's side to find it stained red. For a moment, I can only stare at it, frozen.

"What?" He turns, then blanches. "Oh, God. Is *that* ...? What do we do?"

Casper's leaning into me now, obviously weakening. I shake the fog from my brain, willing myself to stay focused. This is no time to panic.

"Get the cat basket out of the cupboard under the stairs, will you? We're going to have to make a dash across town."

***

"What were you even thinking?" I pant as we cross the market square. Rearranging my grip on the basket, which was digging painfully into my fingers, I continue. "*Why* must you get yourself into every fight going?"

Casper looks up at me balefully from where he's nestled on his favourite blue blanket. I know he must be feeling bad because Freddie and I managed to get him into the basket with surprisingly little fuss. Usually, the very sight of it is enough to send him into histrionics.

I longingly watch a car trundle past. There's no point in my owning a car here in Cambridge; in fact, very few people do. Normally, I'm quite content to get around on foot, although this morning that's not so much the case, what with my rather unwieldy cargo.

I'm beginning to wish I'd just bitten the bullet and called a cab. I'd forgotten how heavy Casper starts to feel by the time you've lugged him halfway across town. Failing that, I should have let Freddie bring him.

"Besides, you're not exactly a spring chicken any more, are you?" I point out, stopping on the corner to catch my breath. "Don't you think you should be past all of this by now? Isn't it time to retire to your basket and let the younger toms have it out?"

Actually, that's probably a bit unfair. The truth is, I have no idea how old Casper is. When I first took him in, the vet estimated him to be somewhere between four and twelve.

Which is ... you know, helpful.

In any event, he's old enough to know better. But perhaps not quite at the pipe and slippers stage just yet.

He obviously feels the same because he glowers at me before turning around in his basket so that he's facing the other way.

"Fine, be like that," I mutter. "It was only a suggestion. Ah, here we are."

Thank God the vet opens early, I think as I wrestle my way, cat basket in arms, through the glass doors. Inside the cool grey interior, all is calm. There are a couple of people already in the waiting room, baskets by their feet. Classical music floats through the air. Behind the curved steel desk, a receptionist taps away efficiently at her keyboard.

"Good morning," I say, still slightly breathless. "I need to make an emergency appointment."

She looks up, a pleasant smile on her face. Then her eyes travel down to Casper, filling with dread. "Oh, no," she says emphatically. "Absolutely *not*. That cat is banned!"

I'd anticipated that we'd come up against this issue, so I'm already prepared with a response. "Look, I know he hasn't always been the easiest of patients ..."

"*Easiest*?" Her voice comes out as a strangled shriek. "He's an absolute nightmare. He can't possibly come in here."

Casper, who's been quietly slouched in the corner of his basket, opens one eye and emits a faint hiss. The receptionist pales, shrinking behind the counter.

"You're not exactly helping yourself," I murmur at him out of the corner of my mouth. "Just work with me here, all right?"

He falls silent, which I take as tacit agreement.

I turn back to the receptionist. "If you could just give him one more chance ..."

"He's already had more chances than he deserves," she retorts. She holds up her hand, beginning to tick off her fingers, and immediately I feel a sense of foreboding.

"There's no need—" I begin hurriedly, but it's too late.

"First he broke the brand new scales."

"That was an accident," I say defensively. "He didn't mean to do it."

She gives me a hard stare. "He *kicked* them off the bench. There was nothing accidental about it."

I notice that the other people in the waiting room are pretending very hard not to listen, but with little success. I feel heat rising beneath my skin.

"Then, of course, there was the time he escaped and ran all around the surgery." She's warming to her theme now. I could swear she almost seems to be enjoying herself. "We had to have half the staff pulled away from their duties to chase him around. Twenty minutes it took us to catch him, and even then we had to throw a towel over him to do so."

"He must have panicked. No one likes to see a thermometer heading towards their rear end. Isn't that right, Casper?" I appeal to him.

He just looks back at me disdainfully. If cats could roll their eyes, I'm certain he'd be doing so right now.

"And then, of course," the receptionist trills, triumph colouring her voice, "the final straw was when he bit poor Stacey. She was traumatised."

I wince. That *was* pretty bad. Who knew a tiny nip from a cat could produce so much blood?

"He sensed that she was nervous, that's all," I reply quickly, with a mollifying smile. "Inexperienced. Perhaps he took advantage a *little*, I'll admit. I'm sure it happens all the time."

She looks at me sourly. "It doesn't."

I feel my face fall. Wow, she's a tough nut. I thought it would be easier than this.

"We had to sign her off with stress, you know," she's saying now. "It was weeks before she felt up to facing another patient on her own."

I sense that I'm getting nowhere with this line of attack. She looks completely and utterly unmoved. If anything, she actually looks even stonier than she did when we first came in. So, flinging my pride out of the way, I resort to the only tactic still available to me: shameless pleading.

"Look ..." I put Casper down on the floor, where he immediately starts terrorising a Jack Russell sitting under the nearest chair. Placing both hands flat on the counter, I look her straight in the eye. "I understand why you don't want him in here, I do. But I haven't had time to find him another vet just yet, and now he's injured. I don't know where else to take him. So will you *please* just see him once more? Then I promise you solemnly that I will take him far away from here, find another surgery, and we will never darken your door again."

For the briefest of moments she looks on the verge of relenting. Then the Jack Russell whimpers from beneath the seat, cowering away from Casper. She purses her lips, and I know that I've lost her.

"I'm sorry, Miss Swift," she declares, not looking particularly sorry at all. "But it's just not possible."

A cold sensation lodges itself in the pit of my stomach as I take in her words. What am I going to do? This was my one and only plan. I look down at Casper. He's lying on his side, panting heavily. I'm willing myself to calm down, but it's not working.

Then, from the doorway through to the surgery, an unfamiliar voice speaks. "I'll take a look at him."

Chapter 8

"Thank you so much for agreeing to see him," I blurt out for what must be the third time in as many minutes.

I'm kicking myself before the words are even out of my mouth. Way to sound like a complete cretin, Clara.

"You're most welcome," he replies, *also* for what must be the third time in as many minutes. Amazingly, though, there's no hint of sarcasm or impatience in his tone. Instead, he just smiles at me, before returning his attention to Casper.

The thing is, the new vet is decidedly *not* what I was expecting. It's sort of thrown me off balance. For one thing, he's quite a lot younger than most of the partners here.

He's quite a lot more attractive too. Just ... you know, as an observation.

Not, of course, that I'm in any state to be noticing that sort of thing. After all, my mind is consumed with anxiety over the welfare of my precious cat. I haven't got the energy left to pay much notice to ... *I don't know* ... say, those warm green eyes or those high, slanting cheekbones or that burnished brown hair falling over his forehead as he leans over Casper ...

Who, incidentally, is behaving most ... well, most *unlike* Casper, for want of a better phrase. That's the biggest shock of all; to be honest, I think I'm still getting my head around it. My cat, sitting quite tamely on the vet's table. He's even allowing himself to be touched without the slightest peep of complaint.

It's like a dream. A very sad, pet owner's dream, granted, but a dream nonetheless.

"He likes you," I say faintly, watching in astonishment as this superhuman being of a vet manages to turn Casper over slightly so he can examine his side, and all without losing a finger in the process.

It's more than a dream. It's a miracle. It's like I've fallen into a parallel universe and everything is the wrong way around. A place where vets are fantastically good-looking and my cat is a model pet.

"I'd like to think I have a vague rapport with animals," he says neutrally. "This would be something of a difficult career path if I didn't, don't you think?"

For a moment, I think I detect the slightest hint of a smile in his voice. But then he carries on with his inspection without further comment, and I decide that I must have imagined it.

"Yes, but Casper's a bit ... different," I say cautiously, suddenly aware that I should be careful what I'm saying. The last thing I need is for him to realise that he's unwittingly taken on the scourge of vets everywhere, the terror of the waiting room. Thank God he's new and that Casper's reputation, for once, doesn't seem to have preceded him. "He's not usually that keen on vets," I finish, tactfully. There. Not exactly a lie, but not the whole scale-kicking, blood-drawing truth either.

He's been waiting patiently whilst I stumbled through that explanation. Now, however, he arches an eyebrow. "I know. I've read his file."

I choke on air. He's *what*?

"Or rather, I should say, files," he amends thoughtfully, as though there's been no interruption. "There were quite a few, you know. They've provided me with an entertaining read on several coffee breaks."

With an effort, I recover my voice, although it comes out as a discordant croak. "And you still agreed to see him?"

"Are you kidding?" He laughs, and the rich sound ripples right through me. "He's the most entertaining patient we have. I couldn't wait to meet him."

I can't believe I'm hearing this. I was joking earlier about the parallel universe thing, but now I'm beginning to wonder. Have I fallen and hit my head or something?

"I'm not sure that your receptionist shares that sentiment," I say slowly. "She didn't seem all that pleased when you let him in."

That's something of an understatement. She looked thoroughly livid. I dread to think what confrontation awaits him in the staff room later.

He raises one shoulder in an approximation of a shrug. "Susan is rarely pleased about anything. It's sort of her modus operandi."

Privately, I wonder if she and Jeremy would get along. Shaking off that thought, I return to the matter at hand.

"Nonetheless, I hope I haven't got you into trouble."

His lips quirk up at the corners. "Fear not, Miss Swift. It was worth it."

I blush, inwardly cursing myself as I do so. Just because someone happens to be charming doesn't mean I have to turn into a simpering idiot. He's probably equally as engaging with everyone who comes in here, whether they're a twenty-something blonde or an eighty-something purple rinse.

For all I know, he could be a serial seducer. He probably uses his position to lure in tender-hearted females, worming his way into their affections with his charismatic banter whilst he runs his hands all over their ...

I look down at Casper and inwardly recoil. Seriously, Clara, what is *wrong* with you? Has it really been that long?

Yes, a small voice in my head replies pertly. *It really has. No wonder you're losing the plot.*

"Clara, please," I say quickly, trying to conceal the fact that I feel like I'm about to burst into flames. Oh, God, this is so embarrassing. Thank heavens technology hasn't yet provided us with the ability to read minds; the day that happens, I'm throwing myself off a bridge. It's the only option. No one can ever find out what weird stuff goes through my head. "I think you've earned that right, after what you've done for Casper."

"I haven't done it yet." He strips off his surgical gloves and leans against the side of the table, folding his arms. I'm momentarily distracted by the favourable effect it has on his biceps, and almost miss the next part completely. "This is what needs to happen next. The wound's quite deep; it's going to need stitches. I'll have to keep him in."

"Wait ..." I surface from the mental fog. "Do you mean ...?"

"It'll be a small procedure, yes. He'll have to go under general anaesthetic."

I feel a swoop of dismay, and something else. Something cold. Fear.

I look at Casper, who's perched on the table, watching us both. I could almost swear that he's following the conversation.

"Isn't there another way you can do it?" I ask desperately.

"Afraid not." The vet's busy disposing of his gloves in the bin, but as soon as he takes a look at my face his expression softens. "Look, he'll be fine. He's a strong, healthy cat, in his prime."

Casper raises his head with a look of approval.

"Stop buttering him up," I scold, dismayed to find that my voice is wobbling a bit. "He's already got enough of an ego as it is."

"I can tell," he says gently. He goes to pick Casper up, then pauses, motioning for me to go ahead. Gratefully, I gather Casper into my arms, dropping a kiss onto the top of his head before popping him into his basket. He gazes up at me, and for the first time I see a flicker of trepidation in his bright green eyes. In that instant, I know that he's well aware of what's about to happen.

"You'll be fine," I say aloud, and I'm not sure which of us I'm trying to reassure most.

Nonetheless, as I snap the clasp on the basket closed, I feel my anxiety get the better of me.

"You will look after him, won't you, Dr ..." I trail off as it occurs to me that I don't even know his name.

"Granger, but I prefer Josh. I don't hold much with formality." He picks up the cat basket and carefully sets it on the table. "And yes, I will. I promise. I'll tell you what, I'll try and get to him this morning. With any luck, you should be able to take him home tonight."

Something about his quietly confident manner reassures me, and I feel the tight ball in my solar plexus unknot slightly.

"Thank you. That means a lot." I hesitate for a moment, knowing that I should just go, but my feet won't move. With a sinking sensation, I realise that I'm about to do something stupid. I'm used to the signs by now, but that doesn't seem to make a difference. I'm powerless to stop it.

"Look, I know you probably think I'm a bit mad, but ... no, don't interrupt," I command as he opens his mouth. Here we go; now I've started. I don't know why I feel like I need to tell him this, but something in me wants to make him understand. Something about him makes me think that he *might* understand, if only I can explain it. "He's very precious to me. He turned up in my life when I needed him most, and ..."

"I don't think you're mad," he says simply.

"He's not just a pet, you see, and ..." I draw up short. "*What* did you just say?"

Humour flashes in his eyes. "I said, I don't think you're mad. Or at least I didn't, until you forbade me from speaking in my own consulting room. Then, I'll admit, I started to have a few creeping misgivings."

"Oh." I'm stunned into momentary silence. Then the implications of what he's said hit me, and I feel hot with embarrassment. Oh, God, he's right. I *did* do that, didn't I? "Sorry about that. I got a bit ... carried away."

Casper buries his head under his blanket, as though he can't bear to watch. I kind of wish I could join him.

"I'm quite sane, I assure you," I joke weakly. "What can I do to prove it to you?"

A snuffling sound comes from beneath the blanket, which I studiously ignore.

"I'd like to get the chance to find out for myself," he says lightly.

We look at each other for what seems like a very long moment, and then, out of nowhere, something amazing happens. Something which I haven't felt for the longest time: a fizzing feeling, sparkling through my entire body like champagne. It takes me by surprise, makes me suck in a breath.

Unfortunately, it seems he isn't similarly afflicted because he's already looked away, occupied in the task of attaching a label to Casper's basket.

"Out of my surgery with you, Miss Swift, before people start to talk. I'll call you later with an update."

***

"You're late, my dear," Eve states in her sing-song voice as I clatter into the foyer in a whirl of frenetic activity.

"I know, I know." I'm in the process of attempting to unbutton my coat, unwrap my scarf and smooth down my hair all at the same time. It's not working. Instead, all I'm succeeding in is getting hopelessly tangled up. "The time has not evaded my notice."

Eve watches me fighting with my own clothing, her perfectly made-up face as benignly impassive as ever. "Is everything all right?" she enquires mildly.

"I had to run Casper to the vet ..." I gasp as my scarf makes a bid to garrotte me. I tug it away from my throat. "Got held up."

Very pleasurably held up, I add silently. Although, of course, my thoughts are still with Casper, I do find them occasionally drifting back to that moment in the consulting room. *Just* occasionally. Not ... you know, once every two minutes. That would be absurd. Except ...

I'd like to get the chance to find out for myself. What did that *mean*? Frankly, it could have meant anything from *I'd like to get the chance to talk to you again* all the way to *I'd like to ask you out*, and everything in between. The fizzing sensation returns as I consider that second possibility, and I bite my lip. Damn it, why do men have to be so obscure, anyway? Why can't they just say what they mean in the first place and have done with it? Then women wouldn't have to waste so much of their time and energy dissecting everything, trying to work out what's going on in their minds when we could be doing other more useful things, like running the world.

Of course, I also have to accept that the alternative to all of this is that it meant nothing at all, save that I'm a hopeless fantasist who's reading far too much into a simple sentence.

That's a deflating thought.

"Jeremy's already been by," Ruby pipes up from where she's

rearranging leaflets on the front desk. "We covered for you, obviously."

"And I knew you would." At last I've succeeded in divesting myself of all malevolent accessories and I reach down to pick up the takeaway coffee cups I left on the marble surround. "Hence why I brought these."

Ruby's eyes go round. "Are those pumpkin spice lattes?"

I nod solemnly. "It *is* pumpkin season, is it not? We must make the most of it while we can."

"Ooh!" Ruby squeals, practically lunging for hers, the leaflets in a forgotten pile on the desk behind her.

Eve accepts hers more gingerly, lifting the lid to peer at the contents with a wrinkle of the nose. "Is this another one of those young person things? Like unicorn porridge and mermaid stationery?"

Ruby and I exchange a knowing look. Eve pretends to be disdainful of all things millennial, but the truth is that she absolutely loves finding out about all of this stuff. It gives her something to boast about at her bridge club meetings. I can already envision her, regaling them all with how she's sampled the ultimate seasonal fad.

"So ..." I take a sip of my own coffee, mentally cursing as I burn the tip of my tongue "... anything I should know about this morning? No disasters of cataclysmic proportions?"

"Not just yet, no," Ruby chirps. "But then, it's only quarter past ten. There's still time. Oh, except ... I meant to tell you, Eve. You were wrong about the Professor Warwick thing. He *hasn't* got a wife. I checked."

I try to keep my choking to a discreet minimum. Honestly,

the man is a plague on my life. Just the sound of his name is enough to give me convulsions.

"It always was an unlikely guess." Eve takes her attention away from her latte to raise an eyebrow. "I've never seen him wearing a ring. But I had to suggest *something*. Ah, well, I suppose I owe you twenty pence, then."

"I'll put it on your tab," Ruby quips. "Although I was wrong about the woman in the picture gallery last week. She really *was* just waiting for her friend. So, to be fair, we're probably about even."

My head's bobbing back and forth as I try to follow the conversation. Ruby and Eve are always making little bets to pass the time. It can be anything: what colour will Jeremy's waistcoat be today; what time will the first water spillage happen; what will get left behind in lost property this week ...?

"What exactly are we talking about here?" I ask hopelessly.

"Rumour has it that Professor Warwick was seen kissing someone in the Roman gallery yesterday," Ruby says in a stage whisper.

Suddenly my throat feels rather tight.

Eve's nodding emphatically, eyes shining. "More than that. Apparently she positively *launched* herself at him."

The word *launched* is uttered with such relish that I long to sink into the floor there and then.

"Really?" I manage at last, although my voice comes out several octaves higher than usual. Luckily, neither of them seems to notice.

"It's all just so wonderfully unexpected," Ruby says gleefully.

"What a dark horse! He looks so stuffy, and all along he has this sordid other life. God only knows what else he gets up to. He probably ..."

"Yes, well, let's not go into that," I interrupt quickly, before the whole foyer is treated to some rather graphic terminology. I know how Ruby's mind works.

I'm actually starting to feel quite sorry for the besmirched Professor Warwick. I dread to think what sort of insinuations are flying around the place, especially now Ruby's got involved with her very ... er ... active imagination. It's a good thing she channels a lot of it into her art is all I'll say.

"This is very sweet," Eve interjects plaintively, having taken a first tentative sip of her coffee. She looks around as though some passerby might offer the answer. "Is it meant to be like that?"

"Stop moaning and drink it," Ruby directs. "The sugar rush will do you good. Anyway —" she turns back to me, pouting "—I just wish I knew what really happened. This surmising is all so unsatisfactory."

She doesn't mean that. She's positively glowing with the thrill of a mystery. I know I should come out with it and burst her bubble, but I can't bring myself to. And so I tell myself that I'm simply changing the course of the conversation with my next question.

"What else do you know about him?"

I fiddle with the lid of my coffee cup, trying to appear casual. Honestly, I don't know why I'm asking anyway. It's not like I'm interested or anything. I have far more important things to occupy my mind, like obscure sentences uttered by handsome vets. Why would I want to know about boring old Professor Warwick?

"Not much." Ruby drains her latte and puts her takeaway cup down on the edge of the desk, where it wobbles precariously. "Just that he's some super-intelligent academic. I've heard Jeremy raving on about him. Apparently he's the youngest professor in his college or something. Sounds pretty one-dimensional, if you ask me."

Eve rescues the cup and deposits it safely in the paper bin. "Or one could say committed," she supplies kindly. "It does seem strange, though. A young man like that. He's always here, and on his own too. One would think he'd have other places to be."

"Why are you so interested in him all of a sudden?" Ruby asks with a suspicious glance at me. "Surely you can't be thinking about it ... I mean, you and *him*?"

Damn it all, but I can feel myself blushing. Why am I always blushing? It just makes me look guilty, even when I'm not.

"Of course not!" I bluster. "What a thought."

"You had me worried for a moment there. Believe me, Clara, he is *really* not your type." Her eyes light up. "Now, if you'll just let me set you up on that app I was telling you about ..."

"And ... that's my cue to leave," I say, scooping my bag up off the floor and making for the stairs.

"Don't run away," Ruby says warningly. "You always run away when I start talking about this."

"Work to be done," I trill, drowning her out.

"Clara!" she yells after me.

But it's too late. I've already gone.

Chapter 9

So, about the online dating thing.

It's not that I'm against the idea per se; after all, how could I be? I have friends who met on dating apps who are perfectly suited for one another. And Ruby seems to be a roaring success across multiple algorithms; she has a new date pretty much every night of the week. So, great. They work. For lots of people. They're just so ... *not me*.

And yes, I *know* lots of people have probably said that in the past. Lots of people who then went on to meet someone and had to admit they were wrong. But I just ... Look, for one thing, I'm pretty old-fashioned. I still use the word *date*, for crying out loud. Nothing about Ruby's cheap and cheerful hook-ups could possibly be described as a date. A date suggests conversation, for one thing, not to mention a beverage which hasn't been bought from the nearest off licence.

I suppose a part of me still thinks it's romantic to meet someone in person. The happenstance of catching someone's eye across a bookshop, or sitting next to one another in a café. Being introduced by a mutual friend at a party; that's how Freddie and Jess met. And yes, I know it was a freshers' party, and it probably wasn't in the least bit romantic, and I know that no one really meets in bookshops because, *come on*, I haven't lost all sense of reality. Although, to be fair, we *are* in Cambridge, and if ever there was a decent chance of meeting someone in a bookshop, then this is the place to do so.

But I'm digressing. I just like the idea of chance, of fate, of bumping into someone and looking in their eyes. Beginning to speak and perhaps not realising that in that moment something has begun. Something magical. Something life-changing. Something like my parents had.

I'm sure I can't be the only person who feels like this.

Can I?

Although I'll admit that sometimes I do wonder if Ruby might be right. Perhaps I'm just too stubborn for my own good. Perhaps the world really *has* changed, and I'm still looking for something that no longer exists. The chance meeting, the moment that you look up, and you see ...

The smile slides from my face. Professor Warwick. *Again*.

Believe me, I'm doing everything in my power to avoid him. But clearly the universe is in a puckish sort of mood because every time I turn around, there he is.

He was in the print room this morning when I popped in to ask the attendants a question. He was on the landing when I took a shortcut back to my office at lunchtime. I even caught a glimpse of him through the banisters at one point; he was downstairs, talking to Eve. It was only the briefest glimpse, and of the top of his head at that, but it was him.

I knew *immediately* that it was him. That was what

maddened me more than anything else. I'd know him anywhere, and he didn't even recognise me when I was sitting right in front of him. It seems unjust; I don't *want* to be so aware of him, but it seems I can't help it.

With a scowl at my own misfortune, I dart behind a pillar, considering my options.

There's only one way across the gallery, and it compels me to pass right in front of the window seat he's currently occupying. So, really, there *aren't* exactly a lot of options to consider. After all, I can't linger here indefinitely. A couple of people have already started to look at me strangely. Which, to be fair, is nothing new, but I feel that as my card is already marked by what happened yesterday, I should aim to keep my eccentricities to a minimum. I've already drawn quite enough attention to myself for one week as it is.

I look thoughtfully back at Professor Warwick. He seems pretty absorbed in what he's doing. Perhaps if I just breeze past him quickly, then he won't notice ...

My thoughts trail off as I find myself absorbed in studying him. Sitting there, with the late afternoon sunlight gleaming in his black hair, he doesn't look half as unapproachable as his reputation would suggest. He's wearing the same battered-looking tweed jacket as before and, beneath it, his shirt collar is askew. So far, so unremarkable. And then I see them.

Bright pink socks with turquoise polka dots, just visible beneath the hem of his trousers when he's sitting down. Something about those socks gives me a feeling of triumph, like I've uncovered a thrilling secret. The bookish young professor, so serious and repressed. And yet look! Those socks suggest the possibility of something else, of redemption, even. Maybe I've been too hard on him. Rude and sarcastic he might be, but I mean, *surely* no one who wears socks like that can be all bad?

Maybe I should go and talk to him. It would put an end to this awkward creeping around, if nothing else. It's somewhat difficult to get on with my job when I can't walk freely about the museum.

Just then he looks up and our eyes meet.

Oh, balls. Automatically, I duck back behind the pillar, then immediately berate myself for doing so. Way to make it all so, *so* much worse, Clara. As if it weren't bad enough that he caught me staring at him, then I had to go and hide as well. Now he'll think that I've got some weird fascination with him or something. Or worse, that I've developed a deep-seated crush after our accidental kiss yesterday. I press a hand to my forehead as my imagination dreams up worse and worse scenarios.

I'll have to leave the museum under a cloud, having been accused of stalking a visitor. And not just any visitor, either. A bloody Cambridge professor, of all things. A bloody superstar *prodigy* of a professor. In this city, that's the equivalent of an A-list actor. It'll be his word against mine. I won't stand a chance. He'll tell them all that I kissed him on purpose, that I followed him around the museum like a lovestruck teenager.

The temptation to slink away to my office and die quietly is overwhelming.

I take some deep, steadying breaths. All right, Clara. Calm down. You're overreacting, as usual. It's not that bad.

I risk another glance around the edge of the pillar.

Professor Warwick raises a hand in a wave.

I bolt back into the shadows.

Okay, so it's *quite* bad. But it's not entirely irremediable if I just go over there, act like everything's normal ... Adopt my cool, professional persona – if I can drag it out of whatever dusty cupboard it's been hiding in all these years. I think I last saw it at my interview for this job. Well, at the beginning of the interview, at least. It abandoned me after I upended an occasional table when they called me in, and I haven't seen hide nor hair of it since.

Leaving the safety of the column, I walk over to the window seat. Quickly, before I can change my mind.

"Good afternoon, Professor Warwick," I say pleasantly.

There, I'm quite pleased with that. I've struck just the right note. No one listening to me would imagine that anything was even remotely amiss.

He looks up, one eyebrow slightly raised in question. "You know who I am."

"Of course I do," I say primly. "It's my job to know what's going on in the museum."

"Yes, you're obviously quite ... actively involved," he says blandly. But something in the undercurrent of his voice makes my eyes narrow.

Why can he not just be civil? Is it beyond him, or something? At least I'm *trying* to be nice.

He must have seen something in my expression, because his face immediately softens. If I didn't know better by now, I'd almost say that he looks apologetic. But it seems I'm destined not to find out because, just as he opens his mouth to speak, a very different, very unwelcome voice fills the air between us.

"Ah, excellent. Just who I was looking for."

I freeze to the spot and, judging by the set of the professor's shoulders, he does the same. But then, I can hardly blame him. Jeremy tends to have that effect on people. He inspires a sense of doomed resignation which is quite unique.

"Good afternoon, Mr Haynes," he replies graciously, although I notice a flicker of wariness in his eyes. "What can we do for you?"

Jeremy casts a perfunctory glance in my direction. "Ah, Miss Swift. I didn't observe you there."

He practically mowed me down in his haste to beat a path to the window seat. I glower at the burgundy velvet-clad back which he turns upon me. But, to my amazement, he almost immediately turns again, including me in the conversation. "Actually, it's somewhat providential that you're here," he continues, in a tone which makes my heart sink. "Clara, my dear, you never told me that you were so well acquainted with the professor."

He never calls me Clara. My whole body tenses in trepidation. What's going on? He's looking exceedingly smug, even more so than usual. This does not bode well.

Professor Warwick doesn't say anything, but that doesn't appear to deter Jeremy in the slightest.

"She tells me that you've known each other for years." He gives a false-sounding laugh. "But then, she can be very modest about these things. Tell me, professor, where *did* you two meet?"

I feel nauseous. So, this is it, then. I swear, after this, I will never lie about anything ever again. I'm officially cured. Never again shall an untruth pass my lips. Even if Heather gets her hair cut into another bob and asks me if it makes her look middle-aged. I'll be honest. I won't spare her feelings.

I screw my eyes up and wait for the inevitable.

"Oh, it's been about three years now, I believe. But time goes so quickly, don't you find?"

My eyes snap open in shock. Jeremy appears to have been stunned into silence, his throat working uselessly. Professor Warwick, on the other hand, looks as impassive as ever. He closes the book in his lap. "Was there anything else? Only I've got an evening lecture across town in half an hour."

"Of course, of course," Jeremy squeaks, looking stricken. "I'm very sorry to have bothered you, professor. I had no idea that you and Miss Swift here ..." he stares at me in something bordering on horror, as if I'm something which has just crawled out of the gutter "... were truly an item."

"We're not," both the professor and I say at the same time.

Now it's *my* turn to be horrified. What a thought.

"Just a professional relationship," I say firmly. Out of the corner of my eye, I detect the hint of a smile cross his lips.

"Indeed. A meeting of minds, one might say."

"But ..." Jeremy looks perturbed. "The ... er ..." He goes delightfully crimson. Clearly, he can't bring himself to utter the word.

Oh, yes. The *kiss*. How are we going to explain that? Even the professor looks momentarily at a loss, although he soon recovers himself.

"A throwback to my Sicilian ancestry," he says smoothly. "It's considered good business practice to embrace upon each meeting. It appeases the gods, you see."

It takes everything I have not to look at him disbelievingly.

"I see," Jeremy breathes. "I never knew. Well, how fascinating."

There's an awkward little quiver of silence, during which we all look at the floor.

"Well," I burst out at last.

"Yes, quite right, Miss Swift," Jeremy says eagerly, despite the fact that I hadn't even posed a statement. "Must be getting on. Can't waste time. Professor, good to see you, as always." He goes to hold out his hand, then hesitates. "I'm sorry. Should we ... er ...?" He steps forward, spreading his arms fumblingly.

"No," the professor says stonily. "A handshake's fine."

Jeremy appears to almost sag with sheer relief, clasping the proffered hand as though it's a life raft of reserved English respectability.

"Don't you dare say anything," Professor Warwick warns in an undertone as we watch Jeremy totter away out of sight. "And if you even *think* about laughing ..."

"I would never," I say solemnly.

"Good. Because this is your fault, you know. And if I now find that my colleagues start coming up to me in the quadrangle and try to kiss me ..."

I decide that now's an excellent time to have a coughing fit.

"I can't legislate for Jeremy," I say at last, when I've recovered sufficiently to speak. I still can't believe he actually lied for me. "But I promise it won't have come from me. I owe you a huge debt of gratitude, Professor ..." I break off with a frustrated sigh, sitting down next to him on the seat. "What *is* your name, anyway?"

He looks at me as though nobody's ever asked him that before. "My name?"

Lord, but he's impossible.

"Your given name? Surely you weren't christened Professor Warwick?"

"Oh, that." He shuffles his feet. "It's Adam. But no one really uses ..."

"Adam." I test it out loud. I like it. It's uncomplicated, not at all what I was expecting. I was anticipating a Matthias or an Ebenezer. Something antiquated and unusual, belonging to another time, a bit like himself.

"Yes, well, like I said, I don't tend to ..."

I cut him off with a quelling look.

"On second thoughts, Adam's fine," he mumbles.

"Good. And you can call me Clara."

He looks pained at the very idea, but at least he doesn't protest.

"Thank you," I say haltingly. "You ... you didn't have to do any of that, you know. You don't owe me anything."

I still don't understand why he did it. After all, it's not even as if he *likes* me. Why would he put himself in such an awkward position on my behalf?

"I hope you'll take it as an apology, of sorts." He looks away, but not fast enough for me to miss the pink tinge which is creeping up his neck. He clears his throat, making a detailed inspection of the ceiling rose above our heads. "For my behaviour yesterday. I've been ... ah ... told in the past that I can be somewhat ... shall we say, insensitive?"

"Surely not," I murmur before I can stop myself.

Luckily, my sarcasm seems to bypass him completely.

"I'm not always very good at reading a situation, you see. I'm afraid I can come across more harshly than intended." He turns his head and I find myself looking deep into his cobalt eyes. From this close, I can see the grey flecks in them, the paler blue halo round the pupils. I don't think I've ever really studied someone's eyes like this before. It's strangely fascinating. Also ... sort of intense. I half want to look away, but another part of me finds that I can't.

"Shall we call it even?" I manage.

"Fair enough. Although I imagine the balance will tilt again before long. You seem to be a magnet for trouble."

I draw back with an accusing glare. "I thought you were going to be nicer to me!"

A smile touches the edges of his mouth. "I never actually said that. Not in so many words."

"Clara—" Ruby materialises breathlessly in front of us "—your brother's been on the phone for you. He couldn't get through on your mobile, so he rang the front desk instead. He's heard from the vet."

With a lurch of guilt, I picture my phone sitting upstairs on my desk. Here I am, sitting around with Professor ... sorry, *Adam*, and all the while my poor beloved Casper has been undergoing surgery. I sit bolt upright.

"Is everything okay? What happened?"

"What?" Ruby looks confused. Then her face clears. "Oh, no, it all went fine. In fact, they've said he can go home this afternoon. That's what Freddie was calling about. He was asking if you wanted him to go." Her gaze slides across to Adam, who's following the conversation with a detached air. "Shall I tell him you're busy?"

Something about her assessing tone of voice pricks at me. Suddenly, I'm all too aware of how close together we are, squeezed into the window seat. It didn't seem at all strange whilst we were talking, but now ... Feeling uncomfortable, I scramble to my feet, forcing myself not to look at Adam.

"No, it's all right. I'll do it myself."

Chapter 10

"Home sweet home," I say merrily to Casper, as at long last our house comes into view. And not a moment too soon either. Is it just me, or has this cat got heavier in the past eight hours? If it weren't for the neat row of stitches across his side, I would begin to wonder if he hadn't had an operation at all, but instead spent the day flirting with the nurses and being fed cat treats.

A disgruntled snuffling sound is the only response I get.

"Are you *seriously* still sulking?" I hoik the basket up so I can look him in the face. "I came to get you, didn't I? What more do you want?"

Two green eyes glower at me from the shadows.

"I mean, I could have sent Freddie, but *no*—" I'm on a roll now "—no, I, loving owner that I am, made a twenty-minute detour across town to come and fetch you myself. But are you grateful? Not a bit of it."

He cocks his head to one side and gives me a hard stare.

"Okay, so perhaps it wasn't *entirely* for your benefit," I admit reluctantly. "The very attractive vet was something of an incentive. But it was mostly about you."

He flops down at the bottom of the basket with a sceptical huff.

He's so dramatic sometimes. I roll my eyes as I flick the catch on the wrought iron gate which leads to our house.

I still love coming home, even after all these years. My house might be little, but it's one of my favourite places in the world. It's a narrow Victorian structure, wedged in between two others in a space which, frankly, wasn't really big enough for a house at all. These days, they'd never get planning permission. Only one room wide across the front, with three storeys and a steeply pitched roof, the whole thing looks like it's been squeezed into shape. Its odd proportions give it a slightly unreal look, like a doll's house, or something a child might draw, but that's sort of what I like about it.

My landlady is a lovely old woman who's owned the place for decades. Every year, she hikes the rent by about ten pounds a year. I half wonder why she bothers, but it suits me so I keep quiet about it. I'd never be able to afford a place like this by myself otherwise.

When the front of the house needed repainting a couple of years ago, I offered to do it myself, on the proviso that I could choose the colour, and now it's a pale sugar mouse pink, with a white door and window frames. We've continued the arrangement inside, enabling me to have a sunshine yellow kitchen with sky blue cabinets, a lilac bedroom and an apple green bathroom. God knows what she'll think when I finally move out and she sees what she's let herself in for.

I squeeze through the gate, taking care to stick to the garden path. I've planted the front lawn with a mass of bulbs and, although it doesn't look like much at this time of year, it's a riot of colour in the spring and summer. There's no method to my planting scheme, only madness. I just chose everything I liked and put it all in together. I like to think it has a certain whimsical vibe, like an enchanted meadow.

I'm halfway to the front door when a voice stops me in my tracks.

"Miss Swift. Just who I was on my way to see."

I look longingly at the door, some two feet ahead of me. So near, yet so far. What else can anyone possibly want from me today?

Apprehensively, I turn my head to see the head of the local fire department advancing along the pavement towards me, a determined look on his face. Automatically, I plonk Casper down unceremoniously behind a rosebush, earning me a faint hiss of complaint. Luckily, though, he's still too groggy from the anaesthetic to protest more volubly.

"Hello—" I plaster a smile across my face, edging sideways so I'm half obscuring the rosebush "—Captain ... er ... Officer ..." I've never known how to address him. What titles do firefighters have, anyway? "*Mr* Trueman. What a surprise. To what do I owe this honour?"

"Thought you'd be wanting this back." He produces a red cat collar from his pocket. Casper's collar: I recognise the frayed edges where he chewed the bells off. I bought it in the hope that maybe it would stem the death toll of small, furry rodents which found their way onto the kitchen floor of a morning. Within half an hour of me putting it round his neck, the bells had mysteriously disappeared and three mangled shrews lay mockingly upon the doormat.

Since then, I've never tried to interfere with his hunting habits again.

"Oh, yes, thank you." I take the collar from Trueman's hand, hoping that now he's run his errand he'll be on his way. But he doesn't move.

"How is that cat of yours, anyway? Keeping out of mischief, I hope."

"Oh, yes." I nod vigorously, mentally pleading with Casper to stay quiet. "He's a reformed character these days."

Perhaps that was a step too far. Trueman's heavy brow thuds down over his eyes. "Somehow, I doubt it. There's no reforming a wild animal like that, Miss Swift, none at all."

A growl emerges from the depths of the rosebush and, for once, I agree with the sentiment. Wild animal, indeed. I feel rather affronted on Casper's behalf.

"You'd be best off giving him to one of those shelters," Trueman's saying now, clasping his hands behind his back. "They'd know what to do with him. Then you could get yourself something nicer to have around. A guinea pig, maybe." He gives me a pointed look. "Something which doesn't cause my finest men to be scrambling about in trees. Jennings' ankle is almost recovered, by the way."

Ah, so now we've got to the point. I *knew* he wouldn't be able to resist.

Casper and the Cambridge fire department do not get along. Much like Casper and the vet. And Casper and the postman. And Casper and the neighbours. And Casper and ... Oh, look, you get where I'm going with this. It's a good thing that I'm on his side, because he's made enemies out of pretty much everyone else in the city.

"I'm pleased to hear that," I say tightly.

Of course, I *am* sorry about what happened. I can still hear the crunch that ankle made as it hit the ground. But, at the same time, it was his own fault that he fell out of the tree. He didn't hold onto Casper tightly enough; what did he expect to happen? You'd think one of the things they'd train firefighters to do is hold a cat properly, at the very least.

I did try and suggest that to Trueman afterwards, but one look at his face told me that it wasn't the time. Maybe I'll try again at a later date. When it isn't all quite so recent.

There's a pause in the conversation, and I allow myself to feel hopeful that he might take his cue and leave, but then he says, with a sort of forced casualness, "Just out of interest, where is he at the moment?"

I feign innocence. "Who?"

"Your *cat*," he says, more sharply. "Where is he?"

Ah, now it all makes sense. This was never about simply bringing back a collar. He's checking up on us.

"Inside, I should expect," I reply tartly. "As I said, he's been lying low recently."

Should I be worried at how easily lies seem to slip off my tongue these days? Before Casper came into my life, I scarcely even knew how to lie. I'd always give myself away, or trip up somehow. Now look at me. I could go into politics.

The rosebush rustles. Trueman glances at it; for an awful

moment I think he's about to go over and look, but instead he steps back with a resigned shake of the head.

"Let's just hope it stays that way, then." He purses his lips ominously. "But if I find that he's been causing any more mayhem ..."

"He won't," I say quickly, as the bush begins to vibrate with more intensity. Casper's obviously grown bored of his confinement, and is trying to break his way out of the basket. "I promise."

"Did you hear that?" I say to Casper as I yank him out from behind the foliage. Now I'm making promises for you. Promises which we both know I'm in no position to keep. You're a law unto yourself."

He butts the roof of the basket with his head.

"Yes, fine, I get the message. I'll let you out." I forage in my coat pocket for my house keys. "But not until we're inside. I've had enough drama for the time being. For once, you are going to have a quiet night in. *No* arguments," I say sternly, as he opens his mouth to yowl in dissent. "That's my final word."

He glares at me venomously, before burying his head beneath the blanket.

I sigh as I turn the key in the lock. It's going to be a very long evening.

***

"Do you think he looks peaky?" I ask, peering around the side of the kitchen table. Casper's dozing in his basket, one paw over his eyes. He looks so adorable that I can almost be lulled into forgetting about the vengeful offering which was waiting in my slipper this morning when I got out of bed.

"He's fine," Heather says shortly, without even turning around to look. "He was running up and down the curtains half an hour ago. Hardly the sign of a cat who's at death's door."

With a small frown, I pick up the cafetière. "More coffee?"

"Please." She sits back in her chair, looking around the room approvingly. "It looks nice in here. Have you tidied up?"

She makes it sound as though I usually live in squalor. Although, by her standards, I probably do. While I've tried to explain to her that the mismatched china and faded old velvet sofa are all things I actually *chose*, I'm not sure that she really believes me. To her mind, everyone should want nothing more than to live in a haze of minimalist neutrals. She probably thinks I've dragged half of my stuff out of a skip. In fact, I *know* she does. I once caught her sterilising my cutlery with boiling water from the kettle before using it.

"I might have rearranged a few things." I busy myself spooning sugar into my cup.

All right, so maybe I have tidied up just a little. Something about seeing Heather's house the other day shamed me into making more of an effort. I even got Freddie to reach right to the back of the cupboard for the cafetière. That hadn't seen the light of day in years. It was a moving in present, I think, although who from, I can't even begin—

"And you've got the cafetière out which we gave you," Heather says, turning it around to admire it. "I've never seen you use it before. I'd begun to think you didn't like it."

I take an overly large gulp of coffee. "I just ... save it for special occasions, that's all."

"Oh, right." She cradles the cup between her palms, motioning towards the living room doorway with her head. "Do you think they're all right in there?"

"Don't worry about it. Freddie's really good with kids. Oscar will be absolutely fine."

"It wasn't Oscar I was worried about," she says drily.

As if on cue, there's a yelp from next door. Whether it came from man or child, I honestly couldn't say. I half wonder if we should go and check, but Heather doesn't stir a muscle. She just carries on sipping her coffee serenely.

Casper stretches in his basket, blinking indignantly at the sudden disturbance.

"Are you sure he doesn't look just the tiniest bit peaky?" I try again, hopefully.

"Clara, if you want to call your vet, just call him," Heather says with uncharacteristic impatience. "There's no need to develop a case of Munchausen by proxy over it. He gave you his number, didn't he?"

"Yes, but ..."

"And told you to call him?"

"And told me to call him *if* Casper showed any signs of going downhill," I correct her. "That's not the same thing."

Heather emits something which can only be described as a harrumph. "Yeah, right. Because it's your *cat* he's really interested in."

I reach for a biscuit, shaking my head. "You'll have to give me a moment to respond to that. I'm still getting over the fact that you just *harrumphed* at me. I didn't know people really did that."

"They do when there's a valid reason for it," she says pertly. "What are you so worried about, anyway?"

I pause, the biscuit hovering halfway to my lips.

"I have no idea what you're talking about." Even to my own ears, it's a pathetic-sounding denial.

"You know what I mean." I watch in astonishment as she selects a biscuit and proceeds to dunk it forcefully into her coffee. I've never seen her do that before. She really must be rattled with me. "Let's face it, you've hardly lived the life of a nun, Clara."

My head shoots up. "Thanks a lot!"

"You know what I mean. It's not like you've never played the dating game before. You know when a guy's flirting with you. You know how to read between the lines. So what's the real problem here?"

I stuff a biscuit in my mouth, playing for time. The truth is that I know exactly what the problem is. Unfortunately, it seems Heather does too.

"You're overthinking it again, aren't you?" she says sternly, putting her cup down on the table with a thud. "Look, Clara, it's not as if you have to marry the man. You promised me that you were going to take things more steadily; well, here's a chance to practise. You go out once, see how it goes. If nothing comes of it, then fine. Chalk it up to experience and move on."

She pushes the card across the table till it's resting next to my hand. "*Call him*. What's the worst that can happen?"

I look up at the ceiling. Where do I start?

"Rejection. Abject humiliation. A waste of a good bra ..."

She smiles. "Nothing new, then."

I'm not even going to pretend to be affronted. After all, she does have something of a point there.

"All right, then." I hold up my hands. "As usual, you're right. I bow to your better judgement."

"I should start charging by the hour for this," she mutters into her cup. "I'd make an absolute fortune."

Chapter 11

"All right," I say to Casper as I plump the sofa cushions for about the third time in as many minutes. "Now, you remember the plan?"

He looks up at me with a bored expression.

"No running up the curtains. No leaping off furniture. And certainly *no* bringing in of dead animals. Just try to look ... subdued, okay?"

He hops up onto the sofa, flattening the cushion I've just plumped so carefully. I narrow my eyes at him.

"Seeing as I require your co-operation in this, I'll let that go." I point a finger. "But *only* if you hold up your end of the bargain. I'm relying on you here."

He just yawns, needling the cushion with his claws. I regard him dubiously. "You're not exactly filling me with confidence."

In retrospect, putting my fate in the paws of a raging sociopath wasn't perhaps the wisest move I've ever made. But in the end I didn't give myself much of a choice. As soon as I heard Josh's voice on the other end of the phone, all of Heather's prudent advice just whooshed straight out of my head, replaced with a kind of woolly panic. I totally froze up. So when he asked if Casper was all right ...

I said no.

Or, rather, I heard a voice which sounded like mine say no. It's all still a bit fuzzy, even now.

I cast a glance at the cat in question. He looks as far from ill as you can get. In fact, he's recovered so admirably from his operation that I've had a hell of a time trying to keep him inside over the past couple of days.

"How do I look?" I ask, checking my make-up in the over-mantle mirror. Honestly, you'd think I'd never had a man in the house before, the way I'm jittering around the place.

I'm not usually this nervous before ... well, I suppose I can hardly call it a date. I believe that the term *date* would imply a willingness, or at least an awareness, between both parties. As far as Josh's concerned, this is a professional call.

So a date that's not a date. Which, incidentally, is really hard to dress for. My bedroom looks like a tornado's been through it. I had just about every item of clothing I own out in a bid to achieve an *I'm-just-hanging-out-at-home-but-looking-really-glamorous-while-I'm-at-it* kind of vibe. God bless whoever invented jumper dresses is all I can say. They have my eternal gratitude.

Like I said, I'm never usually this nervous. As Heather so charitably put it, this isn't exactly my first rodeo. But something's different this time; there was a spark between us, a natural yet unexpected alchemy. I felt it in the consulting room, despite the less-than-romantic surroundings and the hindrance of a cantankerous cat watching our every move. I felt it again later, when he handed me his card and asked me to call him. And when his fingers accidentally brushed mine, electricity seemed to tingle all the way up my arm.

It's been so long since I last felt anything of the kind that I suppose I'm almost afraid of it, somehow. Like it's such a rare, fragile thing that it might break if I get too close.

I daren't tell Heather any of this; she'd kill me. I'm supposed to be taking it slowly. But I can't help how I feel, can I?

The knock on the door makes me jump, even though I've been expecting it for the past ten minutes. "Showtime," I say to Casper, tucking a stray strand of hair behind my ear. "Let's do this."

A disinterested flick of the tail is the only movement he makes.

I skid across the polished wooden floor of the hallway, almost wrenching open the front door in my haste. Already, not the finest of starts.

"Hello," he says with a lopsided smile which makes my stomach flip. For a moment, I can only blink back at him. I'd almost forgotten how good-looking he is.

"You're not wearing your scrubs," I blurt out, already despairing of myself before the sentence is even finished. *Really, Clara? That's your opening line?*

"I stopped in at home to change," he says. "That's why I'm a bit late. I hope you don't mind?"

"Not at all," I say shyly. It was a good choice. He might be one of the few people who can make bright green scrubs look good, but he looks even better in a shirt and jeans. Particularly when the shirt's a soft cerulean blue which complements his golden skin tone and picks out the blond tones in his hair. He looks more like he belongs by the sea in the Californian sunshine than a residential street in Cambridge on a dim October night.

Belatedly remembering that I need to at least try and behave like a normal human being, I shake myself free of my thoughts and stand back to let him pass. "Come on in."

Through the doorway to the living room, I see Casper's head pop up at the sound of a new voice. His ears are pricked and he's staring intently at Josh. That's not a good sign. For the first time, I start to have misgivings. I was so wrapped up in how I felt about Josh coming over that I never really stopped to think how Casper might react. What if I've made a terrible miscalculation? After all, behaving decently while we were at the vet's is one thing; he might have liked Josh well enough in that setting, but what about when his territory is being invaded?

"Evening, Casper," Josh says cheerfully, bending down to scoop him up.

I lurch forwards. "Wait, perhaps you shouldn't—"

I break off. Casper's already lying happily on his back in Josh's arms, purring like an engine.

Josh glances up apologetically. "Sorry, what were you saying?"

"It doesn't matter," I say faintly as Josh scratches Casper's tummy. Normally, that's something he'll only let me and Freddie do. What is happening to my cat?

"I have to say, he doesn't look too bad," Josh says thoughtfully.

Bugger. I'd forgotten about that.

"Er, yes ... amazing how they can suddenly pick up, isn't it?" I manage in a strained voice.

"Quite," he says. His tone is perfectly serious but his eyes are glittering with amusement. "Having said that, I'd perhaps better stick around for a while. Just in case he relapses, you know?"

My heart flutters in my chest. This is definitely *not* standard procedure.

"Oh, yes," I say breathlessly. Then, striving for a more normal voice, "Would you like a drink?"

"I think it could be more serious than that," he says mildly. "Have you had dinner yet?"

That's an unexpected question if ever there was one.

"No, I haven't."

As if I could eat with the prospect of him turning up on my doorstep. I'd forgotten how slimming a crush could be.

"We'd better fix that, then. How about I cook something for you?" He turns to look at me and laughs. "You don't have to look so worried, you know. I *can* cook."

"I don't have a lot in," I say hesitantly, watching as he begins to rummage around in the cupboards. I hope he doesn't come across anything too out of date.

"I'm sure we can manage." He extracts a tin of olives from the top shelf. "It's amazing what you can do with store cupboard ingredients."

"It's usually better stocked." I feel the need to defend my domestic capabilities. "But it's all been somewhat chaotic around here lately. My brother turned up out of the blue about a week ago and ..."

Hang on, come to think of it, where *is* Freddie? I didn't hear him go out, but then I haven't noticed him thundering about upstairs either. Surreptitiously, I back towards the doorway, poking my head out into the hall. His coat's not on the rack. And his shoes, normally kicked haphazardly across the mat, are conspicuous by their absence. I breathe a sigh of relief as I move back to my original position in the centre of the kitchen. That could have been uncomfortable.

"And then, of course, there's Casper," I continue easily, hoping Josh won't notice the pause. "He's been keeping me on my toes."

As though summoned by the sound of his name, Casper comes trotting into the room. I reach down to stroke his head but he bypasses me completely, winding around Josh's legs instead.

"Traitor," I mutter under my breath. He'd do well to remember who feeds him.

Josh drizzles oil into a pan and adds some finely chopped onions.

"I seem to have taken over your kitchen," he says sheepishly when he catches me looking. "Sorry. You get used to cooking at rapid speed when you work the hours I do."

"No, honestly ... it's nice." I'm still a bit dazed at the sight of him making himself at home so confidently. It's like he's been here a hundred times.

Belatedly becoming aware that I'm staring, I open the fridge and survey the contents. There was a newly opened bottle of wine in here yesterday which I'm hoping Freddie hasn't got to in the interim. "So, where were you before? Before you came to Cambridge, I mean?"

I feel I should know something more about the man standing in my kitchen than simply that he's dashingly handsome.

"London." He tosses the onions in the pan with a flick of the wrist. "A huge practice. I didn't like it much. Everything always had to be rushed. I prefer to take the time to understand my patients."

He calls them patients. That's so sweet. It's almost enough to give me a warm glow. Although, of course, that could just be the wine.

"Animals aren't like people," he's saying now. "They can't just tell you what's wrong. Not in so many words, at least. You have to be patient, coax it out of them in other ways. Learn to speak their language. Of course—" he casts a meaningful look down at Casper, who's rubbing against his shin lovingly "—some are more voluble than others."

"Oh, really?" I wander over to the oven on the pretence of stirring the sauce. In truth, I just want to be nearer to Josh. Somehow, he just seems to draw me closer like a magnet. I can't stay away. "And what is he saying right now?"

He leans back against the kitchen counter, surveying me over the rim of his wineglass. "He says that he likes his new vet very much."

"Does he now?" A little thrill runs through me, and I bite my lip. I wonder if it's a concerning sign that he's such an accomplished flirt. He always knows how to say exactly the right thing. "And what else does he have to say?"

"That he wants his dinner."

Casper finally begins to look interested in our conversation. I hide a smile. "It's not his dinner time yet."

Josh shrugs. "He thought it was worth trying his luck. He says it often works. Apparently you're a soft touch."

Casper miaows in agreement.

"I most certainly am not." I tilt my chin. "I'll have you know that I have a resolve of steel."

Is it just me, or are we suddenly very close? I can practically feel the heat radiating off his body.

"That's a shame," he says softly. "It wouldn't be worth me trying *my* luck, then?"

I look up into his eyes. They're an amazing shade of green in this light, and filled with something which makes my breath hitch and my pulse leap. And in that moment I know that I'll be breaking my promise to Heather. I couldn't go slowly right now if I tried. I'm already all in.

"I wouldn't say that, exactly." I close the gap between us. "I'm not completely impervious to persuasion."

"Good. Then let me persuade you."

And the next thing I know, his lips are on mine.

Chapter 12

I wake up slowly, as I always do, taking my time to stretch luxuriantly before my eyelids flutter open. Sunlight streams through a gap in the curtains, pooling across my blossom-patterned duvet.

I roll over onto my side, pulling the covers with me with a sigh of deepest content. I *love* Saturdays. No hurry to get up, no rushed breakfast, no museum. No *Jeremy* ...

Wait, what was that? My eyes pop open as I become aware of a sound drifting up through the floorboards. I lie there, ears straining to pick up on the faint melody.

Music. Coming from my kitchen. I reach for my phone, tension coiling in my stomach: half past eight. Freddie still exists in an owl-like mixture of student and barman time. I've never known him to surface much before nine-thirty. So, either I have a very audacious burglar down there, or else ...

Very slowly, I turn my head to look across at the pillow next to me. There's a dent in the centre of it.

Suddenly, it's all there, a blur of recollection jostling for space in the front of my brain. First the wine. Then the kiss. Then ...

I prop myself up on my elbows as I recall that particular part. Did I really *do* that?

Almost of its own accord, a rising bubble of hysterical laughter rises to my lips and I clasp a hand across my mouth to stop it bursting out. Oh, yes, I most certainly did. And he did.

Oh, the things he did …

Ahem. On second thoughts, perhaps you don't need to know the details. Suffice it to say, I had a *very* nice time.

And he's still here.

Rolling out of bed with such enthusiasm that I almost land flat on the floor, I snatch my kimono from its hook on the back of the door, pausing only to scrutinise my appearance in the full-length mirror. I've never been sure what people mean when they talk about a post-sex glow; personally, I always just look rumpled and faintly exhausted. I run a hand over my hair in an attempt to reinstate some sort of control, before accepting that it's a losing game and purposefully tousling it instead. Sexy bedhead it is, then.

I gallop down the stairs, skidding to a halt in the kitchen doorway and trying to adopt an insouciant air. As it turns out, it's a wasted venture because he's got his back to me as he stands at the oven. I look around in amazement; rarely does my little kitchen see such industry of a morning. Coffee brews in the cafetière, bacon sizzles in a pan on the hob and sitting on the bread board is an artisan-looking loaf, already cut into neat slices.

"Morning," I say shyly.

He turns, and warmth flickers in the depths of his green eyes. "Morning. Do you want some breakfast?"

I wander over to pour myself some coffee, passing close by him as I do so. I kind of want to put my arms around him, but I can't quite bring myself to be so bold. What's the etiquette in these situations? I've never had a one-night stand cook me breakfast before.

Then again, I've never met anyone quite like Josh before. He has a way of making everything seem too easy and natural; there's none of the usual awkwardness that comes after a spontaneous sexual encounter. It feels totally normal, somehow, that he's here, pottering around in my kitchen. Like he's my boyfriend, not someone I only met three days ago.

Hang on ... was it really only three days ago? Okay, when I put it like that, this does all sound rather precipitate. I'm kind of beginning to see Heather's point.

I'm saved from my own thoughts as he snags me by the waist and pulls me against him, bending his head to brush a kiss across my lips. It fairly takes my breath away, and I sound decidedly wheezy as I ask, "How long have you been up?"

"A while. I wake up at six every morning, whether I like it or not. Yet another hazard of the job. You were still sleeping; I thought I might as well make good use of the time."

He flips the bacon, and my stomach responds with a low growl.

"This looks amazing. I'm absolutely starving."

He smiles knowingly. "I thought you might be."

I'm about to reach up and kiss him again when a movement catches the corner of my eye, and I spin around to see Freddie sitting at the far end of the kitchen table, a half eaten bacon sandwich in front of him.

"*Freddie*," I splutter, automatically springing away from Josh. "I didn't think you were up and about yet."

"Evidently," he says, with a barely disguised smirk.

I glare at him.

He looks back at me with raised eyebrows.

"My fault, I'm afraid." Josh's transferring the bacon onto a slice of bread, so has missed our silent sibling exchange. "I opened the kitchen door when I came downstairs and Casper got through. I had no idea he could be so quick."

"He came straight upstairs and jumped on my bed," Freddie adds petulantly.

I smile privately to myself. Casper's bad behaviour does have its occasional uses.

"You did get breakfast by way of apology," Josh points out good-naturedly.

"True," Freddie muses. "Why don't we ever have bacon sandwiches in the morning, Clara?"

"Because this isn't a hotel," I retort.

Josh slices the sandwich into triangles and puts it on a plate, which he hands to me.

"Are you not having one?" I ask in surprise as he starts putting the things away.

"I ate earlier. Besides, I'd better get going. I have hockey practice at half nine."

I bite into my sandwich and try to swallow my disappointment. Although I suppose I get to carry the image of him scampering around in brief shorts for the rest of the day, which is some consolation.

Vaguely, I realise that he's still talking.

"I'm sorry to rush off like this, but I'll give you a call later, okay?" he's saying as he grabs his jacket off the back of the chair, checking the pockets for his phone. And then, just as soon as he appeared, he's gone, only pausing to brush a kiss across my lips before he's off into the cold, bright morning with a slam of the front door.

Silence reigns in the kitchen for several moments. Then, with a sharp intake of breath, I force myself to look at Freddie.

"He was just ... I mean, that was nothing ..."

He doesn't look impressed by my bungled attempts at an explanation.

"Clara, you're a twenty-five-year-old woman. You can do what you like. You won't hear any judgement from me."

For a second, I don't know how to respond. I'm actually quite touched that he's being so understanding. Maybe he really *has* started to grow up lately.

My train of thought comes to an abrupt end as he proceeds to ruin it by adding, "Even if it *is* with the local vet. What next? The milkman? The man who delivers fish on a Friday?"

He's impossible. Usually, I could take the joke, but suddenly a strange mood has come over me. Josh's kiss is still tingling on my lips; now he's gone, I feel listless and fidgety. How am I ever going to concentrate on anything else today?

I need a distraction. But what ...?

I'd begun to stalk out of the room in umbrage, but now I slowly turn on the spot as an idea begins to form in my mind.

"What are you doing today, dearest brother of mine?"

He immediately looks suspicious. "Why are you asking?"

I'll take that as nothing, then.

"Upstairs," I command, whipping his empty plate away before he can protest. "You can have the first shower."

Now he just looks wary. "Why, what are we doing?"

I drop the plate into the dishwasher and close the door. "Get dressed and you'll find out."

***

"*Punting?*"

The incredulity in Freddie's voice is palpable.

I roll my eyes in exasperation. "Yes," I explain slowly. "It's involves a boat, a river and a pole."

"I *know* what it is. But why?"

That's about the twelfth time he's used the word *why* already, and it's barely eleven o'clock in the morning. It's like having a small child with me.

"Why not? We used to do it all the time when we were kids."

Dad used to take us. I don't say that part out loud but, by the beat of silence which follows, I know that Freddie's thinking it all the same.

He points at a nearby punt, which is bobbing gently on the surface of the water. "That looks like a reasonably sturdy craft."

I clamber in tentatively, only to be followed by Freddie jumping on after me. I clutch at the sides as the boat wobbles precariously. "Freddie! I don't want us to capsize."

"I think it's pretty hard to capsize one of these." He retrieves the pole and passes it over to me. "Come on, then. You can do the first leg. If I remember rightly, you'll be whingeing for me to take over before we've made it to the second bridge."

I stand on the back of the boat, trying to keep my balance. The smooth surface of the wood is wet and the rubber soles of my plimsolls struggle to gain much purchase. I prod at the riverbed with the pole.

Nothing happens.

"We're causing a queue," Freddie points out, somewhat unhelpfully.

"It's harder than it looks!" I snap.

With a gargantuan effort, I try again, jubilant when the boat inches forward slightly.

Okay, so here's something I'd forgotten about punting. The boats apparently have a mind all of their own. No matter how hard I try, it's almost impossible to make it go straight. Instead, we zigzag along the river in a disjointed, lurching fashion for several painstaking minutes, Freddie looking less and less impressed as we go on.

"Do you want me to take over?" he asks at last.

"I'm fine," I say, feeling hopelessly flustered. "I'm just ... reacquainting myself with the technique, that's all."

We go under a low arched bridge and I duck, almost losing control of the boat altogether in the process. *Why* did I have to suggest this? I think despairingly. I'd thought that doing something nostalgic would be a good chance for us to bond, maybe even get him to open up to me about what's on his mind. Now I'm wondering if we couldn't have bonded just as well over a drink in a nice warm pub somewhere.

As we emerge from beneath the bridge, though, the sight

which greets us immediately makes me take it all back. How could I have forgotten about this view?

There's a reason they call this stretch of the river the Cambridge Backs. All along the bank, flanked by manicured lawns and terraced gardens, is a part of Cambridge which can only really be seen from the water. The backs of the colleges rise up out of the ground in towers of honey-coloured stone, every piece as impressive as the frontages which face onto the street. We pass King's College chapel, its unmistakable outline reaching for the heavens. Clare College sits solidly next to it, a rigid block of pure Classical architecture, softened by serene walled gardens with views out across the river.

"Best view in Cambridge," Freddie and I both murmur in unison, before looking at one another in surprise.

"You remember that?" I ask.

"Yeah, but I didn't think you did." His eyes glaze over wistfully. "Those were some of the best days of our childhood. Dad loved it out here."

"It was a lot of fun, even when it was going wrong," I agree. "Do you remember the time when the pole got stuck in the mud on the riverbed and Dad ended up clinging onto it while the boat drifted away with us in it? We weren't very old at the time."

Freddie smiles in recollection. "And he made us swear never to tell Mum about it."

"She'd have killed us all if she'd found out. I suppose we're lucky that it turned out the way it did. It could have been much worse."

"We'd have been fine. Dad always knew what to do." Freddie

sighs deeply. "Sometimes I wish there was a way that I could still ask him stuff. Get his advice, you know?"

He's gazing out across the surface of the water, looking totally lost, and in that moment I know that we're talking about something specific here.

This is the moment. I might not get another opening.

"Freddie," I venture. "You know, if there's anything you want to tell me ..."

A heavy thud makes us both jump. The boat, left to its own devices while we were talking, has lodged itself firmly against the side of the riverbank. I try to push off, but it won't budge.

"Are we stuck?" Freddie asks, watching me beadily.

"Er ... no."

"We *are*, aren't we?" He stands, causing the boat to rock from side to side. "Here, hand it over. I'll fix this."

His patronising tone makes me bristle. "I'm perfectly capable of doing it myself."

"Don't be stubborn, Clara." He's grabbed the pole and is trying to wrench it out of my grasp. "Just give it to me."

"No way." I yank it back towards me. "Let go."

"*You* let go."

"No, *you*—"

My feet slip backwards. The momentum's against me and for a split second I'm in mid-air.

Then I hit the water. It crashes over my head, submerging me in its icy embrace. I surface, gasping with cold and shock.

"Clara!" Freddie's peering down at me from the safety of the boat. "Are you all right?"

"All right?" I screech, flapping my arms around wildly in fury. "No, I am bloody *not* all right. I'm in the river!"

He actually starts to laugh, the swine.

"Are you crazy?" a voice bellows from somewhere along the bank.

The next thing I know, there's a splash as someone takes a flying leap into the water. I go still, watching in astonishment as they emerge, dripping wet and furious.

"What the hell?" Adam splutters as water cascades off his head. Then his eyes lock with mine. "It's *you*. Why am I not surprised?"

Chapter 13

"What are you doing here?" I yelp, my voice coming out several octaves higher in surprise.

"This is my college." He gestures towards the sweep of lawns behind him as he struggles to his feet. The water only comes up to his waist. "I was on my way back from a tutorial. I thought you were drowning." He glares at me accusingly. "Obviously, I was wrong."

A tutorial? On a *Saturday*? I feel for his students.

"Well, no," I say lamely. "The Cam's not very deep around here. Didn't you know that?"

"No, because, believe it or not, I've never had cause to dunk myself in it before."

Freddie stifles another laugh, and I shoot him a warning glance. Adam doesn't look in the mood to find humour in the situation just yet. In fact, he looks positively thunderous.

"This is my brother, Freddie," I say speedily. "Freddie, this is Adam. He's a professor at the university."

"Hi." Freddie stretches out a hand. Adam stares at him like's he's totally mad.

"Charming as these introductions are," he says acerbically,

"don't you think we'd better get out of the river first? Before we freeze to death?"

I suppose he has a point. But, then again, he doesn't need to be so damning about it. It's not like it's *my* fault that he came hurtling into the water like a hero in a Victorian novel. And what kind of person lives in Cambridge and doesn't know anything about the river? Has he never *been* punting, or something?

I take another look at his stern face and immediately conclude that no, he hasn't. I don't imagine that a workaholic professor has much time for such frivolities.

"Come on." Freddie pulls me back into the boat. Immediately, I start to shiver as the wind bites into my wet clothes. He gestures to Adam. "Do you want a lift back into town?"

Adam shakes his head, eyeing our boat distrustfully "It's all right. I have my bike."

"You can't go home on that," I protest, between my chattering teeth. "You'll catch your death. Come back with us. It's the least we can do." I'd never forgive myself if he caught pneumonia on my account. "We only live on the other side of the park, and I'm sure Freddie's got some spare clothes you can use."

He still looks reluctant. But then the breeze picks up and he shudders. I can practically see his resolve crumbling.

"All right." He allows Freddie to help him onto the punt.

It's a quiet journey back. The cold has completely sapped my energy, and Adam doesn't look much better. His pale face is in sharp contrast to his black hair. I've never been so relieved to see my house as I am this afternoon. I almost cry with joy when the front door closes behind us and I'm enveloped in warmth. I will *never* complain about Freddie turning the heating up ever again.

Adam insists that I have first use of the bathroom, and I don't put up much of a fight. By this point, I'm so numb with cold that I can hardly feel my legs. I stand under the shower, letting the jets pummel me with hot water, thawing me from the outside in. After that I feel better, but nonetheless I pull on my warmest jumper and stuff my feet into my fluffiest socks. Right now, glamour is not high on my list of priorities.

Even Freddie's obviously taken pity on us because when I come down there's a cup of tea waiting and a saucepan of tomato soup on the hob. Above us, I can hear the sound of the shower turning on.

"Here—" he hands the mug to me, and I cradle it in my hands, revelling in the hot steam curling off it "—this will help."

"Thanks." I take a large gulp, not caring that it's too hot. As far as I'm concerned at the moment, there's no such thing as too hot.

We stand in companionable silence for several minutes.

"So, who is he?" Freddie demands suddenly.

I almost splutter my tea everywhere. "I *told* you. He's a professor at the university."

Freddie leans back against the counter, folding his arms. "Yes, but who is he to *you*?"

I frown at him over the rim of my cup. Why does everyone keep assuming that there's something going on between us? It's utterly perplexing. "Since when did you get so nosy?"

He gives me an arch look. "What, because nosiness is solely the prerogative of sisters?"

"No," I shoot back. "But brothers never normally bother to ask."

"Am I interrupting something?" Adam appears in the doorway. His hair is damp and curling at the ends, and he's wearing a grey T-shirt and jeans, both borrowed from Freddie. It's a good thing they're both tall because they fit ... Well, they fit very nicely, as it happens. I've never seen him out of his tweed jacket, so the sight of his toned arms is a surprise. He's more athletic than I'd expected.

It's so strange, seeing him in clothes which don't age him by about thirty years. He looks different. Younger, somehow. I mean, of course, I *knew* he was young, but something about him usually makes you forget.

"Not at all." Freddie beats a less than subtle retreat. "I'll ... er ... leave you to it. Places to be, you know."

Great, now my brother's got it into his head that I'm some sort of temptress, with a man in every port. Or at least every district of Cambridge. I sincerely hope that this doesn't get back to Dominic. I'll never live it down.

"Here." I thrust a cup of tea at Adam, who's scanning my bookshelf of romantic novels and spiritual self-help guides with a dubious expression. "Freddie made it. I warn you, it'll be vile, but at least it's hot."

He takes a sip, then visibly tries not to pull a face.

"Does your brother live here with you, then?"

"No, he's just squatting temporarily. Not that you'd know it; he seems to have taken over the whole house." I fidget with the handle of my cup, trying to gear up to what I want to say. "Look, I'm sorry about what happened. I know you were just trying to do a good deed. You must feel like I'm a plague on your life."

"Like I said, trouble *does* seem to follow you around," he says lightly. "Although it provides a certain degree of entertainment."

There's a slight curve to the corners of his mouth as he says it, which causes me to look at him sharply.

"Are you laughing at me?"

"Do I look like I'm laughing?"

I tilt my head and regard him for a few moments, trying to make up my mind.

"I don't know," I admit at last, putting my cup down on the counter behind me. "You're not easy to read."

"It has been noted in the past," he acquiesces. "Apparently it can be very frustrating."

He says it easily enough, but the faintest of shadows crosses his face, making me long to ask more. But of course I can't. Something about him is so enclosed, so self-contained, it positively repels intimate questions. Irked, I throw out a challenging line.

"It doesn't matter, anyway. I know exactly what you think of me. You've made it pretty obvious."

He looks entirely unmoved. In fact, he almost looks bored. "I highly doubt that."

The soup has started to bubble violently, and I'm grateful for the excuse to turn away from him. How does he *do* that? One minute we're having a perfectly civil conversation, and the next thing I know, he's managed to push all my buttons.

"There's no point lying about it." I stir the soup, horrified to find that my hand is shaking with emotion. Why does this bother me so much? "You can say it, you know. Let's clear the air between us once and for all. You think I'm a liability."

"Not at all. In fact, if you must know, I think you're fascinating."

I drop the spoon into the soup, my head whipping around in amazement. "Believe me, I'm not fascinating at all."

He walks towards me and, for a disorientating moment, I'm unsure of what's about to happen, but then he simply reaches past me and takes the neglected soup off the hob. Belatedly, I notice that it's hissing and spitting like a volcano.

"That's a matter of opinion," he says softly. "For my part, you're unlike anyone I've met."

I wish I could be sure that he means that as a good thing.

All of a sudden it seems odd, having him here. Like he doesn't fit. He belongs in the museum, in the hallowed halls of the university colleges. But definitely not here. Not in my little yellow kitchen, surrounded by my flea market finds and crystal grids. When Josh was here I wasn't self-conscious about any of that, but with Adam ... He's too observant; I feel his eyes taking it all in, judging me for it, no doubt. I busy myself pouring the soup into bowls, wondering how I can move the conversation onto safer ground.

"So," I begin, hoping he won't notice the brittle note in my voice, "I didn't realise you were with Alexandra College. How long have you been there?"

"Since I was an undergrad." He accepts the bowl of soup from me and sits at the table. "But it's been mapped out for me since I was born. It's sort of a family tradition."

He utters all of this without the slightest inflection, as though reciting some particularly dull piece of factual text.

I pull out a chair, unsure what to say. Yet again, I sense that there's so much more going on beneath the surface. But I don't dare reach out. So instead I keep it light.

"I was at Alexandra for my masters degree, you know." I pause, my spoon hovering over my soup. "Come to think of it, it's a wonder we didn't bump into one another."

"I might have been on my year abroad," he offers. He gazes dreamily off into the middle distance. "I spent it in a remote part of Tuscany on an archaeological dig."

"Tuscany sounds nice," I venture politely. Archeological dig ... Let's say no more about that part. I prefer to view my art from within the comfortable confines of a plush gallery. Ideally one with a café.

Somehow, though, I get the sense he wouldn't appreciate that sentiment.

"I was investigating the influence of Etruscan death culture on the Romans." He looks at me then. "That's my subject, you see. Death in Roman society. That's what I'm doing in the museum at the moment; I'm writing a paper on your sarcophagus. It's shocking how little detailed research has been done on it thus far."

"Oh." I try not to look too appalled. I should have guessed that his specialism wouldn't be something appealing, like decorated pots or marble statues. I've never liked that sarcophagus much; it gives me the creeps. I always try and give it a wide berth.

"You know, I could probably use some of your expertise."

He stirs his soup thoughtfully. "My paper would benefit from an art historical angle."

I start, knocking my bowl with my hand. Hang on, *what* did he just say?

"Me?"

"Yes, you." He looks vaguely entertained by my reaction. "You *are* an art historian, aren't you?"

"Well, yes, but ..."

"Good. Maybe next week at the museum, I can talk you through my thesis. See what you think."

For a moment I stare at him stupidly, wondering if I'm hallucinating. But he just sits there, calmly eating his soup. Surely, if I were hallucinating, he'd be doing something more exciting than that. Dancing on the table, maybe? Or singing an aria?

Of course, I shouldn't be so surprised that someone values my professional opinion. After all, I'm an intelligent woman, aren't I? I have a postgraduate education, and an important role at a prestigious museum.

But the truth is—and this sounds really sad now I'm saying it—I've kind of started to get used to being underestimated. It seems that people take one look at my long blonde hair, my vintage tea dresses, my sparkly nail polish, and they think that I can't possibly have a spare brain cell in my head. In the dry, dusty world of academia, I am *not* the norm. And over the years I've been made to feel it. Acutely.

The worst thing is, when Adam said he wanted to consult me on his thesis, I was half waiting for him to qualify it with, *Of course, it's complicated. I'll simplify it for you.*

But he didn't. I should feel elated, but instead I'm just confused.

"Is this a truce, then?" I venture.

"Certainly. From what I've experienced over the past week or so, I've concluded that it's far safer to be your friend than your enemy."

Friend. The word is so wholly inadequate for the spiky, uneasy, strange relationship which exists between us.

Obviously my thoughts are showing on my face because he quirks an eyebrow. "What, you don't think you could ever be friends with me, is that it?"

He doesn't sound offended, merely curious. I swirl a figure of eight in my soup, trying to work out how to phrase my reply.

"You have to admit we're pretty different," I say eventually. "You're so ... so ..."

"Charming? Gregarious? Conversant on the subject of classical burial sites?"

"Er ..." I wish I'd never started this conversation.

"We were talking earlier about what I think of you, or at least what you believed me to think of you," he says, leaning back in his chair. "Now, what about what *you* think of *me*? Let's see if my guesses are more accurate."

He's enjoying this far too much. I have the unnerving sense that I'm not going to like what he's about to say next.

"Let's see ..." He pretends to consider. "You think I'm cynical ..."

I open my mouth to object, then shut it again.

"... sarcastic, abrupt ..."

"*Stop*!" I put my spoon down with a clatter.

"Am I wrong?"

"Well … I mean, perhaps initially …"

"You're right," he says simply, cutting my feeble meanderings short. "I *am* all of those. And I'm not ashamed of it either. Why should I be? At least I call things as I see them."

I have no idea how to reply to that but, as it turns out, it doesn't matter because he's already rising to his feet, signalling that the conversation is closed.

"Thank you for the clothes. And for the soup. And, of course, for insisting that I stop off here to change," he adds with a reluctant smile. "I'll admit that it would have been foolish to attempt to ride home in those wet things."

I take the bowls over to the dishwasher, trying to adjust to the sudden change of gear. I'm starting to get used to his mercurial nature, but it still catches me out from time to time.

"Is it far?" Now I find myself wondering where he lives.

"Twenty minutes. Usually," he says ruefully. "It's longer now that my wheel's been bent out of shape."

I freeze, my head buried inside the dishwasher. No *way* am I going to ask why.

"Some mangy cat ran in front of me into the road the other night," he continues bitterly. "Bloody thing made me crash."

It's a good thing he can't see my face at this moment. Who's he calling a mangy cat? My cat is *not* mangy.

"Fancy that," I manage through gritted teeth. At once, it hits me what I've done. What was I *thinking*, bringing him back here?

The simple answer is that I wasn't thinking. I was so preoccupied with us not turning into popsicles that it didn't even occur to me that I'd essentially brought Adam right back to the scene of the crime. I'm lucky he hasn't recognised the street.

I need to get him out of here. If he catches sight of Casper ...

"You know, it was around here that it happened," he's saying, looking out of the window. "I'm not familiar with this part of town, but it might even have been this street."

Okay, he *definitely* has to go. Now.

"Well, that's great," I say desperately, shoving the bag containing his clothes at him and hustling him towards the door. "I'll see you at the museum next week. We can talk over the ... er ... tomb thing."

He looks down at me, a frown creasing his brow. "Are you all right?"

"Yes, yes, fine," I gabble, pulling an old coat of Freddie's down off the hook. At least, I think it's an old coat. I'm too worked up to care. "Here, take this for the ride home. You can give it back to me next week. No rush."

He still doesn't look convinced but, to my immense relief, his hand is on the door handle, already starting to turn it.

"Okay, well, if you're sure ..."

And of course that's the exact moment that Casper comes bounding down the stairs.

Chapter 14

"Wait—" Adam lets go of the door, uncertainty clouding his features "—I'm sure I recognise that cat."

Casper promptly arches his back and hisses menacingly.

Adam's eyes widen in comprehension. "I *do* recognise that cat! It's the one that caused me to crash my bike. And you ..." He turns to me, and the expression on his face makes me go cold. "*You* ... " He breaks off, shaking his head. Then he yanks open the door and sweeps out.

For a moment I just stand there, dazed. Then the door slams back into its frame, jolting me into action.

"Adam, wait!" I run out after him. It's rained while we've been inside and my slippers are probably getting ruined, but that's the least of my concerns right now.

Of course, this is *totally* my fault. And it's not as though the possibility of him finding out the truth hadn't crossed my mind. Several times it even seemed fairly inevitable.

But I never realised it would feel as awful as this. And I certainly never realised that I would care so much.

"No, I won't wait!" He whirls to face me. "I think you've

had plenty of chances already, don't you? Why should I give you another?"

Casper has followed us outside, and now he jumps up onto the wall, watching our exchange with interest.

"Look, I know I should have just told you," I say desperately. "But somehow it was never the right moment."

"Never the right moment?" He gives a bitter laugh. "Are you serious? There was *never* going to be the right moment. That's no excuse."

He has got a point. But that doesn't make his caustic tone sting any less.

I can see our new, fragile connection rupturing before my very eyes, and it makes me want to scream in frustration. Why are we even having this stupid argument, anyway? I ball my hands into fists at my sides.

"Why does this matter so much?" I cry.

He stops dead. "Excuse me?"

"I said, why does it matter? So I told a white lie or two. It hardly warrants this kind of reaction."

Anyone would think he was actually *hurt* by my deception. But that's impossible; the man's practically made of granite. It must be something else, something far more logical and less emotional.

His face is half turned away from me. His next words are so quiet that I almost miss them altogether.

"I don't like to be made a fool of."

And then, all at once, it becomes perfectly clear.

"This is about pride, isn't it?"

By the way he flinches slightly, I can tell that I've hit the nail on the head. Oh, I don't *believe* this.

"I'm right, aren't I?" I press. "That's the real issue here. You're so used to knowing everything, you just can't bear to be out of the loop."

"Do *not* try to turn this around," he says in a low voice. "You can't just—"

I cut him off. I'm not finished yet. "You're not angry with me, not really. You're angry with yourself for not working it out sooner."

He sighs deeply. "You're wrong about one thing, that's for sure. I am most definitely angry with you."

The words are damning enough, but there's no real malice there any more. I take a step closer, relieved when he doesn't back away.

"You don't have to be right all of the time, Adam," I tell him gently. "Can't you see that?"

We just stand there for a moment, looking at each other and not speaking. For the briefest of moments, I think I see his eyes soften.

Then Casper flicks out a paw and knocks a potted succulent off the edge of the wall. It lands squarely on Adam's foot.

For half a second nothing happens. Then all hell breaks loose.

"Bloody hell!" Adam hops up and down amongst the broken shards of terracotta. He points at Casper, his face white with pain. "He did that on purpose! You saw him. That cat should be locked up."

"Don't be ridiculous," I say dismissively, although I rush forward to grab Casper before he can do any more damage. "He's a *cat*, Adam, not a criminal mastermind. Clearly, that was just an accident."

From within my arms, Casper emits a self-satisfied growl. Adam gives him a savage look.

Any hopes I was entertaining that we could go back to where we were a minute ago are dashed by one glance at his face. It's pale, with an angry dent between his brows. He wrenches open the garden gate, not looking at me.

"I'll return the clothes next week." He makes to stalk off down the street, then winces and settles into a laboured limp.

"Casper," I mutter reproachfully when Adam's finally out of earshot. "We both know that was deliberate."

He nuzzles me lovingly under the chin.

"Stop trying to charm your way out of it," I command, holding him at arm's length. "I think you might have really done it this time. That must have been the shortest truce in modern history."

He twitches one ear and then the other, looking at me intently. I almost begin to wonder if he's actually listening for once. But then he leaps out of my arms onto the wall, where he starts swatting at a troupe of ladybirds trying to make their way across the brickwork. Clearly, for him, the whole episode is already forgotten.

But then, life is so much simpler when you're a cat.

***

"Okay, Clara, *enough*," Ruby demands. "It's time to spill the beans."

I look up from behind the glass cabinet, where we're rearranging the display of portrait miniatures. I like to move them around every now and again, give different ones their chance in the limelight. Just another sign that I'm turning into a crazy museum lady with a tendency to anthropomorphize the artworks. Next I'll be giving them all names, and making up conversations between them.

Ruby offered to help. With hindsight, perhaps I should have been more suspicious of her motives. After all, who *really* wants to spend an afternoon dusting the frames of over three hundred tiny paintings? Even the most ardent of art lovers would struggle to summon up much enthusiasm.

Now, with a sinking heart, I realise that it was just an excuse to get me alone for an interrogation. I wouldn't be surprised if she and Eve have been plotting this all week.

"Nothing to report," I lie, shoving a portrait of a lady in a spectacular hat into her hands. "Don't drop that, by the way. It's early eighteenth century."

She pouts, dangling it from her fingertips. "Maybe I will if you won't tell me what's going on."

"Ruby!" I try to snatch it from her grasp, but she whips it behind her back.

"Oh, calm down, it's perfectly safe." She places it carefully back in the case. "There, everything as usual. You, on the other hand, have been acting weird for the past fortnight and you won't tell us why. It's no fun at all."

"We're not supposed to be having *fun*, Ruby. We're at work."

She stares at me, her purple-lipsticked mouth hanging open. "Now you sound like Jeremy! What are you hiding?"

Jeremy squints at us from across the room, where he's regaling a couple of tourists on post-revolutionary French portraiture.

"Stop it, or you'll bring him over here," I hiss out of the corner of my mouth. For someone who pretends to be half deaf most of the time, he has a bat-like ear for the sound of his own name. "All right, *fine*, I'll tell you. I had no idea you were so tenacious."

"One of my finest qualities." She preens, admiring her reflection in the side of the display cabinet.

Honestly. If only we could all have just a little bit of her confidence.

"If I had to guess, I'd say it was something to do with that gorgeous vet," Ruby says slyly, slanting a look out of the corner of her eye. "Am I right?"

I almost drop the miniature I'm holding. "How did you know about that?"

"I have eyes," she says simply. "And I have sources. Your brother's *such* a darling, by the way. We had a lovely chat when he stopped by on Tuesday afternoon."

I groan inwardly. Poor Freddie. I bet he didn't know what had hit him.

"So ..." She puts her hands on her hips, showing off her sequinned mini dress to full advantage. How does she get away with wearing these things in broad daylight? "Now we've got the formalities out of the way, the most important question is ... *why the hell didn't you tell me?*"

"Well ..." Actually, that's not a completely unreasonable thing to ask. Why *didn't* I tell her? There's no doubt that she and Eve would have been overflowing with support. They would have wanted to know everything.

But, then again, maybe that's just it. Things with Josh are so good. And it's just been so ... *easy*, I suppose is the only word. I never imagined that it would be so easy. Somehow, our relationship has developed naturally, without us even having to think about it. I've seen him almost every night for over two weeks now, and I still think about him all day long. We've spoken for hours, and still I feel like we'll never run out of things to talk about. I've told him all kinds of things which I've never admitted to anyone before; I explained to him how Casper turned up on the doorstep that night, when I was having one of the worst days of my life. I'd had to sign the exchange of contracts on my parents' house –my childhood home, the last real link I had with them. There was no way we could have held onto it; believe me, I tried, but the death duties were impossible. The weather outside seemed to match my mood; it was blowing a violent storm, the rain lashing against the windows.

I'd been signing my name, trying not to smudge the ink with my tears, when I'd heard a sound, barely audible above the howling of the wind outside. Without thinking, I got up and opened the back door ... and there he was. Soaking wet and shivering on the step was one of the largest, ugliest cats I'd ever seen. I dried him off with a towel, making his bright ginger fur stand up in tufts. He put his paws on my lap and nestled against me. I could feel the rattling vibrations of his purr right through my chest. And as I held him it almost seemed as if something eased within me. Just the tiniest shift in my sorrow, but it was something. And in that moment I knew that the next day would be better. And the next after that. In that moment I knew that I was going to be all right.

Which leads me onto the most amazing thing of all: Casper ... well, he just *idolises* Josh. It's almost impossible to believe that this is the same cat who drove away every other man who dared to set foot in the house.

I looked at Casper the other night, curled up on Josh's lap, and Heather's words came back to me from that day at lunch.

Find someone who can actually win round that cat of yours; now, that really will be someone worth having.

Obviously, I didn't share that thought with Josh. It's best to save the full extent of my madness for further along the road. But I'm falling hard and I know it. It's like I'm on the outside looking in, and I'm willing myself to slow down, not to throw my heart on the line, but I'm powerless to stop it from happening.

Right now, our relationship exists in this fantastic, fragile bubble; it's just the two of us. I'm afraid that if I share it with anyone else, I might jinx it somehow.

"Actually, forget it, that's not the most important question." Ruby makes a dismissive swipe with her hand, sending the colourful bangles on her wrist jangling. "The most important question, by far, is ... how was it?"

Sadly, I was not unprepared for this query, so the answer trips lightly from my lips.

"No comment."

"Don't be such a spoilsport." She prods my upper arm with a bejewelled talon. "It's so obvious you've done it. I know the look of a woman who's having great sex, and you've been floating around with a dreamy expression on your face all week."

"In which case, you already know the answer to your question," I say tartly, rubbing my arm. Her nails are *sharp*. "And you're definitely not going to get any more details, so quit while you're ahead."

"Fine," she huffs, flopping down onto the nearest velvet-covered bench and crossing one leg over the other. "Eve said you'd be like that, but I thought it was worth a try. Good gossip is so hard to come by in this place. Proper gossip, I mean," she adds with a note of disdain.

I know what she means. After all, if it's academic gossip you're after, the museum is a veritable hotbed. Whose latest book has bombed, who's angling for more funding, who's resentful of their associate lecturer's greater popularity with the students – it's all been whispered about here, within these walls. All thrilling stuff, no doubt, if you're a member of that world, but for the rest of us ... Well, let's just say that we all look forward to the occasional inter-departmental fling. At least that has some human interest to it.

In this city, what goes on in books, and paintings, and in the lofty reaches of the mind, is far more real and immediate than anything which might be happening in the real world. It's simply the way it has always been, and probably always will be. It's both ethereally wonderful and suffocatingly bizarre; I've got used to it, but some people never do. Ruby is one of them; I suspect that as soon as her course is over, she'll pack her bags and move on to brighter lights. London, maybe, or Brighton. I could see her in Brighton, with the kaleidoscope of life unravelling all around her.

The thought of her leaving is unexpectedly painful and I busy myself at the cabinet, wondering when I started becoming so woefully sentimental.

At that moment Eve appears in the doorway, almost knocking Jeremy sideways in her haste to get across the room. She's holding something at arm's length and, as she gets closer, I realise with a stab of horror that they're Freddie's clothes.

"Clara, what *is* going on? Why has Professor Warwick given me these men's clothes to return to you?"

Chapter 15

Ruby's head spins around in unbridled delight.

"So *this* is why you were being so cagey! Professor Warwick, hey? I suppose he has a certain intellectual aura about him, although I didn't think you went in for that sort of thing." She gives a long, low whistle, earning an admonishing look from Jeremy, who's still flattened against the doorframe. "Two men at once, then. I never knew you had it in you."

Eve looks scandalised, a finely boned hand fluttering to her throat. "Clara, dear, is this true?"

"What? *No*!" How did this get out of hand so quickly? I look down at the miniature I'm holding. Even the fifth Earl of Kemble seems to be casting a judgemental expression. As if he's in any position to throw stones, I think darkly. He was reputed to have had seven mistresses at one time. I restore him to his rightful place on the green baize backing and close the case with a click. "There's a perfectly innocent explanation, I promise."

They both look at me expectantly. Eve even takes a seat.

"I lent him some of Freddie's clothes after he fell in the

river." I hold up a hand as Ruby opens her mouth. "*Don't* ask. He's just returning them, that's all. So you see, all very dull, I'm afraid. Nothing salacious whatsoever."

Eve doesn't appear satisfied with my account of events. "And why didn't he give them to you himself?"

"Because we sort of ... had a disagreement," I admit, albeit reluctantly. "It's a long story."

As it turns out, my fears of an awkward encounter between us have proved unfounded. I've barely seen Adam at all since it happened; in fact, I'm pretty certain he's actively been avoiding me. When I say I've seen him, what I really mean is that I've seen *parts* of him: an arm disappearing here, a blur of tweed jacket there.

Yes, he's back in that jacket again, I can tell you that much. Regrettably, it must have survived its immersion in the sludgy waters of the Cam.

Of course, I still feel guilty about what happened. He was within his rights to be annoyed; I should never have lied. I'd quite like the opportunity to tell him that, if he'd let me get within twenty yards of him.

On the other hand, I'm pretty annoyed myself about the way he reacted, not to mention the way he's *still* reacting. That feeling has only intensified as the weeks have gone on. The more he avoids me, the less sympathetic feelings I entertain towards him. And the less I feel inclined to apologise. It's almost getting to the stage where I'm thinking that *he* ought to be apologising to *me*.

If it were the other way around, I'd be over it by now. I would. Totally over it.

But then again, *I'm* not an arrogant know-it-all, am I?

The vehemence of that thought pulls me up short. Why am I so bothered about this, anyway?

"Ah, so that explains why he's been behaving so strangely," Eve says knowingly.

"He's an academic," Ruby scoffs. "They behave strangely all the time."

"Something of a sweeping statement, dear," Eve chides.

I let their debate fade into the background as I lock the display cabinet and give the glass a final polish. It's no good; I'm still fuming about this whole Adam thing. So, he'd rather use Eve as a go-between than have to speak to me directly, would he?

Well, that's fine by me. I'll gladly let him have his wish. What is he to me, anyway? He's just another academic in a museum filled with them, in a city filled with them. I didn't like him when we first met. I didn't like him much the second time either. Whatever brief moment of understanding we might have had in my kitchen, a fleeting glimpse of someone more human, more real, it ultimately doesn't mean anything. It doesn't *change* anything.

I was right when I said that we could never be friends.

"Whatever it was about, I wouldn't like to be him right now," Ruby says with a wary look in my direction. "If the expression on Clara's face is anything to go by, he's about to burst into flames at any moment."

I quickly school my features into something more benign.

"It's probably just as well, dear," Eve says practically. "It couldn't have carried on, could it? You spending all of that time with the professor, I mean. Not now that you have a proper man in your life."

For some reason, that statement piques me.

"Why not? It's purely platonic between us, always has been."

They exchange a disbelieving look, which only serves to make me more annoyed.

"It is! Why will no one believe that?"

Do they not know me better than that? Clearly, Adam is *not* the kind of man I'd be interested in. He hasn't a romantic or impulsive bone in his body, for starters. I've never even *thought* of him in that way. And since when did we revert to this outdated attitude, where a man and a woman are unable to form a simple friendship without a cascade of gossip and innuendo?

Okay, so Adam and I aren't *friends*, exactly, but we're certainly not ... well, whatever they're implying. From Eve, perhaps I can excuse it. But Ruby ... she's surprised me. And not in a good way.

"Well, whatever," Ruby says artfully. "You don't want to waste time worrying about him anyway. You've got far more exciting things to occupy your mind. Or should I say, people."

She waggles her eyebrows suggestively. I try not to scowl. No way are they going to get anything out of me *now*.

"Nice try, but I'm not going to tell you any more about him."

"You see?" Eve looks smug. "I said she'd play her cards close to her chest, didn't I? It means she's smitten."

Ruby looks aghast. "You're not, are you?"

She sounds exactly like Heather. At times like this, I can understand why men never tell their friends anything. It's infinitely simpler that way.

Ruby interprets my silence as an affirmative. "Seriously? It's been *two weeks*, Clara!"

"And four days," I add defiantly, folding my arms.

She gives me a disparaging look. "What are you, twelve?" Then her shoulders drop in an exaggerated sigh. "All right, well, in that case, please at *least* tell me that you've had the conversation."

"I know how babies are made, thanks, Ruby. I had that talk over a decade ago."

My sarcasm simply bounces off her.

"I meant have you defined your relationship yet?" she persists. "It's important to categorise your status."

She makes Josh sound like a new species of fungi. I glance across at Eve. She appears as baffled as I am.

"Can't we just ...?" I venture. "Let it happen? Does it really require a discussion?"

Ruby claps a hand to her forehead in despair. "No, no, no! Do you not know anything, Clara? Not everyone is looking for a relationship; you can't just *assume*. He might simply be after a fling."

I shake my head. "Not Josh. He's not like that."

She puts her hands on her hips. "Are you sure? What's his place like?"

I know this is a test, and I feel smug that I can answer. "Not bad. He hasn't had much chance to unpack yet."

"Oh, so you've stayed over, then?"

At this, I waver. "No," I admit. "He says he likes it better at mine."

Actually, I've never really got that; after all, his place has the distinct advantage of privacy, which mine certainly lacks. But I haven't wanted to push the issue; it's not like it really matters, anyway. It's such a small thing, on the face of it.

"And have you met any of his friends?" Ruby presses.

"Ruby, he's only just *moved* here. His friends are all back in London."

All right, so that's not strictly true. There are his hockey teammates; they often meet for a drink in the evening, and he's come over to mine afterwards a couple of times. I've half wondered if he'll invite me to join them, but he never has. I just assumed though that, like me, he's enjoying this period where we have one another to ourselves.

Ruby doesn't appear convinced by my answer. "Look, if you really like this guy, you *have* to find out where he stands. Before you get yourself hurt."

I know that she's trying to be helpful, but all I can hear is condescension in that sentence. I dig my heels in.

"I know how to handle myself, Ruby."

She just looks at me pityingly.

"Of course you do, dear," Eve ventures kindly.

Ruby ignores her, fixing me with a piercing gaze. "Promise me that you'll talk to him about it."

"Sure," I say airily. "Whatever you say."

Honestly, sometimes I despair of my own generation. No wonder people are struggling to find a decent relationship, if they're trying to categorise everything into neat little boxes.

Life just doesn't work like that. *Love* doesn't work like that; it's about knowing someone, trusting them.

But I'm not about to explain that to Ruby. She'll find out for herself one day.

She obviously senses that I'm humouring her, because she frowns. I'm serious, Clara. I really don't want to see you get hurt by this guy."

I look up in surprise. She really *isn't* joking, is she?

"All right," I concede at last. "I promise."

***

I didn't really mean it the second time either. But somehow, over the next couple of days, what she said keeps coming back to me.

Not because anything's wrong. Far from it, in fact. Josh continues to be wonderful, Casper continues to adore him, and my heart continues to flutter.

I only begin to worry that it might be fluttering a little *too* much.

In a way, this was bound to happen. I've always been an all or nothing kind of girl, an old-fashioned romantic, falling fast and struggling not to show it. And how can I *not* fall for Josh, with his laidback charm and sun-drenched good looks? Not to mention his skill set in both kitchen and bedroom.

And, of course, the approval of a very discerning cat.

Everything's rosy. So why am I lying here this morning, in what ought to be a delicious post-coital haze, locked in a mental argument with myself?

It's the weekend, the bed is cosy and Josh's arm is flung across my body, its heavy warmth pressing me into the mattress. Everything is inviting me to drift off into a hazy half-sleep, but I can't relax. My thoughts just won't leave me alone.

It was last night that did it, I decide. He called to tell me that he was going out with his teammates, and that he'd be over afterwards.

"Maybe I could come and meet you all," I suggested.

There was silence on the end of the line.

"You wouldn't enjoy it," he said at last. "It's just a load of guys ... It'll be far too rowdy for you."

"I'm fairly sure I can hold my own," I replied, trying to keep my tone jaunty. But in reality I was beginning to feel a touch uneasy. "Don't you *want* me to meet your friends?"

There was another pause.

"Look, they're calling for me in surgery," he said quickly. "I've got to go. But I'll see you later, okay?"

Obviously, I didn't believe him for a moment about the surgery. I know evasion when I hear it; I can be pretty evasive myself when I want to be. I stalked around the house for the next two hours, unable to settle to anything. Casper and Freddie, clearly sensing my mood, made themselves scarce.

In the end, when Josh did eventually turn up on the doorstep, he was so full of contrition that it swept all of my carefully rehearsed lines out of my head.

"I'm sorry if I sounded strange on the phone," he said. "It's just ... I like having you to myself, that's all. Can you understand that?"

I'd been forced to admit that I could. After all, hadn't I been thinking just the same thing a couple of days previously when I was talking to Ruby and Eve?

Last night, it all seemed to make sense. And yet this morning that nudging feeling is back with a vengeance.

The thought of turning to him and asking him to 'categorise our status' seems beyond risible. But then again, maybe Ruby's right; I don't protect myself enough. It's not like this is my first relationship, and I've been burned before by not asking enough questions in the beginning. I learned the hard way that it doesn't pay to assume; do I really want to risk making the same mistake again?

But this is different. It's Josh. And it feels right. Isn't that enough?

Besides—and this is what I'm really afraid of—what if I ruin it by asking? What if he thinks I don't trust him?

But then, if he's the kind of guy I think he is, then surely he won't take it personally. Surely he'll understand.

Won't he?

Great, now I don't even know what I think. This is why one should never listen to other people. It just opens up a whole world of confusion.

"All right, what is it?"

I start at the sound of his voice. His head is turned away from me on the pillow.

"I thought you were asleep," I stutter.

"With you fidgeting away like that? No chance."

"Sorry. I've just got a lot on my mind, that's all."

He rolls over, propping himself up on one elbow, his head

slanted against his hand. "Anything you want to share?"

Suddenly, I'm afraid. I really want to just say no, to cuddle up against him and pretend that none of this had ever crossed my mind. But I can't.

"Maybe." I fiddle with the edge of the duvet cover. "I suppose I was just wondering ..." Great start; just the worldly, assured approach I was aiming for. Like I ask this question of lovers all the time. I carry on with an effort. "Are we ... well, *you know*?" I finish lamely.

He raises a brow in amusement. "Amazingly, no, I don't. You'll have to give me a bit more to go on."

I make another attempt. "What are we?"

There's a beat of silence. Then he laughs.

"*That's* what you've been so worried about?" He begins to trace languid circles across my bare collarbone. "Really?"

"It's something that should be discussed, apparently," I murmur thickly. His touch feels so good; it's making it hard to form a coherent thought. I sink deeper into the bed.

"How very modern." His hand slips beneath the covers, grazing across my navel as it travels downwards.

I gasp as his fingers find their target. It would be so easy to get swept away, to lose myself in the moment and forget all about this conversation. But I don't. Instead I sit bolt upright.

"So?"

At my abrupt demand, his eyes darken with confusion. He sits up too, leaning back against the headboard.

"Something I said?"

"Something you *didn't* say." I pull the duvet up to my chin, wanting the sense of protection. This hasn't taken the turn I'd expected it to. Despite all of my reticence to raise the subject, I realise now that I only ever expected one answer from him. And what I got was no answer at all.

That's simply not enough.

Comprehension dawns across his face. "Wait ... you're serious about this, aren't you?"

"Of course I'm bloody serious!" I snap, the tension getting the better of me. "Why else would I be asking?"

He takes my chin in his hand, looking into my eyes. "I thought we were having fun. Aren't we?"

"Yes, but ..."

"Aren't you happy?"

"Yes, of course I am, but ..."

"But you want to know." He sighs. "Why do women always do this? Why do you always have to make everything so heavy? Look, Clara, I like you. You like me. We enjoy each other's company. Isn't that enough for now?"

He looks so earnest that I immediately feel ashamed of my outburst. Of course, when he puts it like that, it all sounds eminently reasonable. It makes my demand seem desperate, clingy, paranoid. I cover my face with my hands as he continues.

"And before you ask if I'm seeing anyone else ..."

"I wasn't going to!"

"... Oh, no, please do. Such an estimation of my stamina levels would be immensely flattering."

I peep out from between my fingers. There's a smile curving at the edges of his mouth.

"Stop it," I say, my voice muffled. "You can't make me feel better."

The fact that he's taking it all so well only makes me feel more mortified. I wish I could just shrink into the bed and disappear for good.

"I disagree." He pulls me against him. "I think there's plenty I can do."

From downstairs, I hear the doorbell ring. I freeze, but Josh doesn't seem to notice. He just carries on trailing kisses down my neck.

It rings again, reverberating throughout the house.

"Leave it," Josh says against my skin. "If it's important, they'll come back."

There's nothing I'd rather do at this very moment. But my conscience tugs at me, refusing to let it go.

"I'd better get it," I say apologetically. "It might be something to do with Casper. It often is. Just ... stay there, okay? I'll be back in a minute."

Turning away from his disbelieving face, I pull on my kimono and run downstairs, trying not to entertain murderous thoughts about my own cat. But mark my words, if he has anything to do with the fact that I've been dragged away from what promised to be a particularly spectacular making up session, then I won't be answerable for the consequences.

Casper chooses that moment to miaow a greeting from his position on the hall rug.

"So, *not* you then," I say, surprised. "In which case ..."

I open the door, and anything I was about to utter next dies on my lips.

"Hi," Adam says simply.

Chapter 16

"Hello," I reply warily. "What are you doing here?"

He puts his hands in his pockets, rocking back and forth on his heels.

"Your house is very ... *pink*. I didn't notice it properly last time."

"I like pink," I say defensively. "More people should paint their houses pink, in my opinion. It would enhance national wellbeing immensely." I regard him for a moment. He looks edgy. "But I'm guessing you didn't come here specifically to comment on my paint choices."

"No, I didn't. Actually, I wanted to say sorry. I'm afraid I somewhat overreacted the last time we met. It wasn't my finest moment and ... Look, can I come in for a minute? It's freezing out here."

It crosses my mind to say no, but it occurs to me that would be churlish. Also, he has a point; it is freezing, and I'm standing here only in my kimono.

Literally, *only* in my kimono, I suddenly recall. Surreptitiously, I pull the wrap front more tightly around my throat. It feels slightly wrong, standing here with Adam having one of our strange conversations while Josh languishes upstairs in bed, but what else can I do?

"I've been under a lot of pressure lately." He's talking quickly, as though now he's started he can't wait to get it off his chest. "Mostly self-imposed, I grant you, but not entirely. You see, the head of my department is due to retire next year, and his successor is yet to be announced."

I fold my arms. I suppose I owe it to him to listen, if nothing else.

"And you're in the running?"

"We're all in the running." He shoves a hand through his hair, and I notice how tired he looks. "Of course, I should be well out of it. At my age ... Whoever heard of anyone making head of department at twenty-nine? But there have been hints ... suggestions ... that I might still be considered. I'm viewed as something of a prodigy, you see." He coughs, looking awkward. "But, naturally, my CV isn't as advanced as those of my colleagues. I need to work twice as hard." He sets his jaw. "I won't lose out on the opportunity of a lifetime, not due to lack of application, at any rate."

"And the museum?" I prompt. Upstairs, I hear a floorboard creaking and I fervently pray that Josh stays put. I don't know why I care so much; it's not as if I'm doing anything wrong. Why shouldn't Adam know that I'm seeing someone? Maybe he's seeing someone himself; I've never asked him about it.

For some reason, that last thought corresponds to a funny tight feeling in my stomach, which I swiftly attribute to a lack of breakfast.

"I have a lot of papers to my name, but what I really need

is a book. I think my research in the museum could form the cornerstone." The light dims in his eyes. "But there's so little time. I'm afraid the pressure has been getting to me of late. I'm not acting ... Well, I'm not myself. I thought you deserved an explanation. I didn't want you to think badly of me."

He really looks like he means it. The realisation makes me feel off-kilter, somehow.

"It doesn't matter what I think," I say softly.

"Yes, it does." He pulls a brown paper bag out of his satchel. "I'm afraid I was rather unfair on Casper as well. I've brought him a peace offering, by way of apology."

"Oh." I don't know what to say. "That's actually very ... sweet."

Sweet. Professor Warwick. Who'd have thought it?

"Here." He produces a fluffy white mouse from the bag and tosses it at Casper, who watches it land with disinterest, before batting it away beneath the coat rack with a challenging stare.

"I'm sure he'll grow to love it," I say weakly.

"Hmm." Adam doesn't look convinced. "He doesn't appear ready to forgive me just yet."

"You *did* call him mangy," I feel compelled to point out. "You're going to have to work hard to come back from that."

"Then I will." His eyes meet mine, and there's an unexpected warmth there. "So, you and I ... Is the truce back on?"

I never get the chance to answer because, to my dismay, Josh comes cantering down the stairs, pulling his T-shirt on over his head.

"Everything okay? I heard voices."

I find myself attempting to spring away from Adam, which is both ridiculous and impossible. Impossible because of the sheer lack of space in my narrow Victorian hallway, and ridiculous because ...

Well, because it just *is*. Because it's Adam, and nothing could be more above reproach. Yet I'm acting like there's something illicit going on.

They're both looking at me, and I realise that I'm going to have to say something.

"It's just ... someone from the museum." My mouth has gone dry, and I swallow. "Josh, this is Adam."

"Hi." Josh shakes his hand, not seeming at all aware of the oppressive atmosphere. "So, you two work together, then?"

"Just someone from the museum," Adam reiterates quietly. "Like she said."

What does that mean? I dart a glance at him, but his expression is shuttered.

Casper is scratching at the hem of Josh's jeans, begging to be picked up.

Something flickers in Adam's dark eyes, but it's gone before I can catch it.

"I'll leave you to your Saturday." He seems to look past me then, to where Josh stands with Casper in his arms. "I can see that you have everything you need."

And then, just like that he's gone. And I'm left standing there, unable to shake the feeling that something just happened. Something I should probably understand, but I can't work out what.

"Bit of an odd chap," Josh remarks mildly. "Is he always like that?"

"No," I say slowly, more to myself than anything. "No, he's not."

***

"Jeremy?" I poke my head tentatively around the door to his office. "Do you have a moment?"

I can't believe I'm actually resorting to this. Normally, I avoid him like he has fleas. Which is ironic, really, because if anyone's likely to have fleas around here it's me, what with Casper's incessant wandering and frolicking.

Not that ... I mean, for the record, I don't *actually* have fleas. I just ... Oh, never mind.

"Ah." Jeremy doesn't look in the least surprised to see me. "Of course. I'd quite forgotten. Thank you for reminding me."

I blink. "Excuse me?"

"Our monthly patrol," he says cheerfully, rising out of the cracked leather office chair which looks to pre-date the office itself.

Ah. I'd forgotten about that too.

Every last Thursday of the month, Jeremy and I go on a walk around the museum and reassess our plans for the place. Or, rather, I should say, *his* plans. We look at how the exhibits are arranged, what's gaining the most attention and if everything's working as it ought to be. No paintings falling off walls and onto heads, and suchlike. It would probably be quite enjoyable if I could get a word in edgeways but, as it stands, it generally equates to me trailing around after him for two hours listening to his incessant droning.

"Nothing I'd rather do," I say resignedly. "But first there was something I wanted to ask you ..."

"Walk and talk, Miss Swift." He slings on his most jaunty waistcoat, a brown and rusty orange floral pattern which makes me feel bilious every time I have to look at it. "Walk and talk! There's no time to be lost."

Where he gets this sudden urgency from, I've no idea. This is a museum; the default pace is glacial. Nothing's changed here in almost two hundred years; it's unlikely to in the next five minutes.

"Have you seen Professor Warwick this week?" I puff, following him along the corridor.

He draws up, spinning around to look at me beadily. "Why ask me? I thought you were such *good* friends."

I bite back a retort, pretending to make a study of a nearby watercolour.

The truth is, I'm not sure what Adam and I are at the moment. Our relationship has always been an odd, uneasy one but I thought we'd got back onto a reasonably steady footing. Now, I'm not sure what I think.

I haven't seen him much in the past few days; the one time I did manage to catch him, he looked like a startled rabbit. He mumbled something about being late for a lecture, and off he went. But the thing is, I *know* that he doesn't have lectures on a Monday; he's told me that in the past. If I didn't know better, I'd wonder if he was still avoiding me.

But he can't be. Why would he? We sorted things out, didn't

we? We reinstated our truce. I mean, the only thing I can think of which has happened is that scene in my hallway last weekend. Which ... well, it was a bit awkward, I suppose. But more for me than anyone else. I can't see why it would make him want to keep away from me.

It doesn't make any sense. I'm beginning to worry that something is seriously wrong. Hence why I'm here asking Jeremy about it. The last person in the world I want to have to rely on, but my last chance. No one else knows what's going on; even Ruby's normally invincible spy network has let me down. Perhaps Jeremy can shed some light on the matter.

"I found some old notes on our sarcophagus in the archives," I say quickly, not wanting Jeremy to think that there's anything personal in my asking. The last thing I need is more of his insinuations. "I thought they might be useful for Adam ... I mean, for Professor Warwick. For his book," I add hopelessly.

"Ah, yes." Jeremy's eyes gleam. "His *book*. A great coup for the museum, wouldn't you say?"

"He told you about it?"

For some reason, that makes me feel a little hollow. Which is totally unreasonable, of course; why shouldn't it be common knowledge amongst his colleagues? I suppose I'd assumed that it was a confidence, that he told me because I was special. Now I just feel foolish.

"Oh, yes, he told me about it," Jeremy says cryptically. "Which reminds me, there's something I need to run past you."

For a second I think I've misheard him. But then he carries on, and I realise that I can't possibly have done.

"... I think it would be prudent ... an introduction, you understand. An opportunity to elucidate on the qualities the museum strives to embody, going forwards ..."

"Jeremy ..." I move around so I'm in front of him, stopping him in his tracks

"... simple English, *please*."

He looks distinctly put out by the suggestion, but obliges. "What would you think about making the introductory speech at the gala unveiling next week?"

My mouth falls open. Literally, I'm ashamed to say.

"Don't gawp like that." He tuts, straightening a framed embroidery. "It's terrible manners."

"But ..." I search for my voice. "That's your thing. Not mine."

Jeremy always does the speeches. Much, I have to say, to the dismay of the audience. But this time even I wouldn't begrudge him his moment in the limelight. The acquisition of the new Holman Hunt took months of haggling, endless back and forth negotiations. Luckily, that's one area where Jeremy appears to come into his own. He pulled it off with aplomb. And, knowing Jeremy, I bet he can't wait to tell everyone all about it, in minute detail.

It makes no sense, but then nothing makes any sense at the moment. Adam, Jeremy ... even Casper, who can normally be relied upon to be unwaveringly himself. Maybe I should be getting used to it by now.

"It needn't require in-depth discussion, thank you," he says briskly. "A sensible answer will suffice. What's it to be?"

I'm momentarily speechless.

"I don't need to point out that this is a big opportunity,

do I?" Jeremy says with more than a trace of impatience.

"In which case, she'll take it." A deeply amused voice reverberates from just behind me. "Does it come with a pay rise too?"

I don't turn around, but then I don't need to. My skin is already tingling with awareness.

"Professor Warwick." Jeremy raises an eyebrow. "How unexpected. We haven't seen much of you of late."

"I made the mistake of setting a three thousand-word essay for my third year students on the Classical Civilisations module. It seemed a good idea at the time."

"I would be honoured to," I say, recovering my voice. I'm aware that I seem to have dropped out of the conversation. Or, rather, it's been hijacked by an unwelcome interloper. I direct my comments purposely at Jeremy. "I'll have a draft by early next week."

"Good, good." Jeremy's already distracted. His mind never lingers on one topic for long. "Well, let's be getting along, then. Museums don't run themselves, you know. Unless ..." He looks up at us through his half-moon glasses. He's the only person I've ever met who actually possesses a pair; prior to that I thought they only belonged in fiction.

"Actually—" Adam steps in smoothly, taking the cue "—I was wondering if I could steal Clara away for a moment?"

I instantly bristle. What am I, some baggage to be passed around?

"I have no time to be stolen away, Professor Warwick," I say stiffly. "I have work to do, in case you hadn't noticed. Work which *you're* interrupting."

Jeremy's watching our exchange with unabashed fascination. "You go," he says at last. I glance at him in surprise, but he's looking at Adam instead. I frown. I can't help but feel that there's something going on here, something I'm missing. "I can manage the rest."

I can barely wait until he's out of earshot before whirling to face Adam. "What did you do that for?"

He looks surprised at my vehemence. "It's called saving you. Unless you really wanted to spend the afternoon with Jeremy?"

Not massively. But somehow that doesn't seem to be the point right now.

"I do *not* need saving from my job! Contrary to your beliefs, I do actually have a lot of responsibilities." I pause, then can't resist adding, "If you'd been here lately, perhaps you would have seen that."

He looks at me for a long moment. Then he nods knowingly. "Ah. I see what it is. You're annoyed with me, aren't you?"

"Why would I be annoyed with you?" I scuff my shoes on the polished wooden floor, aware that I sound like a sullen child. "I've no reason to be."

He grins. "Don't say that you've *missed* me?"

"Don't be ludicrous."

Except I have. I've become so used to having him here, both in the museum and in my life. It's just not the same without his presence.

"Come on, don't sulk," he says. "Look, I've brought you something."

He holds out a little mint green box and I accept it from him cautiously. It's small, fitting neatly in the palm of my hand. It's neither particularly light nor particularly heavy. I'm wondering if it would be impolite to shake it, but one look at his face tells me to just get on and open it, so I do.

"Oh," I breathe. Of everything in the whole universe I would have expected to receive from him, this would have been the last thing.

"It's a sunstone," he says.

"You bought me a crystal?" I still can't believe it. I lift it carefully out of the box, holding it up to the light. It's a flat, smooth disc of coral-coloured stone, flecked with iridescent fragments which glint in the sunshine.

"I know you like them."

"*You* went into a crystal shop?"

I'm trying very hard to imagine it, but I'm struggling.

"I went into a *fossil* shop," he corrects me resolutely. "It happened to have some crystals in it."

I smile to myself. If it makes him feel better, then I'll let him have it.

"Thank you," I say softly. "I absolutely love it."

"It's meant to embody joy and positivity." I notice that he looks away from me, like he always does when there's any hint of emotion involved. "It ... I thought it would suit you."

I don't know what to say, so instead I do the only thing I can think of. I hug him.

For half a moment I'm afraid that he's going to back away, or go rigid, like he did last time. But then I feel his arms reach around me.

"It's all nonsense, of course," he begins gruffly. "There's no such thing as ..."

"*Don't* ruin it," I command. When will he learn that it's better sometimes to say nothing?

"Good advice." He pulls away so he can look at me. "Actually, I do have a confession to make. While I've got you on side."

Immediately, I'm wary. "What?"

"It wasn't just intended as an olive branch. It's also a bribe." His lips twist in a rueful approximation of a smile. "There's a favour I need to ask of you."

Chapter 17

Adam's office is much as I'd expected. It's a narrow room, the walls an uninspiring sandy colour, the carpet scuffed and worn. At the far end, a tiny window looks out over a small courtyard. It's a slightly prettier view than the one from my own office in the museum, but only just. The window is ajar; I suspect it's permanently that way. The room's vastly overheated, as all university buildings are. I remember going for meetings with my own university lecturers in rooms just like this one. Apparently, nothing's changed.

Adam seems to have made the best of it, though. The walls are lined with bookshelves, all teetering with hefty-looking tomes. There's a highly polished brass lamp and the obligatory globe—the mainstay of any self-respecting study. A large oak desk takes up most of the space, and provides just about the only surprising feature of the room: it's littered with coffee cups and screwed up pieces of paper.

"Sorry about those." He obviously notices me looking because he begins to sweep them hastily into the wastepaper basket next to his desk. "I'm normally quite tidy."

As if I'm one to judge. I peer into an open cabinet, filled with curious artefacts. Bits of stone, mainly. I pick one up; it looks like a piece of scrollwork which has been chipped off something.

"Ah, that." Adam looks up from where he's arranging some journals into a stack. "It came from the dig in Tuscany that I told you about. They gifted it to me when I left."

"Really?" That seems very nineteenth century. It brings to mind people hacking tiles off the Alhambra to keep as souvenirs. "They just let you take it?"

He shrugs. "They have so much stuff there, they almost don't know what to do with it all. They don't see it the same way we do."

I recall a trip to Rome several years ago. The crumbling churches, the Colosseum with a raging road around it, the cars passing within a hair's breadth of the ancient stonework, the thunder of lorries shaking its very foundations. Coming from Britain, where we're so fiercely protective of our heritage sites, it was quite a shock to the system. I put the stone down and pick up a hammered piece of metal. "And this?"

"That's part of the breastplate of a high-ranking general. He was buried in it."

I quickly put it down.

"They had to prise it off his skeleton," Adam's saying conversationally. "It had pretty much welded itself on ..."

I shudder, feeling a sudden need to wash my hands.

"Do you have anything which *isn't* ghoulish?"

"It's only ghoulish if you choose to look at it that way," he says a touch defensively. "Personally, I think it's fascinating."

"Hmm." I elect not to give more of an answer than that. Personally, I've seen too much of death to ever think of it as fascinating. "Is this what all the conversation is going to be like tonight?"

If it is, let's just pray there's an open bar.

"Afraid so. It is the faculty of Classical Studies, after all. Expect to hear a lot about the Romans."

"And the Greeks, I presume," I say glumly.

"The Greeks will seem like a welcome relief after you've been trapped in conversation with the current head of department, believe me." Suddenly, he looks sincere. "Thank you, by the way, for doing this. I couldn't face it alone. I hate all of this stuff."

"No worries." To be honest, when he said he needed a favour I was imagining something much worse than an evening spent at a drinks reception in the company of a few academics, even if they *are* in contention with one another for a promotion. I was anticipating something more along the lines of moving a body, or giving him a false alibi.

All joking aside, I'm relieved that we're back to our usual bantering mode of communication again. And strangely triumphant too; I kind of wish that Ruby and Eve could hear us now. Then they'd see how ridiculous it is to suggest that our friendship isn't sustainable.

I mean, look at us. We're *fine*. Nothing to see here. Whatever reason there might have been for Adam's distance of late, it appears to be in the past now. Perhaps I'll never know what it was really all about, but at the moment I don't care. I'm just glad to have things back to normal.

Wait ... Normal? Since when did Adam become part of my normal? It's an alarming thought.

"Do I look all right, by the way?" I twirl on the spot, arms outstretched. "I didn't know what the dress code is for this sort of thing."

In the end I went for my midnight blue velvet dress, with the wrap front and angel sleeves. Digging around in the bottom of my wardrobe, I rediscovered a pair of vintage-style T-bar shoes overlaid with silvery lace. I bought them for a wedding two years ago and had forgotten all about them. I wound my hair up into a topknot, letting some wavy tendrils dance around my face, and applied a slick of cherry lip gloss. I would have liked to have painted my nails too, but there wasn't any time left, so I decanted everything haphazardly into my silver clutch bag. God knows what I've got in there. Probably three tampons, an old cereal bar and no house keys, knowing my luck. Let's hope Freddie's at home to let me in later.

"You look lovely," Adam says, staring resolutely at a spot on the wall. I hide a smile.

"And you, er ..." I cough delicately. "You're going to wear that, are you?"

He gives me a dry look which tells me I wasn't as subtle as I'd hoped.

"As it happens, no, I was planning to change my jacket." He reaches into a slim cupboard wedged into the corner of the room. "I keep a supply in here for this sort of thing."

I feel I ought to look away, which of course is ridiculous. He's only changing his jacket, not his trousers. I feign interest in the globe on the desk, spinning it around until everything blurs into a big blue mass.

"There. Will I do?"

I look up, and my breath catches. He's wearing a navy blue blazer, tailored so that it fits the lines of his body, emphasising his broad shoulders and contrasting with his crisp white shirt.

He looks ... good. Really good.

At my obvious surprise, he raises both brows. "I'm not a complete sartorial ignoramus, you know."

Apparently not. I bite my lip, surveying the overall effect.

"There's just one more thing." I move towards him. "If you'll let me."

I reach up and loosen his tie, sliding it off his neck. Then, without stopping to think, I unfasten his top button. My fingers graze the warm hollow of his throat and it seems that we both simultaneously go very still. All of a sudden, the intimacy of it hits me. I feel his pulse jump and snatch my fingers away.

"There." I scuttle backwards, taking refuge behind the desk. I hope the shadows hide my heated face. Unfortunately, they can't do much to disguise the squeak in my voice. "All done."

He takes a long, deep breath.

"Thank you," he says at last. He sounds almost normal, but I notice there's a slight shake between the words. There's a pause, and I almost think he's about to say something else, but then he just gives the faintest shake of his head, as though he's changed his mind. Instead, he straightens the cuffs on his jacket and reaches for the door.

"Come along, then. Let's get this over with."

***

"Don't say I didn't warn you." Adam smirks as I stagger back towards the safety of the bar. He holds out a glass. "Champagne? Or, rather, slightly warm fizzy wine from the supermarket?"

"Right now, anything will do." I take a gulp, the bubbles dancing down my throat. "I thought I was never going to get away."

What I now know about catacombs could fill an entire book. If only that very book hadn't already been written by the head of the classics department at Alexandra College. Shame. As it stands, I won't need to rush out and buy a copy; I think I must have had every chapter recited to me in the last twenty minutes.

"He's obviously taken with you." Adam lounges back against the bar, which is in fact a rickety row of tables, behind which nervous-looking undergraduates are pouring wine into glasses. I wonder if they're actually getting paid for this, or if they've simply been intimidated into doing it by their lecturers. "And he's not the only one. You're quite a hit."

Quite a hit. With a load of tweed-clad academics. What an accolade. I take another healthy swig of my champagne.

"In all seriousness, though," he murmurs, and I get a thrill down my spine when I realise that he's moved much closer. "Thank you for this. I knew I could count on you."

He makes me sound like a faithful hound. For some reason, that makes me feel faintly depressed.

To be fair, I can see why Adam didn't want to do this on his own. Oh, it's all very pleasant on the surface; the Great Hall, with its vaulted ceiling and stained glass windows, the slightly dusty canapés, the rumble of erudite conversation. So far, everyone's behaving themselves.

But there are definite undercurrents of hostility. Pointed glares here from over rims of glasses, sharp comments there from behind sleeves, jibes pinging around beneath a thin shroud of false jollity. Sly allusions to past failures. I even overheard someone accusing one of the others of involving themselves in an affair with a student. In a veiled way, naturally, but the implication was there. And they said it in front of the Dean as well. Who knew the world of academia could be so cut-throat?

Everyone obviously knows that Adam's a frontrunner; in fact, most of the glares have been aimed in his direction. My heart goes out to him; Jeremy might be a pain, but he's a picnic compared to this lot. The least I can do for Adam is take some of the attention off him tonight.

And I've done a pretty good job of it, if I do say so myself. I've listened attentively to the subject of various papers, sympathised over the lack of available grant money and deflected any negative comments before they made it to Adam's ears. I am, frankly, exhausted, and beginning to remember why I stuffed these shoes right to the back of the wardrobe in the first place. My toes are squashed together like sardines.

"The way you sold it to me, I was expecting a punch-up by now." I attempt to wiggle my toes, only to be rewarded by red-hot pain shooting through my foot. I wince. "I'm a bit disappointed, truth be told."

He smiles. "That can still be arranged. Would you like me to start one?"

"Sure." I play along, pretending to scan the room. "Who shall we pick?"

"Professor Fitzharris has always been something of a pompous twerp," Adam remarks mildly.

I nearly choke on my wine. "Sounds like this isn't the first time you've thought about it."

"It isn't. Plus, I saw him look you up and down when you were talking to him. That cemented it."

He almost sounds protective. I feel strangely warm, which I attribute to the wine I've just downed. I'm losing track of how many glasses I've had. Too many, in all likelihood.

At that moment the heavy wooden door opens and a man walks in. By my side, I feel Adam go still.

"What's the matter?" I whisper, nudging him with my elbow.

"I was hoping he wouldn't come tonight. I thought he was still in Athens."

I watch as the man makes a beeline towards us, scooping up a glass of champagne on the way.

"Adam." He nods a greeting, although there's little warmth in it.

"Professor," Adam returns stonily.

My head's bobbing between the two of them in confusion. What's going on here? They're staring one another down like prizefighters at a weigh-in. The older man notices me, and a mocking smile touches his mouth.

"Aren't you going to introduce me to your lady friend?"

"Clara Swift." I step forward quickly, holding out my hand. Adam seems to have temporarily lost the power of speech. "I work at the Montague Museum."

"I know it well. It used to be one of my favourite haunts, although I haven't been there of late." He sidles a glance at Adam. "Perhaps I ought to start coming back. What do you say, Adam?"

Adam's knuckles have gone white around the stem of his glass. "I think we're causing a scene," he says tightly.

Indeed, the volume of chatter in the room has died down, I notice now. Everyone's making a concentrated effort to pretend to be absorbed in their own conversations, but I can tell that their attention is really directed towards our little group.

"Always so uptight," the older man tuts. "It's just a joke, dear boy. Can't you make him loosen up a bit?" he asks me with a wink. "It would do him no end of good."

"I like him as he is," I say lightly, but with deliberate meaning behind my words. I'm starting to dislike this man; what's he got against Adam? And *why* isn't Adam standing up for himself? I've never known him stay silent before. "And we're just friends."

"Ah." Our unwelcome interloper runs a hand through his black hair. It's tinged with grey at the temples but, other than that, it's hard to guess at his age. "That makes more sense."

I'm not sure what that's supposed to mean, but I don't think the insinuation was a positive one. I'm about to make a retort when Adam finally speaks.

"Leave Clara out of this. She has nothing to do with our petty squabbles."

The man drains his glass. "Of course, it's always work with you, isn't it?" He gives me a look as if to say, *No wonder you're not getting anywhere.*

"I think we should go," Adam says quietly to me. "Before I say something I'll regret."

I take one look at his face and immediately concur. I've never seen him look so furious, not even with me. At least then he could vent his anger; now, it's tightly leashed, etched into his face in stark lines.

"Back to your book, is it?" The man leers, grabbing another glass of champagne. "Yes, I've heard about that. Pulling out all the stops, aren't you? Ingratiating yourself very nicely with the powers that be."

"I am *not* going to enter into conversation with you," Adam says shortly, taking my arm. "We're leaving. The stage is all yours. Enjoy it."

"Adam," I gasp as he drags me away. I'm painfully aware of about fifty pairs of eyes burning into our backs. "What's going on? Who *was* that?"

"That," he says grimly, still looking straight ahead. "Was my father."

Chapter 18

One look at Adam's face after we left told me that he needed a drink. A proper drink, preferably in multiple hues and with a swizzle stick in it. If I were to choose a motto, it might well be, *When life knocks you for six, have a cocktail*.

Or even six cocktails.

Actually, scratch that. I've been there before. Six cocktails is *not* a good idea, believe me.

I've brought us to my favourite bar. It has pink suede seating, a drinks menu which stretches to over seven pages and a wraparound terrace from which you can see pretty much the whole of Cambridge. On the horizon, the sky is melting into a rainbow of sorbet-coloured stripes, and a crescent moon peeps out from behind a crenellated spire. On a night like this, the city looks more otherworldly than ever, like a lost kingdom suspended in the half-light of an enchantment.

I'm not sure Adam's even noticed the view. In fact, I'm not certain that he's ever been to a cocktail bar before either. He looked so baffled by the menu that in the end I ordered for him.

He watches warily now as the waiter places a tall, slender glass in front of him.

"What did you say this was called again?"

It's about the first full sentence he's uttered since we left the college.

"It's a Long Island Iced Tea," I reiterate, sharing a sympathetic look with the waiter. "It's a classic."

He picks up the glass, but doesn't take a drink. "And what, exactly, is in it?"

A lot of alcohol is what. That's basically why I chose it. But he doesn't need to know that.

The waiter looks at me questioningly, and I give a minute shake of the head. With a shrug, he puts down my strawberry daiquiri and moves away.

"And what is *that*?" Mercifully, Adam seems to have been distracted by my own drink.

"Strawberries and rum, mainly," I answer, talking a sip. Heaven. "Plus it has the distinct advantage of being pink. And if you ask nicely they'll arrange the strawberry slices in a flower shape on top."

He rolls his eyes. "That's the most ridiculous thing I've ever heard. What's the point? You're only going to drink it."

"Not everything in life has to be purely functional." I twirl the cocktail umbrella between my finger and thumb. "Like these. Completely pointless, and yet wouldn't our planet be a much bleaker place without them?"

The expression on his face suggests that he thinks I'm thoroughly mad. I nudge his own glass closer towards him.

"Come on, drink it. You'll feel better."

Frankly, I think a bit of whimsy would do him good. At least after this evening I can begin to understand why he's so uptight. I can't imagine what it must be like, having to exist in that environment day in, day out. I'd have lost the plot long ago.

"I'm so sorry about tonight." He scrubs a hand across his face with a sigh. "I honestly didn't know he would be there. I never would have subjected you to it otherwise."

"Has it ... always been like that?" I ask tentatively. A part of me knows that I shouldn't pry but, at the same time, how can I not? I still can't believe that was actually his *father*. The way he treated Adam ... It was almost like he hated him.

"Not as bad as that, no." Adam's lips twist ruefully. "He's always been fiercely competitive—with everyone—but he's become so much worse since this whole head of department thing came up. He always expected that the role would be his, you see. But there was never an opening until now, and suddenly he's having to face the prospect that it might skip over him altogether." He takes a long draught of his cocktail. "It's not like I don't understand that but ... I don't know, it's like he just can't separate the fact that I'm his son from the fact that I'm also his colleague."

"And now his rival," I add softly. I've never heard Adam talk like this. He's always so reserved, so self-contained. Sometimes, it's easy to fall into the trap of assuming that he doesn't have feelings. But now the pain in his voice is so audible that it makes my chest clench.

"Exactly." He slaps his hand on the table, making me jump. His eyes look a bit glazed, I notice. Perhaps I should have ordered him something a little less potent. "I don't know what to do any more. It's becoming intolerable; as it stands, I'm not sure if our relationship will ever recover. But perhaps I should stop now while there's still a chance to salvage it."

I'm so busy marvelling at how intoxication hasn't affected his vocabulary that it takes me a moment to realise that he's still talking.

"He drove my mother away, you know," he says suddenly. "She just wanted to teach; she wasn't interested in being a star. Even so, he could never resist the opportunity to turn everything into a competition. In the end, she couldn't take it any more."

I poke at the ice cubes in my glass with the end of the cocktail umbrella. I wonder if he's ever told anyone this before. It doesn't sound like it.

"Where is she now?"

"Wales. She works for a small university on the coast. There's no pressure, no hierarchy. She loves it. She didn't say much when I applied for Alexandra College. But then, she didn't have to. I knew what she was thinking." He screws up a paper napkin in his fist. "I promised myself that it would be different this time. But it isn't, is it? It's happening all over again."

He looks so dejected that I place my hand over his.

"These past few weeks, I've begun to wonder if I didn't make a big mistake, all those years ago. Maybe my mother was right; I should have gone somewhere completely different, broken the chain in this whole preposterous Alexandra lineage." He scrubs a hand across his face. "Maybe it's not too late. I could hand in my notice, go somewhere new. It's not like I have many friends left here; I've been so caught up in my work ... no one would miss me."

I feel a lurch of dismay, and the words are out of my mouth before I can catch them.

"*I'd* miss you."

"You would?" He looks at me intently, and I feel myself shrinking.

"Of course." I attempt to keep my tone jocular. "Who would I have to annoy at the museum? It'd be no fun at all."

He looks away, out across the skyline. "Oh, I think you'd be all right. You'd find someone else."

There's an extra meaning in his voice, something left unsaid, hanging in the air between us. But, for the life of me, I can't work out what. I wait for him to continue, but instead the pause stretches out indefinitely.

Hopelessly confused now, I decide to move us back towards a less contentious topic.

"You know, I still can't understand why Jeremy's offered me the opening speech at the Holman Hunt unveiling next week. I've been racking my brains over it."

Adam leans back in his chair. "It's about time you had more of a chance to shine. He's been keeping you in the shadows for too long. You pretty much run that place."

I stare at him. Was that actually a *compliment*? He's so matter-of-fact in his way of speaking that it's almost hard to tell.

"You think I don't know how much you do?" He looks amused now. "Cambridge is a very small bubble, Clara. Everyone knows everything."

It *was* a compliment. Somehow, the fact that it was hard won makes me feel strangely elated.

My empty glass is frosted with condensation and I run a finger through it, trying to gear up to what I want to ask next.

"Will you be there, by any chance?" I'm hoping I've kept my tone casual, like I don't care much either way.

"Would you like me to be?"

As usual, straight to the point. I should have known better than to try and get anything past him.

"Yes, please," I say in a small voice.

"Then I'll be there."

I look up at him, letting my gratitude show in my eyes. Gratitude that I don't have to explain, that he makes everything so uncomplicated.

"You know, you weren't wrong about these iced tea things," he says, holding up his glass. He drains his drink, beckoning over the waiter. "Shall we have another?"

Chapter 19

I've always loved Cambridge at night, when most of the tourists have gone home and the city feels like it can breathe again. There's no one else in sight as we walk along the river-side. The punts are safely lined up in their moorings, the water lapping gently against the edges of the bank, providing a rhythmic backdrop to our conversation.

I've long since let my hair down, and it dances against my shoulders in the evening breeze. At least the pain in my feet has subsided, something I'm hoping is down to the gloriously numbing effect of alcohol and not because the nerves in my toes have given up and died.

I have no idea what time it is, and I don't want to know. I don't want to be anchored in reality just yet. Everything has a beautifully dreamlike quality to it tonight, the glassy surface of the water reflecting the starlight above like fire-flies. The rustling of the trees, hushed in the quiet air. And Adam ... well, talking. Actually, properly *talking*. That's the most unreal thing of all. And I sense that, like any spell, it will be all too brief. Come the morning, this will just be a slightly hazy, tipsy memory. This new side to him will be gone, locked away behind his inscrutable facade once more.

"I've always known that this was where I wanted to be." He looks out across the water, where lights glow like orbs along the edges of the buildings. "And not because of the legacy, or what was expected of me. Because *I* wanted it. Because this place felt like somewhere I could belong. But perhaps I was wrong." He turns to me, and the resignation in his face is heartbreaking. "What do you think? You believe in all this fate business. Is something telling me to drop out of the running?"

I hesitate, chewing my lip in indecision. I'm always reluctant to give advice, even when asked. In my experience, people need to come to their own conclusions. But I find that I can't keep quiet this time.

"No."

Something flares in his eyes. "You don't?"

I have the full force of his attention; it's almost tangible, a heavy presence in the air around us. With a jolt, I realise that what I say next actually matters. Adam doesn't ask questions like that idly.

"No, I don't." I sigh deeply. "Look, it's not your fault that this is happening. You should be proud of what you've achieved, and so should he. I'm sure if he knew you were actually considering giving up on your dreams because of him he'd be horrified."

"I wouldn't be so sure of that."

I frown at the bitterness in his voice.

"Adam, he's still your father, even if he's not acting much like it at the moment. Parents aren't perfect; they're fallible like anyone else. But, at the end of the day, isn't all they ever want the best for their children?"

"Your faith in human nature is touching. The truth is that my father is a selfish bastard who always puts himself first in the end." He pushes a low-hanging tree branch out of our path. "But then, I'm guessing your parents are warm, adoring types who support you in everything you do. The kind who comfort you when you get a bad exam result rather than yell at you and let you eat cake for breakfast. Who tell you over and over that you could never disappoint them." He shoves another branch out of the way, this time more savagely. "How could you *possibly* understand?"

Suddenly, my chest feels constricted. I stop, placing a hand over my heart, trying to breathe normally.

"Clara?" He's looking at me quizzically. "Are you all right?"

"Yes, I'm fine." My voice sounds dry. "It's just ... you're right; that's exactly what they were like. They used to say that to me all the time."

"Oh, crap." Even in the dark, I can see the colour draining from his face. "I'm so sorry, Clara. I didn't realise. I never would have said anything—"

"What, and pretend they never existed?" I shake my head, which swims alarmingly in response. Okay, still very much on the tipsy side. No wonder I feel like bursting into tears. Usually, if I have to talk about my parents, I put my defences up beforehand. In this state, though, I can't even begin to construct them. "No. I'd rather they were spoken about. That way, it feels like they're still present."

We walk on for a few moments in silence.

"When …? How …?" He breaks off, looking annoyed with himself. "Sorry, bad questions. A historian's habit, to always look for the facts."

Watching him chastise himself for wanting to ask the natural questions is almost touching.

"Three years ago. A plane crash. They were visiting an isolated group in the Norwegian mountains. Mum wanted to experience their spiritual rituals as a way of connecting with her own ancestral line." At the ill-disguised look of disbelief on Adam's face, I find myself laughing. "If you think *I'm* mad, you should have met my mother. She was something else."

His lips quirk in a reluctant smile. "Did she paint the house pink too?"

"She painted the house a different colour each season. Or sometimes just one wall. Inside, all the ceilings were blue, like the sky." Remembering my childhood home should make me sad, but oddly, it doesn't. Not tonight. "She'd hang wind chimes everywhere too. She said they cleared the energy. Every time Dad walked into a room, he'd hit his head on them. It used to drive him crazy. At least, outwardly it did; secretly, I think that's what he loved most about her. Her sense of spontaneity, her belief that life was an amazing gift which should be savoured. She was so full of joy."

"Something she's passed on to you," Adam observes gently.

"I wish." I pull his jacket closer around my shoulders. I hope he's not cold; I felt it would wound his male pride if I refused to take it. "No matter how much I try, I seem to lack her sense of serenity, her absolute unshakeable faith that everything would turn out for the best. A part of me believes but, at the same time, another part ..." I break off, looking at the floor. "Sometimes life just feels so hard, doesn't it?"

I can't believe I'm talking so freely about this. But then, I guess I *am* rather the worse for wear; three strawberry daiquiris will do that to a girl. And Adam ... There's just something about him, something so reassuring and steadfast. Once, I might have found that dull, but I would have been wrong. It's actually one of the most wonderful things about him.

Wonderful. He *is* wonderful. How have I never noticed that before?

"Do you know what my mum would do at this moment?" I ask suddenly. "She'd tell us to stop being so maudlin and to look up at the stars. She'd say that the stars put everything in perspective."

I kick off my heels and sink my bare feet into the cool grass, spinning wildly on the spot. Above my head, the pinpricks of light begin to blur into one.

"Hey—" Adam catches me, laughing "—I think you're a bit far gone to be doing that, don't you?"

He has a point. Right now, he has three faces. I blink hard, trying to regain normal focus.

"I'm *such* a lightweight," I moan, leaning into him. He feels solid, perhaps the only solid thing in the world right now. "Why aren't you as drunk as I am?"

"I am. I just don't show it." He slips an arm around my waist, supporting me. "I'm more of a quiet drunk. There's a reason I never get invited to parties any more; I usually just sit in the corner, growing more and more morose."

"You do that when you're sober," I murmur, resting my head against his shoulder.

"I'll let that slide, given your current state of intoxication. Come on, let's go over the bridge."

Normally, Alexandra Bridge is off-limits to the public as it leads straight onto the college grounds. I watch, still swaying slightly, as Adam produces a key and unlocks the wrought iron gate. His hands are enviably steady.

I twizzle the cocktail umbrella between my fingers, leaning across the stone balustrade to gaze into the black watery depths.

"I just wish that life was really as simple as Mum believed it was. Sometimes, I think I'm doing all right, and then other times ..."

I hold the umbrella out over the water. A light breeze tugs at it, asking to snatch it from my fingers.

"Other times I feel like I could just ... drift away."

"Don't do that." All of a sudden, he's next to me. He takes the parasol from my hand and tucks it behind my ear like a tropical flower.

"Why not?" I'm gazing up into his eyes. They're a fathomless shade in the dark.

"Because *I'd* miss *you*." His fingers linger fleetingly against my cheek, then drop to his side.

I can't tell if he's teasing or not. I tip my head back; up above, the moon is as bright as I've ever seen it, piercing through the ink of the sky, encircled by a scattering of stars. On a night like this, how can I feel anything other than lucky to be alive?

"Isn't it magical?" I whisper.

"Not in the slightest." His response is instantaneous. "It's hydrogen and light particles."

My chin snaps downwards and I scowl at him. Does he have to ruin *everything*?

He moves closer, cupping my face in his hands.

"You, on the other hand, are another matter."

And then his lips are on mine. And the world starts to spin all over again, except this time for an entirely different reason.

For a few seconds it's perfect. Then he tears himself away and the look of absolute horror on his face is enough to sober me up immediately.

"Oh, God, I'm sorry." He presses a shaking hand to his forehead, his breathing ragged. "That was a terrible thing to do."

Despite the fact that I know he's right, I can't help but feel a prickle of indignation. Does he have to sound *quite* so emphatic about it?

He grips the balustrade, staring out over the water. "That was unforgivable of me. You're with someone, and I'm..."

"Very drunk," I say, my calm voice belying the thudding in my chest. "We both are. Let's not blow this out of proportion."

Even as I say it, though, I'm feeling nauseous, the reality of it hitting me in a wave. Is that really any excuse? What am I going to tell Josh?

Because I have to tell Josh, that much is clear. I can't possibly keep this from him. I couldn't live with it if I did.

"I never meant to make things difficult for you, Clara.

Please believe me." Adam looks thoroughly wretched. Instinctively, I go to place a reassuring hand on his arm, but stop myself just in time. We both look at my hand, hovering in mid-air, then at one another, and in that moment the shift which has occurred between us feels unbearably apparent.

In just a matter of moments our relationship has irretrievably altered. Whatever friendship we had begun to form has taken a sharp swerve into unknown territory. I don't know what's okay any more, how to act.

"I'm sure he'll understand," I say. I'm still aiming for a breezy tone, but instead it just sounds false. "I mean, it was just a stupid moment, right? It didn't *mean* anything."

There's a weighty pause.

"No," Adam says at last. "Of course it didn't. Nothing at all." He looks away, but not before I catch a glimpse of a faint flush across his face. Or at least what looks like a flush; in this light, it could just be shadows. "Would you like me to ... you know, speak to him? Try and explain?"

I can't decide if I'm more touched or appalled. Just the thought of them having that conversation makes me want to crawl into a hole and die.

"God, no," I blurt out before hastily backtracking. "I mean, no, thank you. I'll handle it."

He has the grace not to look wholeheartedly relieved. "All right. But the offer stands. If things get difficult ..."

If things get difficult, then he's more likely to be greeted by a swift right hook than a chance to say his piece. He's a smart man; surely he must know that.

I close my eyes against the swirling thoughts in my head.

Why did he have to choose this moment to be so unbearably sweet? It just makes it so much harder to walk away.

I slide his jacket off my shoulders and hand it back to him. "I'd better go."

He steps forward. "I'll walk you home."

"No." The word comes out more forcefully than I'd intended. "I'll make my own way. Thanks."

He doesn't look pleased, but then he doesn't have a lot of choice in the matter.

"Well, if you're sure."

His voice is distant, coldly formal. I wrap my arms around myself. It's almost like we're going backwards, reverting to our initial awkward exchanges. I hover, not knowing what else to say. That just makes the aching even worse; before, I would *always* have known what to say to him.

"I'll see you ..." When? At the unveiling? Who knows now? At the museum? Maybe. But will we even speak? Oh, God, this is awful. "I'll just ... see you."

And, with that obscure parting shot, I turn and walk away into the dark.

Chapter 20

"So ... you kissed him. Again," Heather adds, somewhat unnecessarily. And somewhat pointedly too, in my opinion. I frown at her, a feat not easily achieved when I'm bending over with my head between my knees and my hands flat on the floor.

"I did not *kiss* him the first time. We've been over this." I straighten up too fast and stars dance in front of my eyes.

"But you definitely did this time." She follows my lead, stretching her arms up above her head. "What's this one called again?"

"Mountain pose. And if we're being technical about it, *he* kissed *me*."

"It doesn't matter who started it." She reaches up higher, wincing. "Did you kiss him back? That's the important question here."

I release my arms, gradually dropping them down to my sides with a deep exhale. Obviously, Heather hasn't grasped the concept that yoga is supposed to be meditative and relaxing. It's anything *other* than relaxing right now, with her firing questions at me. Especially questions I don't particularly want to answer.

"I don't know," I admit. I've replayed it all so many times, I don't even know if I trust my own recollection of events any more. "It all happened so fast."

"Oh. So not a full-on kiss, then?" Is it just me, or does she look faintly disappointed?

"No," I say sharply. "Of course not. We both realised straight away that it was a mistake, and we pulled away. It was a few seconds of madness, that's all."

That's the line I've been repeating in my head, over and over since it happened. And if it's beginning to hint faintly of desperation ... Well, look, it's the truth. Or at least it's the only truth I can handle at the moment.

It *has* to be the truth. There's simply no other option.

"If you say so."

I catch my foot in my hand, placing it against my thigh in preparation for tree pose. I'm trying hard not to feel annoyed with her. Annoyance is not yogic. I'm supposed to be suffused with benevolent thoughts, love to the world and all of that.

"None of this matters anyway, not now," I say crisply, hoping to put an end to this line of discussion. "I've told Josh, and we've sorted it out."

"Wait ... You *told* him?" She wobbles precariously on one leg. "God, this is hard."

"Just concentrate. It'll get easier."

"Easy for you to say." She eyes me malevolently as I gently unfurl from the pose. "You have better balance than I do. Probably because you're not permanently exhausted from running around after a three-year-old all day. Sometimes, I find it hard to stay upright on two legs, let alone one. Most days, I could gladly fall asleep in the supermarket aisle."

I huff disbelievingly.

"Like you ever go to the supermarket any more." Heather's Waitrose delivery slot is sacrosanct; nothing messes with it. Even poor Oscar's needs are secondary.

She ignores my jibe.

"What did he say when you told him?"

"He was fine about it." I hesitate, wondering whether to tell her more. "As a matter of fact, he kind of ... laughed it off."

"He *laughed*?" She loses her balance, stumbling back into the sofa. Her handbag flops onto its side, spilling its contents across the seat. Casper looks up in indignation at the disturbance and she pats him apologetically on the head before turning back to me, aghast. "You told him that you kissed another man and he laughed?"

"Not literally." Actually, he kind of did, but now I'm on the defensive. I'm beginning to wish I hadn't said anything. Heather has a way of latching onto things. "What I mean is that he thinks it's no big deal. And why shouldn't he? He could see that it was nothing to worry about. He said that these things happen."

"Clara—" Heather sits down on the sofa, her face creased with concern "—don't you think that's a little ... odd?"

Whatever she's getting at, I don't want to go there. To be honest, I'm just so grateful that he took it as well as he did; I half expected him to end it there and then or, failing that, for things to be decidedly strained between us for a while. But they haven't been; in fact, anyone could be forgiven for thinking that nothing had happened at all.

He's been utterly wonderful about everything, far more so than I think I could have been if it had been the other way around. So, yes, perhaps his reaction was a little ... surprising. But after the understanding he's shown me, how can I possibly start questioning his motives? It would be horribly unfair. Trust has to work both ways.

I don't want to turn into someone like Heather. That's the difference between us; she's always worrying, always looking for problems. Sometimes where there isn't even one to find in the first place.

"He's just not the jealous type, that's all," I explain. "He doesn't overreact to things. He *listens* instead." How many men can you say that of? "It's one of the things I like best about him. It's why we fit. I thought you knew that."

I'm beginning to feel exasperated. I mean, it was her idea to put myself out there in the first place. She *wanted* me to meet someone who makes me happy.

And Josh does. He really does, I remind myself staunchly. Things are so great between us, I almost have to keep pinching myself to check that it's real. We've almost fallen into the pattern of a relationship without even having to try; he stays over at mine every night now. I've even caught myself referring to him as my boyfriend a few times. Just in my head so far; I haven't actually said it in front of him as yet, but I'm thinking that I will soon. I mean, one of us has to go first, don't they? And the last time we tried to have a conversation about our relationship status ... well, it was about the most awkward it's ever been between us. I don't want to attempt that again.

The truth is, I'm starting to realise that talking about it just isn't our style. It's too formal; it makes it weird, when it doesn't have to be. How much more natural would it be to just drop it into the conversation—at the right moment, of course—and he'll look at me with those glorious green eyes, and something unspoken will pass between us and ...

"Yes, but don't you think there's such a thing as *too* easy-going?" Heather's voice jostles me back into the present. She's playing with a tassel on one of my cushions, looking apprehensive. "Do you really think he's as serious about your relationship as you are?"

I stare at her. I can't believe she's actually asking me this.

"Heather," I say slowly. "What are you doing?"

"I'm not doing anything!" She holds up her hands. "I'm just asking the question, that's all. I want you to be honest with yourself. Why are you being so defensive?"

"I don't need to be honest with myself!" I say hotly. I've given up all pretence of doing yoga by now. Instead I fold my arms across my body, glaring down at her. "And if I'm being defensive, it's because you're trying to make me doubt him. I thought you were *happy* for me."

"I am!" Heather bites her lip, looking anguished. "But I'm worried, Clara. He's not acting like a man who wants commitment. I'm just not sure that you two are on the same page, and I worried you're going to get hurt. You know that you have a tendency to ..."

"To what?" I demand. "Go on, say it."

"You tend to only look for what you want to see," she says quietly. "You get carried away on some romantic daydream and you miss all the warning signs."

"What warning signs?" I all but cry. "There *are* no warning signs. He's bloody *perfect*. Even Casper adores him. Wasn't that the ultimate test? Well, he's passed! What more proof do you need?"

"Casper ..." For a moment, she looks confused, then her face clears. "Wait, you don't mean that conversation we had over lunch? Where I told you ..."

I just look back defiantly. Her blue eyes widen in horror.

"Clara, that was just a joke! I didn't mean for you to take it literally." She gives a forced-sounding laugh. "Cats don't matchmake. Surely even you must know that's crazy."

"No, I don't," I say furiously. "And I'm not a joke, whatever you might think."

Her face falls. "I've never thought—"

"Yes, you have! You *all* have! You think I'm some zany airhead who floats around in floral dresses and fills her house with meaningless coloured rocks. You *humour* me." Suddenly, tears are pricking at the back of my eyes, and I blink them away. Years upon years of being sidelined, patronised and underestimated are all coming to the surface. But then, maybe they've never really been that far beneath it. "At least Josh takes me seriously."

"That is *not* true." Heather shakes her head. "No one thinks that. *I* don't think that."

But there's a faint hesitation before she says it which I don't miss.

How could I not have noticed? Or perhaps I did, and I just didn't want to admit it, even to myself. Heather, my colleagues ... even Adam, I realise with a heavy sensation. All that talk about discussing his thesis; maybe he just suggested that out of kindness, to make me think that he actually respected my opinion. When I'm with him it's easy to forget but, let's be honest; what am I in his eyes? Just a ditzy, frivolous girl. I don't belong in his world. I'm fine for a laugh, a cocktail or two, perhaps even a stolen kiss.

That kiss. My stomach drops to the floor just at the memory. Would he have acted so rashly with someone more illustrious, I wonder? Another academic, someone who was more on his level?

Someone *important*?

No, I don't think he would. The thought alone is enough to make my throat tighten all over again.

And now I'm with Josh, and for once I actually feel like we're on a level. For once, I feel like I'm enough, just as I am. And my best friend is trying to ruin it for me. I don't understand why. Unless ...

"Are you *jealous*?" I ask Heather abruptly. I'm lashing out, speaking before I think, but even as the words are leaving my mouth I know that it's the only explanation. Why else would she be saying all of this?

Her mouth drops open. "*Excuse* me?"

"You are; you're jealous." I jab my finger at her. Which just goes to show how much she's got to me; normally I'd die before doing anything so vulgar. "Because you settled with Dominic, and you know it."

Her fingers grip into the cushion, causing deep dents in the velvety fabric. Other than that, she's completely still. Even her lips hardly move when she next speaks.

"How can you say that?"

"Because it's true!" I throw my hands up in the air. "You tell me to be honest with myself; why don't you take some of your own advice? You knew the truth all those years ago, when we sat up all night talking about whether you should break it off with him. Do you remember what you said?"

She's gone white. "No, I ..."

"Well, I do. You said you didn't think that you could ever love him. To which I replied that, if that was the case, it was better to end it sooner rather than later. And you *agreed*! But you were afraid to do it, and then you found out you were pregnant, and suddenly it was too late." I break off, breathing heavily. We've never spoken about this before; there's always been a tacit agreement between us to pretend like it never happened. After all, what was the point? What was done was done. But now all of those old feelings, that lingering sense of unfairness which I've always been too ashamed to confront ... it's all there, fuelling my words. "You made your mistake, Heather, and you've had to live with it. But now you just can't bear to see *me* get it right, can you?"

There's a tense, awful silence. Immediately, my hand flies to my mouth; I've said too much, and I know it. But I can't unsay it; it's there, out in the open, and there's no taking it back.

"Well," Heather says at last, and her voice is so low that I can barely make out the words. "If that's really what you think ..."

she begins to gather items back into her handbag with shaking hands "... then I suppose there isn't much more I can say."

"Heather, look ..."

I feel like the worst person in the world. She looks utterly crushed, and all I want to do is fling my arms around her and beg for forgiveness. But something stops me— perhaps a sense that if I don't hold my ground now, I won't be doing myself any favours. How can I expect her to take me seriously if I don't take *myself* seriously? So I stop before I can say any more.

She looks at me for a long moment, then hoists the bag onto her shoulder.

"You're better than this, Clara. You might have convinced yourself on the surface that he's everything you've been looking for, but underneath you know that something's not right. But if you won't even be honest with yourself, then I can't protect you. You're on your own this time." She stands. "Don't worry, I'll let myself out."

After she's gone, the atmosphere in the room is unbearable. Even Casper seems to be looking at me accusingly, which in itself is unsettling. Because, God knows, his moral compass is decidedly skewed.

"I don't know what you're looking at me like that for," I snap. Then suddenly all of my anger leaves me and I sink down onto the sofa, dropping my head into my hands. Casper clambers into my lap, wedging himself into the tight space between my arms. I pull him close, burying my face in his fur, and for once he doesn't protest at being squeezed.

At least, if nothing else, I'll always have my cat.

Chapter 21

"You okay?" Ruby smoothes lip gloss over her lips, pouting at her reflection in the mirror. "You look kind of jumpy."

Ever tactful, Ruby.

"I'm nervous, that's all." I brace my hands on either side of the sink. "It's a big thing for me."

"Well, you look great, so you're halfway there."

Even I have to admit that she's right. For once, my nerves aren't showing on my face. In fact, I look pretty glowing, although that might have more to do with liberal application of highlighter than anything. I've left my hair down, with just the front sections pulled back from my face, revealing my high cheekbones, which are further accentuated by said highlighter. Ruby's always telling me to show off my cheekbones more.

I went through my wardrobe this afternoon, trying to find the most sombre garment I owned. Something appropriate for an assistant curator to stand up in front of a room full of academics, museum-goers and art journalists. But instead, almost of its own accord, my hand reached in and pulled out this dress. It's the very opposite of sombre, a halterneck fifties-style frock with a swirly skirt and an all-over lemon print. Usually I keep it for summer weddings and suchlike; I don't know why I chose it for tonight. But somehow it felt right. Perhaps a part of me felt what I always have, that I shouldn't need to change my appearance to be treated with respect. What's the point of standing there and pretending to be someone I'm not?

In any event, I needn't have worried about being the most outlandishly dressed person here. Ruby's wearing an emerald green catsuit. I thought Jeremy might have an apoplexy when he saw, but luckily he didn't. In fact, he seemed to almost take it in his stride. Perhaps he's mellowing.

Ha. That will be the day.

"Just stand there, say your stuff, we'll all applaud, then we can have champagne." Ruby waves her lip gloss as though this were the simplest thing in the world. "Easy."

Easy indeed. Easy, perhaps, when nothing fazes you and the whole world's your stage. But I hate public speaking; I always have, even in school when all we had to do was stand up in front of the class and recite a poem.

I unfold my notes now and stare at them for what has to be the thousandth time. I'm pretty pleased with how my speech has shaped up, if I do say so myself. It's nothing groundbreaking, but then how could it be, with Jeremy as chief editor and censor? The page is covered with his crabbed handwriting: crossings out here, additions there, the odd cryptic comment. My favourite is the one next to a sentence about the accessibility of great art, which says 'too inspiring'. How can something be too inspiring? Then again, I think now, peering at it closely—his handwriting *is* appalling—maybe it actually says 'too insipid'. Or even 'too insufferable'. Either's perfectly likely.

But, even with Jeremy's dampening influence, I still think it's a good speech. And somehow it's still *my* speech. It doesn't just sound like something Jeremy would write, which is what I was afraid of. Hopefully, it will also manage to keep more people awake than one of Jeremy's speeches.

"Okay." I square my shoulders, winding an errant curl around my finger to coax it back into position. "We can't hide in the ladies' forever. We'd better get out there."

Ruby gives me a look as if to say, *Who's hiding?*

Taking a fortifying breath, I push open the bathroom door, only to be hit by a wall of sound. Classical music tinkles tastefully in the background, beneath the buzz of educated chatter and polite laughter. Waiters weave between the crowd with trays of champagne. *Actual* champagne in this case, I happen to know. And since when did our dusty little museum's budget ever stretch to waiters? I mean, granted, the Holman Hunt is a big coup, probably one of the biggest in the museum's history, but still. Jeremy must have had to pull hard on the purse strings for this one.

"Here ..." Ruby snags a couple of glasses from a passing tray with her customary shameless ease. The waiter, who was obviously taking them somewhere, looks annoyed until she flashes him a disarming smile. He smiles shyly back, looking slightly awed; I can practically see him falling under her spell. How does she do that? Perhaps it's the lamé catsuit. "This will help take the edge off."

"Thanks." I take it gratefully, knocking it back rather faster than I perhaps ought to.

"Steady!" She puts a hand on my wrist. "You don't want to be half-cut for your speech, do you?"

Actually, that doesn't sound like a bad idea right now. I look around at my intimidating audience, and my stomach tightens with nerves.

And then, across the room, I see a familiar face. And my stomach tightens even more, but this time it's in a good way. A fluttery way.

Josh crosses the room in long strides. "Hey," he says as he draws closer. "I'm not late, am I?"

He's really here. It took quite a bit of persuading; he kept coming up with excuses, and all I managed to wrest from him in the end was a vague promise that he'd do his best to make it. My heart soars as I take him in; he looks incredible, in a dark suit, the white shirt setting off his golden skin. Like a Greek god.

"No," I manage dazedly. "You're perfect."

And all mine.

He pulls me close and kisses me. It's an amazing kiss, totally romantic, if not a little theatrical.

And if not a *little* inappropriate, considering the setting.

"Josh!" I push him gently away, my face already heating. "I'm at work."

He retrieves a flute of champagne from a nearby waiter. "Not really. Isn't this just an excuse for a party?"

I feel myself frowning. "This is a big moment for the museum. It means exposure and maybe even more funding. It's important that we impress tonight."

I'm aware that I sound like a stick-in-the-mud, but his casual dismissal of this evening has pricked me. I need him to know how important this is. I thought he *did* know how important this is. I told him all about it, and he said ...

Well, actually, come to think of it, he didn't say much at all. We were in bed at the time, and he started doing the most amazing things to ...

Okay. I really *have* to stop over-sharing, don't I?

"No Heather tonight?" he asks lightly, and I jump guiltily.

"Er ... no. She had a last-minute emergency with Oscar."

I haven't told Josh about the argument with Heather. I don't want him to think that we've fallen out because of him; he'd feel terrible, and that wouldn't be fair. The issues which came up the other day were old and deep-set. Josh was just the catalyst.

"Oh?" He's looking at me in alarm. "Nothing serious, I hope?"

"No, just a small case of ..." I search the air for inspiration. This is the problem with lying; once you start, you just get yourself into all sorts of trouble.

"Marek's disease, I think she said."

I have no idea what that is; I seem to remember seeing it on a leaflet somewhere recently. Hopefully, it's something so obscure that he won't even question it.

If anything, he looks even more alarmed, not less.

"Doesn't that affect poultry?"

Oh, crap. Of course, he's a vet. He knows about stuff like this.

Actually, come to think of it, wasn't it *in* the vet's that I was reading that leaflet? (And before you even ask why I was reading a leaflet on avian diseases, they don't change the magazines nearly often enough for such a frequent visitor as myself. I've read them all at least twice.)

"Well, you know, he goes to the farm park sometimes," I say vaguely. "Anyway, Heather said it wasn't serious. Just a bit of ..." What? What would happen? Clucking? Scratching on the floor? "A temperature," I finish weakly.

There. You can get a temperature with just about anything. Surely he can't find anything wrong in that.

Mercifully, I never have to find out, because at that moment Jeremy appears, accompanied by an elderly man I faintly recognise.

"Clara, have you met Lord Boland?"

I find myself standing up straighter. Lord Boland is the head of the illustrious Pre-Raphaelite Collecting Society but, to be honest, that's pretty much just a hobby. He comes from one of the oldest ducal families in Europe, and his vast fortune is always at the disposal of his greatest passion: art. His support, both financial and otherwise, has been the lifeline of many a smaller museum. It's lifted obscure institutions out of near-closure and put them on the map. Any museum with him behind it finds its power and status in the art world permanently heightened. Suddenly, doors are open where before there were only walls. Acquisitions and loans from places which normally wouldn't even give you the time of day. Coverage in the national art press. The list goes on.

Needless to say, Jeremy has been after Lord Boland for years. I think he could die happy if we were to secure his patronage.

We could *all* die happy.

"And are you ready for your speech, my dear?" Lord Boland asks with a benevolent smile.

Why do all old men in the art world think that it's all right to call any woman under the age of sixty 'my dear'? Even so, given the circumstances, I'm prepared to let it go. This time. Needs must, and all that.

"Thank you, yes," I say prettily. "I've been writing it all week."

"Well, we're expecting great things," Lord Boland says genially, leaning heavily upon his stick. He's so slanted, it seems as though he might tip over at any moment. How old *is* he, anyway? He makes Jeremy look positively sprightly. "Jeremy here has been singing your praises to me."

I shoot a disbelieving glance at Jeremy from beneath my eyelids, which he stoically ignores.

"Clara is a great asset," he says simply. He even manages not to sound too begrudging about it. Even though I know it's all for show, I can't help but feel a small twinge of pride at his words.

"It's important to have young blood about the place," Lord Boland agrees. "New ideas, and all of that. Just because we deal in the past doesn't mean we can allow ourselves to fall behind the times. Wouldn't you agree, Jeremy?"

"Indeed," Jeremy says stonily.

"I've had my eye on this place for a while, you know," Lord Boland confides to me, apparently oblivious to the look on Jeremy's face. "But I've always felt it needed something fresh, something to shake it out of its complacency. I suspect that could be you, my dear."

"Oh!" A glow of delight unfurls within my chest. "Well, thank you very much. I hope my speech reassures you."

"Of course it will," Josh says, slinging an arm around my shoulder. "It's fantastic."

I hide a wry smile at his enthusiastic review. He hasn't even heard it yet. I tried to read it to him in bed one night but, five minutes in, he'd gone very still and quiet and, when I looked, I discovered that he'd fallen asleep.

But still, I appreciate his support. I'm so thrilled that he's here; I hadn't realised how tense I'd been, how worried I was that he wouldn't show. I beam up at him and his green eyes meet mine, filled with warmth and affection and ... something else. Something which makes my pupils dilate and my breath quicken.

I recall our earlier kiss, and my pulse skips with desire. I'm idly wondering if there's time to drag him off to my office before my speech is due to start. Or, if we can't make it that far, an innocuous broom cupboard.

"And you are, young man?" Lord Boland booms politely, making me start. "Are you with the museum too?"

I'd forgotten he was even there. Josh has a way of making everything around us disappear when he looks at me like that.

"Oh, no." I laugh brightly, hoping he attributes the guilty tinge which warms my cheeks to the temperature in here rather than improper thoughts. "This is just my boyfriend, Josh. He's here for moral support."

The words trip off my tongue so easily. I almost feel like I'm floating: a combination of nerves, excitement, lust and champagne. I hardly know what I've said, but then it hits home and the most wonderful sense of rightness flows through me.

I've said it! *Finally!* I mean, perhaps it's not quite the moment I'd have chosen, with Lord Boland and Jeremy standing there. Not exactly the spirit of romance, those two. But, even so, right now, I find that I don't care. It's said, and I feel so relieved, and so suffused with happiness, and I'm looking at Josh, who is ...

Standing there. Just standing there. Lord Boland is holding out his hand, asking 'How do you do?', but Josh's not taking it. He's staring at me instead, with a look of utmost horror on his face.

"Clara," he says, very slowly. "What did you just call me?"

Chapter 22

I just look back at him, not blinking. Time seems to have stopped. Lord Boland's hand is still hovering, outstretched. Jeremy has frozen, his champagne flute halfway to his lips. Josh's face is immobile, his skin white as chalk beneath his golden tan.

Except time hasn't stopped at all. For an interminable couple of seconds, nobody moves. Then Josh speaks again, more forcefully this time.

"I'm *not* your boyfriend, Clara. Surely you know that?"

That seems to break the spell. Lord Boland's hand drops to his side. Jeremy takes a half step backwards. And I finally manage the faintest, "*What*?"

"I thought we were on the same page." He runs a hand through his hair, dishevelling it. Which somehow only makes him look even better. "Christ, Clara, I thought we were just having *fun*."

His voice sounds like it's coming to me down a long tunnel. I know I should be feeling something here. I should be reacting. I know what he's saying, but it doesn't make sense. It's like another language.

"But ... I thought it was obvious," I say helplessly. "I thought we both knew ..."

Dimly, I'm aware that we shouldn't be discussing this here. Not in front of Lord Boland. Jeremy. Everyone else, too; heads are beginning to swivel in our direction, with the natural human instinct for a brewing drama. But the haze is pressing close around me; they all seem so far away.

"When did I ever say that we were in a relationship?" Josh demands, his voice rising. "I laughed when you kissed another guy, for Christ's sake!"

Lord Boland's eyebrows shoot up into his hairline at that last statement. It would almost be comical in any other situation. But finally, belatedly, things are starting to hit me. I look around at the sea of faces, all staring with unabashed curiosity. I'm a show— this is all just a show to them. I feel cold, shivery with shock and mortification.

"So, all of that," I say shakily. "It was just ..."

"Nothing!" Josh cries desperately. "It was nothing. I *liked* you, Clara. You were a laugh, but that's all. We're only young; no one settles down at our age. No one actually *wants* a relationship. No one wants to be *tied down*." Panic flares in his eyes as he utters those last words. "What did you honestly expect?"

That was a rhetorical question, I think, but I decide to answer it anyway.

"Romance," I say quietly, with as much dignity as I can muster. I tilt my chin and look him right in the eyes, challenging him to respond.

He laughs bitterly, although there's not much conviction

behind it. "There's no such thing. Not any more. You're a great girl, Clara, but you need to get real. There are no unicorns, or magical healing crystals, or romantic heroes. It's time to stop believing in fairy tales before you really get yourself hurt."

"That's *quite* enough." Ruby emerges from the crowd like an avenging angel, a resplendent Amazonian vision in green and pink. "I think you should leave now."

She links her arm through mine and looks challengingly at Jeremy, as though daring him not to support her.

It obviously works because he leaps to attention. "Er ... yes," he says stridently. Then he turns, and his face falls as he realises that his head only comes up to Josh's shoulder. To his credit, though, he carries on. "As she said, I'm afraid ..."

"Don't worry, I'll go," I hear Josh's deep voice respond. "I've no reason to stay."

My heart thuds against my ribs. I wish I could turn back to look at his face, but Ruby's already steering me away, pushing through the throng to reach the door.

"What a weasel," she's saying furiously. I get the impression she's deliberately moderating her language. The Ruby I know would find a much more descriptive word than that. "How could he *do* that to you? And tonight, of all nights, when he *knows* ..." she rants on, but I've already tuned out. I still feel cold and numb, like none of this is real. Like I'll wake up any moment and I'll be in my bedroom with Casper wheezing away on the pillow next to me.

I wish. Oh, how I wish. But there's no doubt about it; this is real. What just happened, how I feel ... it's all too real. The ache in my chest is real. The pain and humiliation is real. It drenches me like a waterfall, making me gasp inwardly.

How could I have got it all so wrong? And after everything I said to Heather, all of those awful things ... I close my eyes against a rising wave of dizziness, trying to breathe.

"... anyway, let's get you to the ladies'. We'll freshen up your make-up, and you'll feel better," Ruby's saying briskly, as though a touch of lipstick will suddenly make all of this go away. "Then you can get out there and smash that speech of yours. That'll show him."

Oh, my God. The *speech*. All of those faces, looking up at me. Panic lances through me, closing in around my throat.

"I can't ..." The words tumble from my mouth in a rush. "I mean, I need some air."

I have to get away. From everyone, even Ruby, with her bright, well-intentioned mien. Somehow, her attempts to pretend it wasn't so bad only make me feel worse.

I wrench my arm from her grasp and, before she can stop me, I'm off, half walking, half running down the corridor. Even in this state, I have far too much self-respect to actually be seen *fleeing* the scene.

I don't even know where I'm going. All I do know is that the further the sounds of the party recede into the distance, the more the pounding in my head eases.

I've reached the end of the corridor. There's only one way out now— the glass door which leads into the gardens. I grasp the brass handle, praying that our infamously lax security guard has left it open. It turns easily, and I practically stumble out into the night air, sucking in a deep, frosty breath. It clears my head, the haze melting away into the dark.

Unfortunately, that's not altogether a good thing.

"Oh, *God.*" I sink down onto the stone steps which lead down from the terrace to the lawn. It's not exactly a big garden, just a square strip of grass planted with wide borders and fruit trees. It doesn't look much at this time of year, but in the spring and summer it's actually very pretty. The whole thing's encircled by a high sandstone wall; originally, this would only have been one small part of the garden. The orchard, I suppose, looking at those old, gnarled fruit trees. But, over the centuries, the space has gradually been sold off until all we're left with is this. We're actually quite lucky to have it; most museums don't have the luxury of a green space to call their own.

Come to think of it, this place has always felt like something of a haven. A quiet spot to escape to on lunch breaks, to listen to the birds, to get away from the unbearably stuffy, over-crowded atmosphere of the museum during the summer months. Well, I need its sanctuary more than ever now.

There's a soft squeaking sound as the door handle turns again, and I'm aware of a presence behind me. For a heartbeat I wonder if it's Josh, and my head spins around.

"Oh," I say flatly. "It's you."

He raises an eyebrow. "Nice to see you too."

Immediately, I feel terrible. "I'm sorry. I didn't mean to be abrupt. It's just been a trying evening, that's all."

He doesn't reply to that, and it all becomes clear in an instant. Of *course* he hasn't just turned up, has he? And he hasn't just wandered into the garden by coincidence either.

I screw my eyes shut. "How much did you overhear?"

"Some of it."

He's being kind, I know.

"You heard it all, didn't you?"

There's a pause, and I can almost hear him deliberating with himself.

"Yes."

I release the breath I'd been holding with a sharp exhale.

"Great. That's just ... *great.*" I screw a fistful of my skirt in my hand. "I should have sold tickets, shouldn't I? Invited everyone in my life to come and watch. See what a mess I'm making of it all. My parents would be so proud, if they could see me now, wouldn't they?"

"Clara ..." He places a hand on my shoulder but I shake him off, scrubbing at my eyes with the back of my hand. I'm probably causing havoc with my eye make-up, but who cares now? It's only me and Adam out here in the dark, and he's seen me looking much worse. He saw me after I'd fallen in the river, after all. It doesn't get much worse than that.

"What are you doing here, anyway?" I demand heatedly. "Why did you even come? You weren't supposed to be here."

"I came because you asked me to," he says calmly. "I promised you I'd be here. I wasn't about to break that."

"Stop it," I say furiously, blinking away tears. "Just stop being so ..." I break off sharply. "You're only making it worse."

He sighs, leaning forward, his elbows resting on his legs. "He's an idiot, Clara. That's all. It's not your fault."

Oh, how I wish he weren't here. I can't stand him being kind, looking at me so pityingly. Pretending our kiss never happened. Pretending that none of this is my mistake.

But I can't pretend any more. And I can't let other people pretend for me.

"Why not? He never promised me anything. I just saw what I wanted to see. I so wanted to *believe* ..." I take a shuddering breath. Because that's the worst of it; Heather was right. A part of me knew that some things didn't add up. But I didn't want to see it; I so wanted to believe that the fantasy I'd created for myself could come true. That I could have that magic which has always evaded me, which everyone else knew could never be real. This was never really anything to do with Josh; it was about me all along. And they all tried to tell me, didn't they? They all tried to protect me from myself. Finally, I can see the truth. "But maybe he was right. Maybe it's time to stop believing in things which don't exist."

"Do you want my advice?" Adam says abruptly. "Don't."

I look up in confusion. That's the last thing I expected him to say.

"Don't change, not for this. Not for anything." His face is close to mine, his eyes inky and intense. "I think you're perfect just as you are. Crazy, but perfect. There are plenty of boring, unimaginative people in the world, Clara. There are plenty of people who are willing to believe that life is a dull enterprise, and that magic only exists in books. However, there aren't many like you." He gives a self-deprecating grin. "I can't believe I'm actually saying this. My colleagues would be horrified if they could hear me now. They'd probably have me committed."

"*I'm* thinking about having you committed," I confess, staring at him. "Whatever happened to the stern professor who told me that he was proud to be cynical?"

Perfect. He thinks I'm perfect. The words chase themselves around my head in an endless, cyclical chant, and I try to swat them away. It was just a turn of phrase, I tell myself. He was trying to make me feel better.

"He's taking a short holiday. He'll be back on Monday, growling at the students and avoiding everyone in the staff-room. But for tonight ..." He puts an arm around my shoulders. "You've got me. I hope that's acceptable."

"More than," I murmur, leaning into his side.

We sit for a while, not speaking, just looking up at the stars. And then a flash of colour catches my eye. I sit up straight.

"Look, that's a firework!"

As I'm speaking, it explodes into a cascade of pink and gold, the light dazzling to my eyes.

"They *are* customary on the 5th of November," Adam replies, sounding amused. "Did that particular history lesson pass you by?"

Of course. I'd forgotten it was Bonfire Night today. Everything's been so hectic over the past few weeks, it had almost slipped my mind altogether. Which is strange because when I was little it was always one of my favourite features of the year. The tang of woodsmoke in the air, the cold biting my cheeks. Dad would lift me up onto his shoulders so I could watch the colours bloom and burst, lighting up the sky. These days, it's more of a bittersweet occasion, a reminder of everything that's gone.

Except tonight, sitting here with Adam, it doesn't feel so sad. It feels like I'm watching it for the first time all over again. The dark sky is luminous, the air filled with bangs and crackles and whizzing sounds as sparks spiral off into the night, radiant and fleeting. And, as I watch, I feel something beginning to build within me, an acute sense of emotion, stretching out until it fills my chest with a pressure which is almost painful.

"I know you think I don't understand how it feels." His voice emerges stiltedly from the darkness next to me. "But, believe me, I do."

"Who was she?" The words are out of my mouth before I can restrain them. Suddenly, I find myself very interested in what kind of woman could hurt Adam.

"An associate lecturer in the Anthropology department. We were together for five years. Eventually, she ended it."

For a moment I think he's going to say more, but he doesn't.

"Why?" I ask gently. I can't stop myself.

"Because, apparently, I have no romance in my soul." Even in the dark, I can see the rueful twist of his lips.

Once upon a time, I would have agreed with her. But now, as I watch the colours reflected in his eyes, I feel a white-hot surge of anger towards this unknown woman. Did she not know him at *all*? Because there's so much more to see, if only you take the time to look deeper. I've learned that in only a matter of weeks; how could she not after five years?

She was wrong.

But I don't say it. I don't know why I don't say it.

Then the last firework disintegrates into the sky, leaving only a smoky outline hanging in its place. And, for a few precious seconds, everything is perfectly silent.

Chapter 23

"How is it possible that this house looks even pinker in the dark?" Adam asks as he nudges open the garden gate. The bemusement in his voice makes me giggle.

"It's growing on you. Admit it."

"I wouldn't go as far as to say that." His lips set in a thin line as he rummages around in my clutch bag. "Where the hell are your keys, woman?"

"In there somewhere," I say vaguely, lolling back against the gatepost. The night air feels so delicious on my skin and I close my eyes, enjoying the sensation.

"Clara!" At Adam's voice, my eyes snap open.

"What?" I say indignantly.

"Don't fall asleep," he commands, eyeing the half-empty champagne bottle I'm still clutching in my hand. "Maybe that wasn't such a great idea."

"It was *your* idea," I point out, bending over to retrieve my house keys, which are glinting from the path. They must have fallen out of the bag. "Here they are. Whoa!"

I've tried to straighten up and almost toppled into the rose-bush in the process. Somehow, that strikes me as uproariously funny, and I burst out into hysterical laughter.

"You'll wake the neighbours," Adam admonishes, unlocking the door and shoving me unceremoniously inside. The house is in total darkness; Freddie's obviously not here. Not that that's particularly out of the ordinary at the moment. I haven't seen him properly in ages. Just something else to worry about then, when I get a chance. At the moment, it's relegated to the bottom of an ever-growing list. "And, for the record, *my* idea was for you to take the edge off a bit, help you sleep. I didn't mean for you to get absolutely plastered."

For some reason, the way he says 'plastered' in that disapproving way sets me off all over again. I lean against the wall, gasping for breath. He waits, arms folded, until my laughter has subsided.

"You shouldn't have stolen a whole bottle then, should you?" I manage archly.

It was quite impressive, actually. I couldn't face going back through the party, so we sneaked round the side, passing the entrance to the kitchens on the way. Adam slipped inside, reappearing moments later with an unopened bottle of champagne. I don't know where he got the nerve from; he did it so confidently. In fact, the whole thing was so out of character that if it weren't for the evidence in my hand, I could easily believe that I'd imagined the whole thing.

Then again, he does sound very much like his usual self now, as he mutters, "What I *shouldn't* have done was trust you to measure yourself and not drink half the bottle."

"I like it when we spar." I lean into his side, enjoying his solid warmth, the crisp scent of him. He's so wonderfully reassuring, like a broadsheet newspaper, or a heritage building. Unchanging. I love that about him. "We haven't sparred in ages. We've been too busy kissing, and suchlike."

"We are not sparring," he says crisply, although I notice he looks a little flustered. He begins to manoeuvre me across the hallway towards the living room. "You're just spouting drunken nonsense and, more fool me, I'm bothering to respond."

He sits me down on the sofa, prising the champagne bottle gently from my fingers. "I'll get you some water. Stay here."

"Yeah, sure." Like I'm going anywhere. Right now, I only have one agenda. I curl up against the cushions, kicking off my shoes with a sigh of relief. Why do I keep wearing high heels? Why don't I become one of those cool women who only wears flats, no matter the occasion? I admire those women; they respect their feet.

"*No* falling asleep!" Adam catches me as I'm listing to the side, propping me back upright. "Not until you've drunk this."

He proffers a large glass of water, which I grudgingly accept. Sobering up doesn't look like a particularly appealing option at the moment. Sobering up means that I'll have to face everything which happened tonight, and I'm not ready to do that.

"Why are you always getting me drunk, anyway?" I shoot at him, putting the glass down on the coffee table. "You're supposed to be a sensible role model. What would your students say?"

"They'd probably be thrilled," he says drily. "They think I have no life. But may I remind you that last time it was actually you who got *me* drunk?" He picks up the glass and puts it back in my hand. "And I had one hell of a hangover the next morning too. I'm just trying to save you from the same."

All right, so he has a point, even if I don't like to admit it. Besides, this is all going to feel bad enough tomorrow, in the cold light of day, without a hangover making it even worse. I raise the glass to my lips, then pause.

"I don't usually drink very much, you know," I say, feeling the need to defend myself. I fear I'm getting a reputation in his eyes as a reckless alcoholic. "But it's not exactly been the best night of my life."

His dark eyes soften as they scan my face. "I know."

And that's all it takes. Whatever has been building inside me snaps, and tears pour down my face and drip into the glass of water, causing ripples across the surface. Wordlessly, Adam takes the glass from me and puts it aside; then he pulls me against him. Somehow, his steady unspoken action is more reassuring than any amount of comforting platitudes. Which, of course, only makes me cry harder.

"*Why* am I such a disaster?" I sob into his chest.

"You're not." He sounds taken aback at my vehemence. "Why would you—?"

"I *am*. I've ruined everything. It's not just Josh. I've said some unforgivable things to Heather; I've wrecked everything with you; I've embarrassed the whole museum, and the speech ..." I sit bolt upright, horror arcing through me. "Oh, my God! The speech!"

How could I have forgotten about the speech? That was my big opportunity; more than that, everyone was relying on me to do it. I was supposed to dry my eyes, steel myself and walk out there. Smash it, as Ruby would say. Make everyone forget about the scene which they'd just witnessed. Remind them all what we were *really* there for: art. Culture. Heritage. And instead ...

Instead, I crept out of the back door and ran away, leaving everyone else to pick up the pieces. And totally overshadowed the entire event in the process. Because, of course, no one's going to forget about it *now*, are they? It'll be all they talk about for weeks. The museum will be a laughing stock.

"It's okay," Adam says soothingly. "I checked before we left. Jeremy was going to do it. I'm sure everyone's dozing off to the sound of his voice as we speak."

For once, I can't even appreciate his attempt at humour. I feel sick and shaky.

"Oh, no." I drop my head into my hands. "I'm going to lose my job, aren't I? Jeremy will never forgive me for this."

"All right, now listen to me." Adam's voice turns firm. He takes my hands in his, forcing me to look at him. "You're *not* going to lose your job, all right? It was just one incident. Don't make it into more than it was."

I know he's trying to be helpful, but his tone strikes my ears as patronising.

"Oh, really?" I say acerbically, wrenching my hands away. "And if you did something like that at an important function for the college? How would they feel about that, do you think?"

"They would be angry, I'm sure," he says calmly. "But I'm sure we could reach an understanding. And you can ..."

"No, I can't!" I snap, exasperated. "How could you ever understand? You're a big star, an academic poster boy. Exalted lineage. Youngest professor in the history of the college. You're an *asset*. They need you more than you need them. Do you even know what it's like not to be important, to be fawned over? Because I do, and ..." Suddenly, I hear myself. I pull back, scrubbing at my face. "I'm sorry, Adam. You don't need this. You'd better get yourself home; it's late."

I feel hot with shame. Why can't I seem to control my tongue around anyone these days? I swear, I used to be a *nice* person. I used to try to make people feel better, not alienate them completely. I don't know what's happened to me, but I wouldn't want to hang around with me at the moment; unfortunately, *I* have no choice, but Adam does.

To my surprise, though, he doesn't move.

"I didn't exactly have the best night myself the other evening, if you recall," he says neutrally. "So I think you know that my life isn't always easy. I'm well aware what it's like not to be fawned over, as you so eloquently put it. By the people who are supposed to be closest to me too. At least you're permanently surrounded by love and support, Clara, even if you don't always appreciate it. Everyone in your life adores you; they'd do anything to make you happy. I've never been blessed with that." His dark eyes bore into mine. "In fact, if either of us has the easy time of it, I'd say it's you."

I just sit there, blinking back shocked tears.

Because the worst of it is, he's right. I might not have my parents any more. I might not have a boyfriend. But I'm far from alone. I have Freddie. I have my friends, especially Heather, if she'll have me back. I even have Adam, or at least I did until I managed to screw that up too. And, of course, I have a constant, if challenging, companion in the form of Casper.

When I look at it like that, it's not so terrible after all.

"Adam ..." I begin.

"I'll stay, at least until Freddie gets back," he interrupts, in a tone which brooks no argument. He stands, divesting himself of his jacket, and it's clear from his body language that the conversation is over. "Do you mind if I make a cup of tea? I never did get any dinner in the end; I rushed straight from the college to the museum. I was worried that I'd be late."

"Oh". The thought of him racing across town to get there in time for my speech, even after everything, makes me feel ... odd. Not very descriptive, I know; I'm not sure what the feeling is exactly, only that it's complicated. Far too complicated for tonight; I'm way too exhausted to decode it. So I simply file it away for later and say brightly, "Use whatever you like; there's a loaf in the bread bin if you want to make toast."

"Great." He loosens his tie. It's pink with blue flowers on it; for a second, I wonder if he wore it tonight for me, and I get a funny fluttering feeling in my stomach, but then the ludicrousness of it hits me and I bat the notion away, feeling foolish.

He looks down at me, mercifully oblivious to my train of thought. "Do you want anything?"

"No, thank you." I sink down onto my side, resting my cheek against the cushions. Tiredness washes over me, a combination of champagne and spent emotion. "I'm just going to rest here for a minute."

"You do that." There's a smile in his voice. He pauses in

the doorway, seeming to hesitate over something. "Oh, and Clara?"

"Hmm?" My eyelids are struggling to stay open.

"You didn't ruin things between us." He pauses, takes a breath. "You could never do that."

His voice seems to be coming from a long way away. Dimly, I want to reply, to say something, but I can't. I'm too heavy, too far away. My mind drifts off into a half-sleep, punctuated by odd snatches of reality. I have a vague sensation of a blanket being put over me at one point, the faint sound of the radio coming from the kitchen, the cat flap clattering. That's loud enough to make me open my eyes for a moment, struggling to focus through the haze.

Casper's standing there, a stoat clamped between his jaws. I wonder if this is all part of a dream, because really, where would he have got a *stoat* from? This is suburban Cambridge, not a wild Scottish heathland.

"Okay—" Adam holds up his hands in a gesture of surrender "—before you gnaw my leg off, just hear me out."

Casper growls, his fur bristling with animosity.

"Put the stoat down," Adam coaxes. "And let's talk."

Casper glares at him for a long moment, but then drops the stoat, which lands limply on the kitchen floor. Cautiously, Adam crouches down in front of him.

"She's had a tough night, okay? I'm just here to look after her, nothing more."

Casper eyes him sceptically.

"Maybe you and I ... just for tonight, could we put our differences aside? For her," Adam suggests. "Normal hostilities will, of course, resume first thing tomorrow. But for now ..." he holds out a hand, palm facing upwards "... what do you think?"

For the first five seconds, Casper visibly considers latching his jaw around the exposed fingers. Adam swallows but holds still, meeting his gaze. And then, very slowly, Casper lifts up a paw and places it on top of Adam's outstretched hand.

"Thank you," Adam says softly. They look at each other, and it seems that something passes between them. But I'm already sinking back into the dark, losing myself to sleep.

I remember nothing more.

Chapter 24

Monday morning is one of the most nerve-racking of my entire life. I've spent the whole weekend simultaneously nursing a hangover (Adam's prescription of water didn't do the trick) and fretting about what was going to happen when I came into work today.

I wake up with the dawn with what feels like a cannon ball lodged in the pit of my stomach. It's there while I shower. It's there while I rifle half-heartedly through my wardrobe (what exactly *does* one wear to get fired? Why don't fashion magazines run useful articles like that, rather than showcasing endless arrangements of Perspex shoes and unflatteringly voluminous jeans?) It isn't there when I have breakfast, but that's only because I couldn't face any, which must be a first for me. Instead, I force a cup of tea past my lips, dust a hint of brightening powder across my face in a vain attempt to hide my sallow skin, and head for the door.

At least getting to the museum early means that I don't have to see anyone. I wander through the echoing, empty rooms, past statues and paintings which have become as familiar to me as the decor in my own house. To think I might never see them again is too hard to bear, and I have to keep my head down, gaze to the floor. Because, of course, I won't ever be able to come back here, will I? It'll be far too painful. This place I love, which has been my sanctuary on so many occasions, will become just somewhere I used to know.

There's nothing to be done. I shut myself in my office, pull up some visitor projections on my computer ... and wait.

And carry on waiting. By ten o'clock, the sun has risen outside my window, streaming across my desk. The visitor projections still sit untouched on the screen—I was never really planning to do much with them anyway; I just wanted the reassurance of pretending I was working—and I'm almost beside myself with tension. Everyone's here; they have been for the past hour. I can hear them moving around in the corridor, the scrape of chairs against floors in the neighbouring offices. But no one's come in.

I don't understand it; I thought they'd be keen to get it over with. What's the point of suspense?

Maybe Jeremy's waiting for me to go to him. And that's what I should have done, I see now. I should have just walked straight in there first thing and dealt with it. Instead, I'm just sitting in here pathetically, too paralysed to act.

My eyes travel to the window. I get up and open it, peering down at the ground. How far *is* that, exactly? There are some shrubs planted against the wall, so if I angled it right ...

Wait ... what am I *doing*? I jerk back from the window, shaking my head in despair at myself. *No, Clara. You are not going to escape out of the window. You're not going to run away at all, not this time. You're going to go out there and face the music, and you're going to do it with dignity.*

Before I can back out, I stride across to the door. At least I might be able to convince Jeremy to let me resign; I mean, my career in the museums sector is over, obviously. No one else will hire me after this, not if they have any sense. But in another field, where I'm not known ... Well, a resignation will look better on my CV. For a moment my heart sinks and my resolve wobbles.

Job-hunting. Oh, my God. I hadn't even thought about that. Just the thought makes me want to reconsider the whole jumping out of the window idea.

No. I set my shoulders, grasping the door handle and yanking it towards me. I will be strong. I will be powerful. I *will* ...

The door flies open and Jeremy comes crashing in, nearly sending both of us into a sprawling heap on the carpet. Grabbing onto the door frame, I just about manage to keep my balance.

"What the—what are you *doing*?"

"I was coming in." He looks puzzled.

Oh. His hand is still on the outer door handle, so that seems like a reasonable explanation.

"I was ... going out," I say weakly.

"Indeed," he says, blinking at me owlishly from behind his glasses. Belatedly, he seems to realise that they've been knocked askew in the scuffle, and reaches up to straighten them. "Might I have a word?"

"Yes, of course." Flustered, I retreat to my desk. Definitely not the best start. The chances of resignation are receding into the distance already. "Please, have a seat."

He casts an eye over the only other chair in the room, which is covered with papers and files.

"Thank you, but I'll stand. I'll only be a moment."

It'll be quick, then. That's a relief, at least. I'd have expected him to revel in the process. Then again, for the first time, I notice that he doesn't look quite as exultant as I'd thought he would. In fact, he almost looks ... fidgety.

Jeremy *never* fidgets. He says it's a sign of poor breeding.

"How are you, my dear?" he asks tentatively.

I almost wonder if it's a trick, but no, he appears to be in earnest. He's peering at me over his now righted spectacles with an expression which I've never seen on his face before. If I didn't know better, I'd venture to say it might even be *concern*.

It really must be bad. I can feel the blood draining from my face. Is it even worse than I thought? Perhaps they're firing us all. Perhaps they think the museum is ineptly run, and they're bringing in a whole new ...

"Such an unfortunate thing," he's saying haltingly. "But you must ... Onwards and upwards, and all of that. These things happen to everyone ..." He pauses, seeming to reconsider. "Well, perhaps not *quite* everyone, but ..."

I watch him bumbling on, dumbfounded. Is he giving me a *pep talk*?

"Jeremy," I blurt out, "I understand that you're firing me, but what about ...?"

"Firing you?" He looks nonplussed. "My dear, what are you talking about?"

"Well, you know—" I flap my hands around desperately, as though that will elucidate "—the scene on Friday. The speech ..."

"Oh, never mind that. I did the speech in the end; it was thoroughly enjoyed by all." He pauses in self-congratulation. "You'll get another opportunity, my dear."

"Another ...?" I trail off faintly, clasping a hand to my forehead. "But ... the embarrassment to the museum ..."

"The only one who should be embarrassed was that young ruffian," Jeremy says hotly, and I notice that the tips of his ears have gone quite pink. "Luckily, I managed to get rid of him discreetly."

He looks so proud and protective that I haven't the heart to point out that it was actually Ruby who did the getting rid of. And that there was nothing particularly discreet about it either.

"But ... Lord Boland ..." I say desperately. I'm aware that I shouldn't be shoring up a case for my own sacking, and I should probably just shut up now. But this all just feels so unreal.

Surely, he's letting me go. I mean, he *has* to, right? This is Jeremy; he's all about honour, and reputation, and not causing a stir.

And that's before we even mention the fact that I might just have cost us one of the country's most coveted patrons.

"I'll deal with Lord Boland. I'm sure he can be made to understand." And then, as if in slow motion, he reaches over and awkwardly pats my hand. "We've all been crossed in love at some point."

For a moment he looks almost wistful. I genuinely consider slapping myself to make sure I'm not hallucinating. But then he coughs and snatches his hand away, his voice returning to its usual strident vibration. "Anyway, that's enough of that. I wanted to talk to you about those revised visitor projections figures the grant committee have asked for."

I realise that I'm still gaping at him, and give myself a mental shake.

"Yes, I've just started doing them now."

"You can send them over to me," he interrupts. "I'll finish them."

He says it so plainly, as though it's nothing out of the ordinary. I want to thank him, but I know that nothing would horrify him more.

"I'll do that," I say formally.

"Good." He straightens his waistcoat, looking embarrassed. "That's good."

I watch him shuffle out, not knowing how to deal with this new information. Jeremy has *feelings*. Who knew? I'm sort of ashamed to admit that I'd long ago stopped thinking of him as an actual person; he's just such a part of this institution, as much as any of the paintings on the walls or the plasterwork ceiling.

Just something else I was wrong about, then. It's getting to be a long list.

I sit there dumbly for a few minutes, unsure what to do with myself. I don't even feel relieved yet; instead I just feel ... stunned. I was genuinely convinced that I was going to be fired. I was ready for it. And now ... Well, I suppose I'm meant to just get up and carry on with things as usual. But something stops me; it doesn't feel the same. I feel like an impostor. Like I'm sitting in an office which is no longer mine.

I shake my head, trying to restore a sense of perspective. It's just a delayed reaction, that's all. Of *course* I'm thrilled; it just hasn't quite sunk in yet.

Mercifully, I'm saved from any further rumination by my phone starting to ring, vibrating across the polished surface of the desk. I grab it before it can attempt a kamikaze leap off the edge into the wastepaper basket.

"Clara?" Heather's voice comes down the line, blurred by static. It cuts out for a second or two, then I hear her say, "Are you there?"

"Yes, it's just ... terrible reception," I garble, before wanting to kick myself. Of course she knows that; how many times has she rung me here? Over a hundred, probably.

How strange it is that one argument can change everything; it's like it rewinds time. Suddenly years of closeness seem to recede into nothing, and you're speaking to one another as if you've only just met. I go back over to the window and wedge my torso through the gap, contorting myself into the bizarre angle I've perfected as the only way to get a decent signal. It's highly uncomfortable, but it's either this or having to trek all the way downstairs and stand outside.

"How's that?" I ask, when I'm finally in position.

There's a pause, a crackle, then her voice comes back on the line.

"Better. Have you got a second?"

The knot of nerves is back in my stomach. Just because I

can hear her voice better now doesn't make it any easier to interpret. The only thing I can say with certainty is that this isn't a gushing making up call.

We haven't spoken once since our spat over a week ago. I think it's the longest I've ever gone without hearing from her and, to be honest, it's felt really weird. My phone is noticeably more silent without her sarcastic texts pinging in throughout the day. I miss being able to call her about anything, even if it's nothing at all. I miss her dropping in for a glass of wine and a chat. Not being able to tell her about Josh has made it all so much harder; I never realised how much I valued her support, her sensible advice. She'd have made it all seem okay, somehow. Or at least slightly more okay.

I so wanted to call her over the weekend. It was like an itch; I kept reaching for my phone, scrolling down until I found her name in my favourite contacts. But I never went through with it; I suppose it was all just too raw. I couldn't face admitting how wrong I'd got it.

And then there was a part of me—a tiny, hidden part of me—which was afraid of what would happen if she didn't want to know. Normally, it wouldn't even be a question; we've always been there for one another. But, this time, it feels different. This time, things were said which can't be forgotten.

What if we can't go back from this? The thought terrifies me.

"Absolutely." My reply is a half-second late and slightly laboured, like I'm trying too hard to be normal. "Fire away."

"The thing is, I need to ask you a favour." Her neutral tone is beginning to crack; I can hear the strain creeping through.

"Mum fell this morning and she thinks she's broken her collarbone. Dad's on a golfing holiday in Majorca, Dominic's away visiting clients up north ..." The words are tumbling out faster and faster as the sentence goes on. I know she'll be pulling her hair back from her scalp at this very moment; that's what she always does when she's stressed. "I have no one else I can ask ..."

"Calm down," I interject before she works herself up into a real state. "Just tell me what you need me to do."

Focusing on the practical seems to mollify her, as I'd anticipated.

"Oscar needs to be picked up from nursery at twelve. He does a half day on Mondays," she adds, as though this insight into his social calendar is somehow helpful. "Could you take him home, make him a sandwich ... just keep him busy until I get back? You still have the spare key, don't you?"

"Yes." I omit the *somewhere* from my reply. That'll just send her into a full-blown panic. I look across at my handbag, gaping open on the floor, and send up a little prayer of thanks that I'm not one of those women who changes their bag regularly, decanting things from one into another. My bag gets cleared out twice a year, if it's lucky, and even then it absorbs all manner of paraphernalia. I tend to operate on the policy that you never know when you might need something. The key will be in there somewhere. "Look, don't worry. I'll sort it out. He won't even notice you've gone."

"Thank you." She exhales gustily, and I can practically hear the tension leaving her. "That's such a ... But wait, I don't know what you'll feed him. I've had to cancel the Waitrose order." She sounds stressed all over again. "I think I've got some smoked salmon in the freezer ..."

Smoked salmon? What kind of lunches is this three-year-old used to getting?

"Heather, we will be *fine*," I tell her firmly. "I won't let him starve. Now, go to the hospital. Oscar and I will see you later."

Sometimes, even Heather just needs telling what to do.

"You're right, of course you're right," she says, sounding much calmer. "I'll ring you when I'm on my way back. And Clara ..." She hesitates. "You know that you and I ... I mean, it doesn't matter. You're still ..."

"We'll talk later," I say gently.

And when I put down the phone I find that the knot of nerves has eased slightly.

Maybe we might just be okay, after all.

Chapter 25

"Come on, Oscar," I say coaxingly, tugging on his sticky little hand. "Let's get home, and then we can have some lunch."

At the mention of lunch, his blue eyes light up. "Is it houmous? Mummy promised me houmous."

"Er ... I don't know." I'd been thinking more along the lines of a cheese sandwich, but I don't dare tell him that. I'll never lure him onwards with so pedestrian an offering. "Tell you what, let's see how fast we can get home. Then we can find out!"

It's not a particularly subtle trick, but I'm growing desperate. God, but kids are *slow*. What should have been a ten-minute walk back from nursery is constantly punctuated by random stopping. Sometimes it's to look at clouds, then at bits of moss growing in the cracks in the pavement ... and then, of course, there are the puddles.

"Look, Auntie Clara!" He bumbles off towards a particularly splendid example, glistening in a dip between two paving stones. If bumbling is an accurate word for such a fast pace; I only just manage to snatch at the back of his hood before we both get a soaking. No wonder all kids' coats have them;

never mind keeping the rain off, they're really just a lead in disguise. And I can see the similarities between Oscar and a puppy. The minute he sees anything of interest, he's off, without the slightest fear or hesitation. No wonder he's broken so many bones.

"Can you see the rainbow?" I point up at the sky, where a watery arc shimmers against the bruised clouds. It's been a day of contrasts, showers then sunshine then showers again. I think there might be another one brewing now, in fact. There's a definite feeling of rain in the air. Just another reason to drag Oscar home quickly. "Isn't it pretty? Do you know all of the colours?"

The rainbow proves suitably distracting, although my last question does prompt a chorus of some dreadfully inane tune about the colours of the rainbow which lasts all the way home. By the time we get back to Heather's house, I'm about ready to blow my brains out. Now I know why parents look so glazed over all of the time; this song would be enough to lobotomise anyone after a while.

I sit Oscar down at the kitchen table with some crayons and a colouring book, and head to the fridge to see what the situation is.

As it turns out, Heather's idea of 'nothing in the fridge' is markedly different to mine. I take the phrase somewhat more literally. I can picture the contents of my fridge right now; it's not difficult, when it consists of half a bar of chocolate, some wine and a tub of coconut yoghurt which is so old that I'm actually torn between fascination and apprehension at the prospect of opening the lid.

Heather's fridge, on the other hand, looks like she's just been shopping. I stare at the stuffed shelves, feeling daunted. There are only three of them, for heaven's sake; how do they get *through* all of this? More to the point, how do they ever choose what to eat?

After some deliberation, I take out ham, lettuce and organic butter. The bread bin proffers an expensively rustic-looking sourdough loaf, which I saw at inexpertly with a serrated knife.

I place the finished sandwich in front of Oscar, who inspects it like a judge at an international art competition.

"It's wonky," he says, in that matter-of-fact way which children have.

"It's unique," I say airily. "Do you want some crisps with it?"

I start opening and closing cupboard doors, trying to work out where Heather would keep them in her complex organisational system, but all I'm confronted with are rows upon rows of flavoured oil and tins of olives. Honestly, it's like a delicatessen in here.

"Mummy doesn't let me have crisps," Oscar pronounces worthily. "She says they're bad for you."

I struggle to keep a straight face. What a hypocrite! I've seen Heather polish off an entire tube of sour cream and onion Pringles by herself in a single sitting.

"I'm sure she's right," I say diplomatically, closing the cupboard door which I've just opened to discover four bags of hand-cut crisps. On the highest shelf too. Ah, well, her secret's safe with me.

I tidy up the kitchen while Oscar picks at his sandwich, chattering away all the while. He tells me every detail of his morning in minute detail, and I'm glad of the opportunity to do nothing more taxing than nod at the appropriate moments. I'm absolutely exhausted already, and I've only been in his company for ... I sneak a look at the kitchen clock ... fifty minutes. How do people do this all the time?

I mean, don't get me wrong. He's adorable and all of that, but he never *stops*. Whilst I can feel myself getting older and more withered with every passing minute.

"I've finished, Auntie Clara," he chirps, and I start. *Already?*

"You ate all of that?" I walk around the island and, sure enough, the plate's empty.

"I even ate my crusts," he says, and he looks so proud of himself that my heart swells.

Okay, so perhaps I *can* sort of see why people want to do this. I rest a hand on his downy head.

"Would you like some pudding?"

His eyes automatically go to the fruit bowl. I want to roll my eyes.

"*Proper* pudding. Here—" I pick up my handbag and feel around for the packet which I know is in there "—what about some chocolate?"

He stares at it in awe.

"These are Uncle Freddie's favourite." I open the bag of chocolate buttons and hold them out to him. "I had to hide these from him so he didn't eat them all."

"I saw Uncle Freddie yesterday," Oscar says, popping a button in his mouth.

"Did you?" I smile. "Where?"

Oscar probably knows more about my brother's whereabouts than I do. Lord only knows where he keeps going, but a part of me has begun to wonder if he might actually be avoiding me. He's certainly less chatty when we do cross paths. My sense of unease is growing with each passing day. Next time I see him, I promise myself now, I'll pin him down and find out what's going on once and for all.

"In the bookshop." Oscar's voice is getting vaguer; he's far more interested in the chocolate than the conversation. "Mummy and I went to look at the train. Uncle Freddie was there."

The thought of Freddie browsing for books in his spare time is surprising enough, but I know the wooden train Oscar's talking about; it's in the children's section of the bookshop. What would Freddie be doing there? There must be some mistake.

"Are you *sure* it was Uncle Freddie?" I ask gently. "Not just someone who looked like him?"

Oscar looks at me unwaveringly, as though affronted that I would call his testimony to account.

"It was Uncle Freddie." He licks chocolate off his fingers. "He was looking at a book with a baby on the front."

Before I can reply, the front door opens and Heather bustles in, her pale blue mac dripping with water.

"I'm back! It didn't take too long, thank God. They were able to see her straight away. Got caught in the most dreadful shower on the way home, though. It came out of nowhere." She shrugs off her coat, hanging it on the hook to dry. "Is everything all right? Did you manage?"

Anyone would think she'd expected to walk in and find utter mayhem. Or, more likely, both of us dead from starvation on the floor.

"We're fine. Oscar's just had some lunch."

Oscar chooses that moment to wave the chocolate wrapper in the air. "Mummy! I had buttons!"

Heather momentarily freezes in horror, then her face relaxes. "Well, it *is* a special day." She picks him up and carries him over to the sink to wash his hands. "Did you have a nice time with Auntie Clara?"

She looks at me properly for the first time then, and I see gratitude in her eyes. Tentatively, I smile at her.

"Why don't you get some of your trains, Oscar?" she asks suddenly, setting him down on the floor. "Your track's still set up in the living room."

As he scampers off on his quest, she puts the towel she was using to dry Oscar's hands back on the rail and leans against the counter, arms folded.

"How have you been?" She still sounds guarded, but not as cold as before. I give an internal sigh of relief.

"Okay." I shrug, tracing circles with a spilled droplet of water on the work surface. "I'm ... actually, no, that's a lie. I'm not okay really."

The next twenty minutes are best glossed over. There's crying on both sides. There's Heather exclaiming, "What a bastard!" before clamping a hand over her mouth as Oscar appears in the doorway. Luckily, he's too excited by his trains to pay much attention. There's plenty of self-recrimination, and not just from me.

"I should have been there that night," Heather says furiously, dabbing at her eyes with a tissue. "I *knew* I should have been there. I felt something was wrong. But I was just too bloody stubborn ..."

"You tried to tell me." I shake my head sadly. "But I wouldn't listen. Instead I just flung accusations at you. I'm so sorry about that. I had no right to say those things."

"You didn't say anything which isn't true." Heather sinks onto a bar stool, looking defeated. "We both know that."

"What? No!" I grab her hand, making her look at me. "Don't set any store by what I said. I was just angry, that's all. You and Dominic ..."

"Are hardly love's young dream," she concludes with a twist of the lips. "Let's not deny the obvious. We're more of a partnership than a marriage. But we have Oscar ..." Her head turns towards the living room, from where the sound of whirring wheels on track drifts through the doorway. "And so that's had to be enough. But that doesn't mean I don't sometimes think about it."

"About what?" I ask, although I already know the answer.

"About what might have been." There's a tremor in her voice, and she pauses to compose herself. "If things had gone differently. I envy you, you know."

My eyes widen. "Me?"

Why on earth would Heather envy *me*? I mean, our lives ... the comparison ... Well, it's not even worth spelling out. There's just no contest.

"Yes, you." She raises an eyebrow. "I look at you, with your career and your carefree single life ... It looks like a lot of fun to someone stuck at home with a three-year-old, you know." She looks weary all of a sudden. "Sometimes I feel like my life has just ground to a halt. All I ever think about are practical things: running the house, organising our lives ... and I think, what *happened* to me? I used to be so vibrant, so full of zest. Everything was exciting. I had so many plans. And now look; I'm twenty-five and I feel more like forty-five most of the time. All of the opportunities I thought I'd have, they're just not there any more. And while I know that if I actually had the choice I wouldn't change a thing, it still doesn't make it easier to accept."

I have the distinct sense of the ground shifting beneath me. Heather's always been so constant, so straightforward. Or, at least, so I'd thought. How did I not realise she felt like this? How could I have missed it, for all of these years?

"You know, I envy you sometimes too," I say haltingly. Perhaps it's time that both of us were completely honest. "With your big house, and your marriage ... and most of the time my life just feels so chaotic; I don't have a handle on anything. I feel like I should be so together by now ..."

"No one's 'together', Clara," Heather interrupts. "And you're doing better than you think, believe me."

Adam told me pretty much the same thing on Friday night. Perhaps it's time I started to listen.

"Maybe we both are," I venture.

She gives a quivering smile, squeezing my hand. "Maybe we are."

Chapter 26

By the time I set off for home later that afternoon, it's almost teatime. My head's pounding and my eyes are sore from crying; I feel totally wrung out, but at the same time so much lighter, like something I didn't even know I'd been carrying around has been lifted from my shoulders.

Heather and I ... we're okay. I think. We've learned a lot from one another this afternoon, at any rate.

Maybe things aren't perfect for either of us. But Heather has Oscar and, no matter what she might say about Dominic, I know that he's her rock. She needs that stability, someone who's always there. She might think my life looks fun but, in reality, she wouldn't be able to hack it at all. She'd be wailing for her 1,000 thread count sheets within a week. And if she had to live with Casper, with everything that entails ...

I allow myself a smirk. Actually, I'd pay to watch that. It'd be *hilarious*.

But, anyway, what I really mean is that, no matter how she might feel sometimes, she's in the right place. I hope she can see that now.

A bus trundles towards me and I stick out my hand.

Normally, I like the walk, but I feel like I've been put through an emotional mangle this afternoon. I think that justifies the bus fare.

I snag myself a window seat and prop my chin on my hand, gazing out at the street. A handsome college frontage rises up in front of me, smothered in vivid red Virginia creeper which seems to glow in the low sunlight. In the doorway, a couple are posing for photographs. She's wearing an Edwardian-looking wedding dress, he's in a tartan waistcoat, and they both look unutterably happy. A bridesmaid throws confetti into the air and it flutters away on the wind, filling the sky all around. A piece of it sticks to the window, which is still damp from the earlier rain. It's a pink heart and, as I press my finger to the glass behind it, the breeze tugs it away, off on its next adventure. I hope it lands on someone who really needs it, who'll cherish it as a sign that life can be beautiful.

Or, at the very least, someone who'll *notice* it. On the pavement, people are scurrying past, heads down, totally oblivious. I wonder if they even know what they're missing. How much there is to see if we just stop and look around us properly.

I've been as guilty of that as anyone, I have to admit as the bus pulls away. The couple are out of sight now, just another memory. I mean, haven't I been walking around my life with my head down? Metaphorically, at least. There's so much I've missed, so much I didn't see, either because I didn't want to, or because my attention was elsewhere.

If the whole sorry situation of the last few days has produced anything positive, it's a new awareness of what's really important in my life. The truth is that while losing Josh might have been mildly painful, the prospect of losing my job, Heather, even Adam ... that was so much worse. Josh was a fairy tale, a dream of what I thought I wanted. But all of those other things ... they're real. They make my life what it is. And what it is ... all told, it's pretty wonderful.

I'm ashamed to think that I almost risked all of it for a fantasy. Especially when the truth is that I never needed that fantasy in the first place. Adam was right after all; everything I ever thought I needed or wanted from a relationship, I already have. I wanted to be treasured, and I am. I wanted to be supported, and I am. I wanted to be loved ... Well, I don't even need to finish that sentence, do I?

I'm not saying that I'm going to give up on relationships altogether. I'll always be the dreamer who believes that magic and romance is out there somewhere. But, all of a sudden, I'm not in such a hurry. It'll find me when it's ready.

In the meantime, there's quite enough magic in my life as it is.

That last sentence makes me wince. I'm getting increasingly mawkish these days.

Just then I see a familiar unruly blond head out of the window, and I stab at the 'stop' button. The driver slams on the brakes, veering into the bus stop we were just about to pass with a bitten-off curse.

"Sorry," I say sheepishly, as I sidle past him.

He just mutters something about punters who can't make up their minds in time and pulls off sharply, leaving me in a cloud of exhaust fumes.

"Freddie!" I gasp, chasing him down the road. He starts to

turn and, on impulse, I fling my arms around him. Someone else I've been taking for granted, I think guiltily. I've hardly spent any proper time with him in the few weeks he's been here; bar that day on the river, it's just been snatched conversations in the kitchen. And who knows when I'll next see him after this? They'll be off travelling, on the other side of the world. I probably won't be able to get in contact with him for days or weeks at a time.

There and then, I resolve to be a better sister. I'll clear my schedule from now until whenever he leaves. We'll spend time together, like we used to. We can even go—

"What's up with you?" he says grumpily. "Has that new boyfriend of yours proposed, or something?"

Of course, Freddie doesn't know about what happened with Josh yet. I scan his face, trying to be surreptitious about it. He doesn't look good, I have to say. There are dark smudges under his eyes, and his cheeks look oddly sunken.

Oh, no, I think, with a spike of alarm. Please don't tell me that he's on drugs, or an alcoholic, or ...

All right, stay calm, Clara. Don't overreact. He's probably just tired, that's all.

"No, nothing like that," I say mildly, trying to keep my voice normal. "I just ... wanted you to know that I love you. That's all. And that I'm here."

We *never* say this stuff to one another. It's kind of a golden rule between siblings. But today, I'm breaking it, I think for the first time since our parents' funeral. I don't care that it's not the done thing. I'm tired of the rules, tired of maintaining an indifferent facade.

To my surprise, he doesn't look appalled. Instead, he hangs his head, covering his face with his hands.

"Oh, God. You *know*, don't you?"

"Er ..." I'm taken aback.

"I should have known you'd work it out." He sighs, and it sounds defeated. "I can't get anything past you."

I feel a fresh stab of confusion, my elated mood fast evaporating. What the hell is he talking about? *Please* don't say I was right about him being an alcoholic.

"Wait ... What?" I grab the sleeve of his jacket, urging him to look at me. "Freddie, what are you ...?" I trail off. Our house has come into sight, and there's someone standing on the doorstep. Someone in a green coat. I'd know that coat anywhere.

"It's Jess!" I exclaim. I didn't know she was coming. Why does Freddie never *tell* me anything? I turn my head to ask him that very question, only for the words to die upon my lips. He's frozen to the spot, staring at the figure in the distance with a look of total dread.

"What's wrong with you?" I hiss, elbowing him in the ribs. He doesn't move and, with an exasperated huff, I advance towards the gate, leaving him standing there uselessly on the pavement. Whatever's going on here, Jess will hopefully be able to shed some light upon it all. She always knows how to deal with Freddie.

"Jess!" I call, and as she spins around it's suddenly my turn to freeze to the spot. She doesn't look her usual polished self either; her hair has lost its lustre, and her nails are bare. Jess *always* paints her nails, it's just one of her things. But that's not what I'm staring at. Her coat is open, and beneath her jumper ...

"Sorry to intrude, Clara," she says softly, then swallows nervously. She cradles the curve of her stomach. "But you see, there's something I need to talk to you about."

***

The next thing I know, I'm sitting on the sofa in the living room with them both peering down at me, concern etched upon their faces.

"Are you all right?" Jess is pressing a glass of water into my hand, her brow crinkled with worry.

"Yes, I'm fine," I say, a bit embarrassed to be the cause of such fuss. "I just ..."

"You swooned," Freddie says bluntly.

"I did not *swoon*!" I snap, although I can feel my face growing hot. All right, so I did kind of swoon. Not properly, but just ... a bit.

To be fair to me, I had just had the most almighty bombshell dropped upon my head. I think anyone could be excused a small swoon under the circumstances.

Freddie and Jess exchange knowing looks. I see Jess mouth, "Shock," at him, and he nods sagely.

"I am *here,* you know," I say tetchily. Honestly. They've already got the whole patronising parent thing down to a tee, at least. They'll have no trouble ...

I can feel myself growing pale. Parents. Oh, my God. They're going to be *parents*.

My little brother is going to be a father. The same little brother who can't seem to pick his own socks up off the floor is going to be in charge of a fragile new life.

Just as that thought hits me, another, even more disturbing, one follows on its heels.

"The baby," I say, gesturing to Jess's bump, which looks even more protruding now she's taken her coat off. "It is ... er ... well, it is ...?"

"Clara!" Freddie all but bellows, looking outraged. "Of course it's *mine*. Who else's would it be?"

"Sorry." Now I really do feel hot. But I had to ask. "Sorry, Jess. No offence. It's just ... he's been moping around here and ..." I narrow my eyes at Freddie. "Wait ... you don't seem surprised. How long have you known about this?"

"I told him the same day I found out myself," Jess supplies quietly. She's settled herself upon the edge of the sofa. Despite her growing bump, she looks more frail and bird-like than I've ever seen her. "Five weeks ago."

"And you've been *here*?" I yell, swivelling round to face him. "What, did you think you could just hide from it and hope it would all go away?"

I can't take this in. It's too much.

"I couldn't face it!" he blurts out. "It was just ... It was never the plan, okay?" He turns to Jess, his eyes pleading. "It was never part of our plan. There was so much we wanted to do. And now ..."

"You don't think I didn't feel all of that as well?" Jess fires back. Her face quivers with barely leashed emotion. I can't even begin to imagine what she's been through these past few weeks. "It was a shock to me too, you know. Don't you think *I* was scared? I needed you more than I ever have before. I needed your support, Freddie. And instead you ran away." She breaks off, looking perilously close to tears.

"I was always going to come back," Freddie says desperately. He looks like a cornered animal; I've never seen him so terrified. "I never meant to stay away, I promise you."

"I gave you the benefit of the doubt," she says sadly. "I said to myself, 'He's panicking; that's natural. I'll give him time'. I *knew* you were immature, Freddie; I'm not under any illusions. But I thought this would make you grow up a bit." She balls her hand into a fist at her side. "And instead I have to come and *get* you! Do you have any idea how that makes me feel?"

"No!" He kneels down at her feet, taking her hands in his. "Jess, don't. You know how much I lo—"

"I don't want to do this on my own." Tears are streaming down Jess's face. "But after this ... What kind of father are you going to be? Perhaps I'm better off by myself."

I've been sitting here all of this time, but now I force myself to move. I shouldn't be listening to this.

"I'll give you some space." I edge out of the room, although neither of them look up anyway. They're just staring into each other's eyes, not speaking. There's a finality about the moment which breaks my heart and I turn away, feeling intrusive.

I pull open the front door and slip out, not even stopping to pick up a coat from the rack. I just need air. I need to think.

"I'd stay outside if I were you," I tell Casper, who's sitting on the doorstep. "It's safer out here."

He just gives me a bored look. I dread to think how many

babies he's fathered over the years. He probably thinks it's no big deal.

I set off down the street, barely aware of putting one foot in front of the other.

How could I not have seen this coming? Of *course* Freddie was behaving oddly; the whole thing was odd, his turning up like that, out of the blue. I *knew* that.

At once, I'm subsumed by guilt. What was it he said to me? 'I can't get anything past you.' Except he did, didn't he? I've been so wrapped up in myself lately, so obsessed with what *I* want and what's going on in *my* life, that I didn't even see what was going on right in front of me.

Even so, I can't understand it. The brother I know would never have done this. He would never have been so selfish and reckless.

This is my own fault; I was *supposed* to be looking after him. I was supposed to make sure that we would both be okay. Clearly, I've failed us all.

Mum and Dad would be so disappointed in me.

My eyes are hot with unshed tears. I look up, trying to dispel them, and realise that I'm next to the gateway to Alexandra College. I have no recollection of how I got here; my feet must have brought me of their own accord.

"Are you coming in, love?" the gateman enquires kindly, leaning out of his glass-fronted booth.

I realise that I'm just standing on the pavement, staring at the facade blankly.

"Yes," I hear myself say. "Yes, I am."

Suddenly, the urge to talk to Adam is almost overwhelming.

It's almost like I subconsciously knew that's what I needed.

I cross the quad, following the labyrinthine corridors which I remember from my last visit. I take a couple of wrong turns, but eventually I find it. His office is tucked away at the end of the row. I knock on the door, feeling strangely nervous.

"Come in." His voice emerges from within.

I poke my head around the doorframe. "Hi."

He's sitting at his desk, next to a stack of essays. I can tell that he's been at it for a while because his hair is all tousled, like he's been running his hands through it. He does that when he's concentrating hard on something. Or when he's exasperated by something, come to think of it. He certainly does it an awful lot when he's around me and, heaven knows, I'm exasperating enough.

He looks up and for a second I see his eyes widen behind his glasses. They're a heavy black-framed style; I've never seen him wear them before. They suit him. As I think that, my stomach does a little flip and I grit my teeth together, trying to quell it.

"Clara. I didn't expect ..." He pushes his chair away from the desk. "I'm sorry, I'm in the middle of marking, hence why it's such a tip in here."

Hence. Only Adam would use a word like hence so casually. It makes me want to smile. I was right; just being in his presence makes the hollow feeling inside me abate slightly.

"I didn't know you wore glasses," I say shyly.

"I do when I've been squinting at first year essays for the past three days. I gave up on vanity yesterday afternoon and took my contacts out."

"Oh." For the first time, it occurs to me that I shouldn't have just waltzed in here like this. Of course he's busy. He has work to do; he doesn't want me interrupting him. "Sorry. I should leave ..."

"Not at all. I could do with a break, anyway." He picks up a small travel kettle which is plugged in on a side table by the window. "Tea?"

I settle back against the desk, feeling ridiculously pleased that he wants me to stay. He has a way of making me feel like I'm always important.

"Obviously. What else happens at four o'clock in this country?"

"You weren't at the museum today?" His back is to me as he picks two tea bags out of the box and drops them into the cups.

"Not all day; I left early. It's sort of ... Well, let's just say it's been an eventful afternoon."

"Nothing to do with your veterinary friend, I hope?" He asks lightly enough, but he's gone very still. There's a tension about his shoulders as he holds the kettle poised over the cups.

"God, no." I actually find myself laughing at the absurdity of it. "Josh is the last thing on my mind, believe me."

Only two days ago, our breakup seemed like the end of the world. But now it just seems infinitely small and unimportant.

Adam places the tea on the desk next to me. "Want to talk about it?"

He seems perfectly earnest, but suddenly I feel reticent.

After all, hasn't he heard enough about my problems? He doesn't need to get tangled up in any more.

"It's a long story," I hedge, picking up my tea.

He smiles wryly. "I'm a Classics professor, remember? I'm used to long stories. The Roman Empire lasted for 1,500 years, after all."

Chapter 27

The next few days are manic. Strange, manic and ... oddly wonderful.

I didn't know what to expect when I finally got home that night. Freddie's severed head rolling down the garden path, perhaps? As it was, I found them snuggled up together on the sofa, lost in each other's eyes. I simply picked up Casper, who was glaring disgustedly at them from the doorway, and quietly made myself scarce upstairs.

The next morning I came down early to find the kettle on and Freddie already up, sitting at the kitchen table reading a book. I had to rub my eyes to make sure I wasn't still dreaming, but no—he even offered me a cup of tea. A changed man, indeed. And it turned out that the book in question was *the* baby book which Oscar saw him reading in the bookshop (it seems that I owe Oscar an apology for doubting his word. Probably best paid in chocolate.); he bought it after all, so at least he *was* telling the truth when he said he was planning to go back. I can't tell you how much that reassured me. I knew he would pull through in the end. After all, whatever his faults, Freddie has a good heart. We all know that. I think it's a large part of the reason why Jess decided to give him another chance.

And, to his credit, he's not wasting it. I've never seen my brother so motivated. He's doing everything in his power to be the best soon-to-be father possible. When he'd finished that first baby book, he went off to the library and came home with a stack more. He's used the money they'd been saving for their travels and gone on a shopping spree; my house has turned into an obstacle course of baby paraphernalia. If I'm not stepping over boxes, I'm ducking beneath the old dismantled cot Freddie managed to reclaim from one of the neighbours, which is propped across the hallway at a drunken angle.

I have to say, I'm rather looking forward to having my house back. To think that I ever bewailed living on my own.

I mean, don't get me wrong. It's great having them here. And, believe me, I'm more pleased than anyone that Freddie is taking all of this so seriously. He seems to have grown up before my eyes in the past few days.

But the *conversation* ... If I have to hear one more debate on wooden versus silicone teething rings, or self-soothing versus a pacifier, or swaddling versus a sleep sack, I'm going to go stark raving mad. When you're having a baby everything seems to be versus everything else. Even Jess looks bemused by most of it. She just shrugs and goes off for a nap.

She went off for a particularly calculated nap yesterday afternoon, leaving Freddie and me alone for the first time since it all happened.

"I should have just told you the truth ages ago." He hovered by the fridge, hands shoved in his pockets. "But I just couldn't ... I didn't want you to be ashamed of me."

"*Ashamed* of you?" I stared at him. "What do you mean? I could never be ashamed of you. You're my little brother, and whatever ..."

"Yes, but you've handled everything so well," he burst out. "After Mum and Dad ... You've got past it, made a life they'd be proud of. How can I admit to you that I feel like I'm drowning most of the time?"

"You think I've got *past* it?" My face was numb with shock. "Freddie, I will *never* get past it. It hurts every day. I'm just doing my best to carry on with life. I get things wrong too, believe me. Josh was a case in point, and that's just a recent example."

"Yes, but you wouldn't have done something like this," he said bitterly.

I looked at my brother, his anguished face, and immediately I saw how much he regretted it. What was the point in making him feel worse?

"Neither of us are perfect," I said softly. "Perhaps we should just leave it at that."

"I would have stayed, you know," he said suddenly. "I still feel terrible that I left you with all of that. It wasn't fair."

I sighed. I'd known we'd come back to this at some point.

"You had to go to university, Freddie. You had your whole life ahead of you. They were holding your place."

"I could have deferred," he said, and I saw that same stubbornness in his face that I recognise in myself sometimes. "I could have helped you sell the house, deal with all the paperwork. You didn't need to do it on your own."

"I wanted to protect you," I confessed. "I saw you as my responsibility."

"Exactly, and you still do. But I was eighteen when they died, Clara. Not a lot younger than you. I was an adult, not a child. You don't need to feel responsible for everything I do."

His words so closely echoed what Adam had told me in his office that day that I could only stare at him in amazement.

"Thank God Jess has taken me back." He sighed gustily. "You know that Mum and Dad split up for a while, before they got married? He told me once, a couple of years before they died."

"Wait ... What? No, I never knew that." I pushed myself away from the counter. "What happened?"

I can't believe it. My parents—their relationship was perfect. They never even *fought*.

Freddie just shrugged. "He didn't go into details. All he said was that it was hard at the time, but ultimately it made them stronger. I hope I'll be able to say the same to our baby about Jess and me one day."

"I'm sure you will." I put a hand on his arm. "And you know I'll be here for whatever you need. Although you seem to have most it sorted out already," I added with a wry glance around my cramped kitchen. "Do you really need all of this stuff *right* now?"

"All right, so I might have been a bit precipitate," he

admitted defensively. "But there's just so little time ... Heather says that you can never be too prepared."

One of the first things I did once everything had settled was send the two of them off to see Heather; after all, she's been in the same sort of situation herself. She's been amazing, although the problem now is that every other sentence begins with "Heather says ..."

"You'll certainly be that," I remarked drily.

I shouldn't have mocked him, really. Because I can see why he's panicking; it turns out that Jess is actually five months pregnant. Five months! Apparently she didn't even realise for the first three and a half, and then, when you add on Freddie's untimely disappearance ...

But never mind that. I promised to put it in the past.

Anyway, the upshot is that I'm absolutely exhausted, and I'm not even the one having this baby. Jess and Freddie seem to be on a high, though. They've taken the whole thing in their stride, whereas I still haven't even had the chance to sit down and process the fact that I'm going to be an aunt.

The only one who shares some of my perplexity is Casper. He spends most of his time outside, terrorising anything smaller than himself. And a few things which are bigger too. I had to stop him from going after a fox last night.

My one anchoring point of sanity is Adam, who calls to see how we're getting on. It's like being a teenager again, lying on my bed talking on the phone for an hour at a time. I don't know why, but I always seem to retreat to my room; I suppose I don't want Jess and Freddie to get any ideas. I know what they're like; they'll be planning our wedding before I've even had a chance to refute that there's anything romantic between us.

And there isn't. We're just friends. That's all. Women and men *can* be friends.

I mean ... there is one small, irritating thing. Every time his name comes up on my phone screen, I get this warm, fluttering feeling in my chest.

But, you know, that's *all*. It doesn't mean anything. Adam and I could never be right for one another. Imagine the arguments, for one thing. And what would happen with Casper? He'd probably leave home in umbrage.

Not that any of this matters. Because we're just friends.

And that's fine. That's all I need.

For the first time since I lost my parents, life feels like it's working out. I hadn't realised just how much I'd been clinging on by my fingernails, forcing myself to believe that I was coping. That nothing mattered. Now, I can see that it's okay if things matter, so long as I keep it all in perspective. If this baby has taught me anything, it's that life is here and now. Even if it's unexpected; sometimes that's how the best things happen, when you're not looking. I don't want to miss any more moments because I'm so busy scanning the horizon for something which, if it's meant to come into my life, will do so in its own time anyway.

And ... that's as deep as I'm going to get. For now.

"What do you think, Clara?" Freddie asks, bringing me back to the present. He turns his laptop around so I can see the screen. A photo of a red-bricked Edwardian house meets my eye. "It's four bedrooms, detached, decent-sized garden ..."

"A new house has just come up here in Cambridge." Jess taps at her phone, her brow dented with concentration. Her nails are painted a vibrant red; she borrowed it off me the day after she and Freddie made up. I take it as a sign that all is well in the world again. "It's a two-bedroom terrace, only a couple of streets away from here. It's pretty; it has one of those little wooden canopy porches above the door. I love those."

"Yes, but only two bedrooms?" Freddie scoots across the sofa, peering at the small screen. "Is that really going to be big enough for the baby?"

"Of course it is! It'll only be a tiny thing; how much room could it need?"

"Yes, but what about afterwards?" Freddie insists. "I assume we'll want more at some point. Then we'll have to move again."

"*More*?" Jess manages in a strangled voice. "Let's get this one out of the way first, shall we?"

I scratch Casper behind the ears, letting their voices wash over me.

When Jess finally told her parents, who live permanently in Dubai, they immediately offered to pay for the deposit on a house as a baby gift. Which, whilst a lovely gesture, has only incited a fierce debate on where to live. It always goes exactly the same way. Allow me to outline:

Manchester is near their friends.

But Cambridge is near me and, seeing as I'm the only family member either still alive and/or living in this country, I'm considered quite important. If I do say so myself.

Ah, but then Manchester is *so* much cheaper. They can get

a family-sized home for the same price as a poky terrace here. A poky terrace much like the one we're in now, as Freddie so graciously pointed out, during one of their more heated discussions on the topic.

Manchester is also bigger and more cosmopolitan. Better to raise children in the city, where there's lots to do.

But *Cambridge* is smaller and more intimate. Better to raise children in the country, where it's a more laid-back lifestyle. (Their words, not mine. If they really think Cambridge counts as 'the countryside', then they really have been living in a big city for too long.)

But *Manchester* …

Anyway, never mind. You get the gist. It only ever goes round and round in circles, anyway.

As if to elucidate my point, they're still going now.

"But Jess," Freddie's saying urgently, "think about the garden. The baby's going to need a garden to run around in."

"Not for a while. And this *has* a garden." Jess stabs at the screen, bringing up a picture of an uninspiring bare lawn. "Yes, it's small. But Cambridge has loads of green space. We'll take it to the park to run off steam."

As if of one mind, they both turn to look imploringly at me.

"What do you think, Clara?" they say in unison.

"Oh, *no*." I disentangle my legs from where they've been curled up beneath me on the sofa and get up, beginning to clear the empty coffee cups off the table. "I've told you. I'm staying well out of this. It's not my decision, it's yours."

Clearly, I would love for them to stay here in Cambridge.

I couldn't think of much better than having my little nephew or niece just around the corner. But, at the same time, I don't want to sway their decision. It's their life; they have to decide what's best for *them*, not anyone else. And if that decision means they might be living almost two hundred miles away, then, well ... there are trains, right? It's hardly the moon.

"Just take a look at them," Freddie urges. "Come on, Clara. We're getting nowhere trying to decide on our own. We need your input."

"No, you don't," I say, gently but firmly. "You're your own little family unit now. When this baby comes, you're going to have to make dozens of choices every day. You might as well start getting used to it."

He huffs, but then he turns to Jess and says, "Tell you what; why don't we make appointments for them both? We can't make any proper decisions without seeing them, can we?"

She nods happily. "That's a good idea."

I smile to myself as I take the cups through into the kitchen and put them in the sink. That's another reason I'm not going to tell them what to do—because they don't *actually* need me to. They think they do, but they don't. I look at Freddie these days, and I see a totally different person. He was right; he's no longer the boy I felt I had to look after, to shield him from the world.

The doorbell rings, reverberating through the house.

"Anyone going to get that?" I holler. Then, when it rings again, I stick my head through the doorway into the living room. Freddie and Jess seem to have given up on the house search entirely; instead, they're entwined upon the sofa, kissing passionately like a couple of teenagers, oblivious to everything around them.

I edge past them, trying not to look. We *really* need to get them installed in their own house, and soon. Much more of this and I'll probably morph into an *actual* gooseberry.

"Hi—" I wrench open the front door breathlessly "—sorry to have kept you waiting. I was just ..."

And then I stop mid-sentence. Because standing on the doorstep, with his hands in his pockets and a familiar crooked smile, is the last person I expected to see.

Chapter 28

Actually, upon reflection, that's not strictly true.

I mean, there are plenty of less likely candidates to find upon the doorstep. Jeremy, for one. Or the Prime Minister. Or the milkman who refused to do our round any more after Casper took to hiding behind the empty milk bottles and attacking his hand when he reached down to collect them. Or even ... I'm warming to my theme now ... my parents, perhaps?

Now, that really *would* be a surprise.

Having said that, I definitely wasn't expecting to see Josh again. I thought we'd ended things between us pretty succinctly.

"What do you want?" I ask warily.

He doesn't seem deterred by my cool reception. In fact, he just flashes me another one of those gorgeous smiles. I wait for my heart to flip, but it doesn't.

All right, so maybe it does a *tiny* bit. I mean, come on. He's still beautiful. And I'm only human.

"How are you?" he says conversationally, leaning against the doorframe in that urbane manner he has.

How *am* I? Is he *serious*?

"Fine," I say stonily. "What do you *want*, Josh?"

That seems to dent his bravado a bit. The dazzling smile flickers slightly. "I wondered if we could talk. Just for a minute."

"Really?" I'm getting exasperated. I'm way too tired and overwhelmed to deal with this right now. And I'm not in the mood to play games either. "I think we covered everything the last time we spoke, didn't we?" My voice grows a jagged edge as I warm to my theme. "You were quite explicit about how you felt. In fact, everyone in the room heard about it, including, by the way, my friends, my boss, and one of the country's top art patrons. I don't need you to spell it out again, thank you very much."

His shoulders drop, his eyes filling with contrition. "I know I'm probably the last person you want to see right now."

I consider that for a moment. In this case, he's probably right. I *can't* think of anyone I'd less rather see at the moment. Even that hostile milkman.

"But just ..." He rubs the back of his neck self-consciously. "Look, let's not do this here. Let me take you out. No pressure, I promise," he adds quickly, as I open my mouth to refuse. "Just for a chat. If at any moment you don't like what I'm saying, you can leave. I won't stop you. And if, after that, you still don't want to see me ever again ... well, I'll respect your wishes."

There's nothing I'd like more than to slam the door in his face. But that would only make me look childish and unreasonable; I'd lose whatever moral high ground I currently possess. Besides which, I *do* still have my pride; I want him to leave regretting what an amazing thing he threw away, not thanking his stars for a lucky escape.

I hesitate. It's only for the briefest of moments, but he sees it.

"Please, Clara," he says softly. "I just want to do something right for once."

His words hit me right in the centre of my chest, making my defences wobble precariously. Damn, but he's persuasive. What can I say to *that*?

I don't owe him anything, I remind myself firmly. And really, he has no right to expect me to listen to him. He has no right to even *ask*.

And yet ... I look into his deep green eyes and I can't deny that a part of me wants to hear what he has to say. If I send him away now, I'm afraid that I'll regret it. I'm afraid that I'll always wonder.

The decision is made for me a moment later as a squeal emits from the living room, followed by a crash which sounds suspiciously like the lamp falling off the side table. I know that sound well; God knows, Casper's knocked it over often enough.

I'm already reaching behind the door for my coat. I might not know my own heart, but at least one thing's for certain: even a walk with Josh is preferable to being forced to listen to my brother having coitus on my sofa.

"All right. I'll come. But just for a few minutes. And this *doesn't* mean anything," I warn him, pulling the door closed behind me. It's a deceptively cold day, all sunshine and frosty air, and I fasten the buttons on my bright red coat, telling myself that it was pure coincidence which led me to grab my most becoming piece of outerwear. After all, I'm not trying to impress him any more. This is just a formality, a *courtesy* even. A means to get some closure. I couldn't care less if he finds me attractive.

You know, technically.

"Nothing at all." He shakes his head in agreement, which is an odd juxtaposition. "Just two friends ..."

"*Acquaintances*," I correct him staunchly.

"... having a walk," he continues smoothly. "Maybe even a coffee, if all goes well."

"Don't get ahead of yourself," I mutter. But I can't help adding, "A hot chocolate, since you're asking. And I want it with all of the trimmings; it's the least you can do. I'm talking whipped cream, marshmallows, sprinkles ..."

"*Sprinkles*?" He looks appalled. "Are you sure?"

"And chocolate sauce," I finish resolutely. "Maybe even some of those little honeycomb pieces if they have them."

"Sounds like a coronary waiting to happen," he says faintly. "But all right. I can hardly say no, can I? Got to pay off the debt. How many hot chocolates will it take, do you think?"

I give him a disbelieving look.

"Too soon for jokes?" He winces. "Okay, just thought I'd try it."

"Not quite seeing the funny side just yet," I say in a strained voice. "I could have lost my *job*, Josh."

"I'm sorry," he says sincerely, hanging his head. "I didn't realise ... I never intended ... well, any of it. Please say that you believe me on that score, at least."

I briefly entertain the notion of tormenting him, but then I sigh in defeat. I'm better than that. "I do."

For all of his faults, I know he didn't intend to do it. He's not a bad person, just a thoughtless one. And, much as I'd like to stay angry with him, I can feel the heat of it ebbing away. After all, it took some courage turning up at the door like that. He must have known that he wouldn't receive a warm reception, and yet he's willingly put himself in the firing line. That must count for *something*, mustn't it?

When it comes down to it, I don't really have the energy in me to carry on resenting him. Too much has happened since then.

While we've been talking, we've wandered down to the park, where there seems to be some sort of fair going on. There's a scattering of artisan food stalls in the foreground (after all, this isn't just any old fair. This is a *Cambridge* fair) and Josh inclines his head towards them now.

"Let me buy you that hot chocolate?"

We settle at one of the rickety metal tables next to the stall while we wait for the promised beverage to arrive. Josh was as good as his word; he made the poor stall owner get every topping off the shelves. Luckily, he's charming enough to get away with it.

He certainly got away with a lot when it came to me. But that was my own fault; didn't I register that charm early on? Didn't I even wonder if it was something to be wary of? And yet I let myself fall beneath his spell anyway. No one could say that I didn't do so willingly.

"Clara ..." he begins haltingly, interlacing his hands

together on the table in front of him. "I want you to know that I never meant to hurt you. I just ... when you came out with that ... I panicked. I was immediately ashamed of how I'd behaved, and I haven't been able to stop thinking about it since."

I shrug. "I did rather spring it upon you."

The truth is that a *lot* of it was my fault; I can see that now. I mean, sure, he could have handled it a lot better; I'm not excusing him from that. But I played my part too. I made assumptions based upon what I wanted to be the truth, not upon what was actually going on in front of me. I twisted his words in my head until they meant what I wanted them to mean. I was never really in a relationship with Josh; I was in a relationship with a vision of Josh I'd created.

And, in doing so, I missed out on a relationship with the real man. Someone who's caring and interesting and funny. I didn't imagine those things. Someone I now find myself wishing I'd let myself get to know.

"But still ..." He leans forward intently, then breaks off as the waitress places our drinks down in front of us. She's smiling at him coquettishly, but he doesn't even look up. His gaze is steadfastly fixed upon me. I suppose I ought to be flattered. *She* certainly thinks so; she shoots me a resentful look over her shoulder as she walks away.

Josh carries on, completely unaware of this byplay.

"The thing is, Clara, I really did like you. I *do* like you. You're fun, and different, and ... well, it was never just about the sex, no matter what I might have said in the ... uh, heat of the moment." He flushes appealingly.

"You don't have to say any of this." I'm feeling pretty embarrassed myself. I poke at my hot chocolate with the spoon; it's a monstrous confection of cream and toppings. I have no idea how I'll manage it all. I only really ordered it to spite him.

"No, I want to." As if on impulse, he takes my free hand, which is resting upon the table. We both stare down at our interlocked fingers for a moment. I'm frozen in indecision. I should pull my hand away, but I don't, and then somehow it seems too late to do it. So I just leave it there, trying to pretend that it's no big deal.

Except ... it is. Because I can feel the warmth of his skin against mine. And it's doing something strange to my insides.

"I've missed you," he murmurs, looking at me with those enthralling green eyes. Those eyes are wasted on a man; any woman would kill for them. "That's never happened to me before. Usually it's just easy come, easy go, but with you ... I can't let go. You make me want to try harder, to try and have something more meaningful for once."

I stare numbly back at him, feeling torn.

A part of me wishes he wasn't saying all of this. Once upon a time, it would have been my every dream come true. But now ... the last thing I need is any more complication in my life.

And who am I kidding? That's not just it. The truth is that I've changed. I'm wiser than I used to be, more wary. Just because a gorgeous man wants to be with me doesn't mean I'm about to leap into his arms.

On the other hand ...

"Let me try, Clara," he whispers. "That's all I want."

Butterflies, definite butterflies. They're still there. I take a breath, spoon cream off the top of my hot chocolate. Hope I'm not about to make a big mistake.

"One step at a time," I tell him. "Then maybe ... we'll see."

His face breaks out into a glorious smile. "I see a coconut shy over there. I was pretty good at that when I was a kid." He points at my still half-full cup. "Tell you what; finish that, and then let's see if I can win one for you."

***

I'd forgotten how easy it is, being with Josh. He's so wonderfully uncomplicated. We spend the rest of the afternoon at the fair. He *does* win me a coconut, and a lurid pink rabbit from the hook-a-duck stall. We take a spin on the teacups, much to the ride manager's palpable disdain, and I manage to persuade Josh to try some candyfloss, even though apparently it goes against his every medical sensibility.

For the first time, I'm not expecting anything more from him. I'm not angsting over the state of our relationship, or worrying about where it's all going. I'm not trying to make him into anything he's not. And that means I enjoy being with him in a way that I never really have before. He makes me laugh. A lot. It's been a while since I've felt so purely in the moment. He makes me feel light again, as if all of the seriousness of the past few weeks has been lifted from me.

I mean, don't get me wrong. I'm not falling for him all

over again. That would be foolish, after what happened last time. I'm keeping my distance. My heart is well and truly guarded.

But that doesn't mean that I can't appreciate his company, right?

To his credit, he seems to respect our new boundaries. He doesn't try to kiss me, although I can tell that he wants to. A couple of times throughout the afternoon he looks at me, and my breath catches at the hungry expression in his eyes. He doesn't hold my hand again either, although at one point he does place his palm against my back to steer me. It's only a fleeting touch, but it counts. I think.

Not that I *want* him to touch me or anything. Because, you know, boundaries. Strong, modern woman and all of that.

Even so, as we grow closer to my house, I find myself deliberately slowing my steps, wanting to prolong our time together. And when we arrive at my front door, I don't reach for my keys. A light rain has begun to fall, lacing my hair with water droplets.

We just stand there, looking at one another. Apparently neither of us knows what to say.

"Thanks for this afternoon," he says at last, pulling his coat collar up around his neck as the rain intensifies. "I had a great time."

"So did I," I say breathlessly. I realise that I'm tilting forward slightly, as though inviting him to kiss me, and I tug myself back. Modern women do *not* throw themselves at men. Especially ones who've hurt them in the past.

But this Josh doesn't feel like the same guy who did all of

that. He feels like someone new, someone I'm just getting to know for the first time, and ... damn it, I *so* want him to kiss me. And maybe that's wrong, after everything, but I don't care. I don't care about anything except feeling his lips upon mine, seeing if we still have that same magic.

"Can we do this again?" he asks, and he almost sounds tentative. "I mean, obviously, not this exactly, but you know ... something else."

He's rambling. Delight blooms within me, and I have to stop myself from breaking out into a grin. Josh's always so self-possessed, so unflappable. And yet, here he is, tongue-tied as he tries to ask me out on a date.

It's adorable. And it only makes me want to kiss him all the more.

"I'd like that," I say simply. I'm aware that we're having about the most clichéd post-date conversation ever here, but so what? I haven't changed *that* much; my heart still skips at the thought of being the girl in the fairy tale. The girl romance happens to. With the rain, and him hovering on the doorstep like this, and maybe even ...

"I'd better get going, before we're both soaked to the skin," he says pragmatically, and I feel a stab of disappointment.

So that's a no to kissing in the rain, then.

"Absolutely," I say brightly. "Just ... give me a call."

"I will." He heads off down the garden path without a backward look. I fish my keys out of my bag, feeling strangely disconsolate, but just as I'm pushing them into the lock I hear footsteps behind me.

"I'm sorry, but it won't do. I can't leave it like that."

And then he spins me around and into a long, dizzying kiss.

At last he pulls away, breathing hard. "See you later."

Before I can catch my breath, he's gone. And I'm left standing on the doorstep, not knowing what to feel.

Chapter 29

"Can we talk?" Ruby hisses, digging her electric-blue fingernails into my arm.

"What about?" I ask innocently.

"Him!" She jabs a finger in Josh's direction. He's standing at the other end of the gallery, looking blankly at a depiction of Lancelot and Guinevere. "What the hell is going on?"

I should have known this was coming. It was always going to be a risk, bringing Josh to the museum. But I figured it had to happen at some point; why not today?

"We're looking at paintings," I say primly, attempting to tug my arm away, but she clings on. "That *is* the accepted activity in a museum, isn't it?"

"Don't try and be cute," she snaps. "You know what I mean. What are you doing with *him*?"

"We're just having a nice time together, that's all. It's nothing serious."

"Nothing *serious*?" Her lipsticked mouth drops open. "Are you *insane*? It shouldn't be anything at all. Have you forgotten ...?"

"No, I haven't. And neither has he. But we've decided to put it behind us." I sigh, my annoyance abating at the worry in her face. She's only trying to protect me, even if she does have a slightly abrasive way of going about it. "Look, I get that you don't approve. But I know what I'm doing, believe me. This time, it's different. I'm the one in control."

I can't fault Josh; he's been as good as his word. I've never known a man try so hard to impress me. He calls when he says he will. He's taken me out to dinner. We've been for walks in the park. We've been for coffee. We've even been ice-skating. There's something gloriously whimsical about it all; it's like old-fashioned dating.

The kind of dating which everyone told me didn't exist any more. I can't say that I don't feel a little smug to have proven them wrong.

And in case you're wondering, yes, we *have* kissed a couple of times. But no, there *hasn't* been anything more. There's something nice about taking it slow. It really is like we've started all over again, and this time I'm determined to keep it in perspective. This time it's on my terms.

Once, I wouldn't have been able to do that. I couldn't forgive and forget, give someone the benefit of the doubt. Once a relationship was over, that was it. If they didn't live up to my high standards, then obviously they weren't the one. I moved on. But Freddie telling me that Mum and Dad had split up once has had an effect on me; it's made me wonder if perhaps I've only hurt myself by being too hasty. Perhaps in the past I haven't given people enough of a chance. After all, if it worked for my parents, then why not me and Josh?

"He's still too handsome for his own good," Ruby says darkly, frowning at his profile.

Isn't he just. I follow her gaze. He's only wearing a white T-shirt and jeans, but he still looks heart-stoppingly sexy. He catches my eye and smiles. My heart flips as usual, although perhaps not as much as I was expecting it to.

In fact, if I'm being honest, nothing's quite as intense as it was last time. The tingles when he touches me. The electricity when we kiss. It isn't that it's not there, exactly, just that ...

Well, it's not *there*. If you know what I mean.

It's the only small fly in an otherwise blissful ointment.

I'm not about to blow it all out of proportion, mind. That's what the old Clara would have done. New Clara is simply putting it down to jaded experience. I'm more measured these days, not as dreamy and idealistic. So it follows that my feelings aren't going to be the same.

After all, real relationships aren't all butterflies and rainbows, are they? No wonder I could never make anything work out before, if that's what I was anticipating.

If only Adam could hear my thoughts now. He wouldn't believe it.

Thinking about Adam immediately makes me feel guilty. I haven't seen him in ages. Actually, I've missed a couple of his calls and never returned them. Slightly accidentally-on-purpose, I'll admit.

I suppose I'm afraid of him finding out about Josh and me.

All right, so not *afraid* as such. But his opinion ... well, it matters to me. Ruby's ire I can take ... Adam's quiet disappointment, I'm not so sure. He won't understand any of this; he'll think I'm weak, that I've fallen into the same trap all over again. And even though I know differently, just the knowledge that he'll be thinking it causes me to squirm.

"Hey." Josh's wandered over to join us. He slings an arm around my waist, pulling me against his side. "So, what was it you wanted to show me?"

"Sounds like she's shown you quite enough already," Ruby mutters under her breath.

I shoot her a quelling look.

Either Josh doesn't notice her hostility or else he's unfazed by it, because he bestows upon her one of his most engaging smiles. The kind which can disarm a woman at ten yards.

"Tell me, have we met? You look familiar."

Any woman, it seems, except Ruby. She's utterly unmoved.

"I'm not surprised you remember me. *I* was the one who kicked you out of here after you broke Clara's heart in front of two hundred people."

"Ah." Josh nods knowingly. "Of course. I can understand that you're furious with me. You probably think that Clara's making a massive mistake in letting me back into her life."

"You've got that right." Ruby sniffs, although she looks faintly surprised at his candour. "You don't deserve her forgiveness."

"You're right; I don't," Josh agrees readily. "And I remember that every moment that we're together, believe me. It's never far from my mind."

"Oh." Ruby's eyes dart between us, uncertainty clouding her features. "Well, that's ..."

"And don't worry," Josh adds with a wink. "She's making me work for it. I'm not getting off lightly."

Ruby emits something which sounds like a titter. I stare at her, incredulous.

"I'm pleased to hear it," she says robustly. But there's a twinkle in her eyes which is unmistakable.

I don't *believe* it. He's charming her! The most ardent feminist I know, reduced to a girlish puddle after just ninety seconds in his company. I wouldn't credit it if I weren't seeing it with my own eyes.

"Now, if you'll excuse us," Josh says gallantly, taking my arm. "I promised my lady that I would accompany her on a tour of the museum. I mustn't disappoint her."

"No," Ruby breathes ardently. "No, you mustn't."

"You shouldn't have done that," I chide as we leave her standing there, apparently still a little dazed.

"She deserved it," he says airily. "Now, where are we going?"

"Through here." I pull him towards a pair of ceiling-high double doors at the end of the main gallery.

"Breaking the rules; I like it." He grins, eyeing the 'Private – no entry' sign which is emblazoned in red ink.

I roll my eyes, even though I'm unfastening the bolts so he can't see my face anyway.

"Hardly, seeing as I work here."

"Still, it's kind of hot."

"You're such an idiot sometimes." I give the last bolt a sharp tug and it releases. "Come on."

I bound into the centre of the room, my footsteps echoing around the bare walls.

Josh follows me at a more considered pace, looking around with a nonplussed expression.

"It's an ... empty room."

"But it won't be." I spin in a circle, arms thrown wide. I'm so excited, I can barely contain myself. "Next summer, it'll be filled with paintings. Paintings *I've* chosen. Can you imagine?"

All of this *space*. Just for *my* exhibition. I feel heady just thinking about it.

I thought I might faint when Jeremy told me that I could plan the summer showcase. At first I thought he was joking. But of course I should have known better. Jeremy *never* jokes. It's not in his programming.

I've envisioned so many themes over the years, I almost didn't know where to start. I was buried under a sea of old notes and vision boards for days. Things I'd never had the courage to pitch, so had just sat gathering dust in my office. But eventually I hit on it. I pulled an old board right out of the back. The paper was faded and peeling, but the idea still shone as brightly as ever.

It's going to be *amazing*.

I have to say, though, Josh's not looking as excited as I hoped he might.

"It's going to be called *Daydream Believer*," I persevere. "A collection of Aesthetic and Pre-Raphaelite art. Maybe even some early Art Nouveau. I want to juxtapose ..."

"Great," he interrupts. "That's great, Clara. I'm glad for you. Now come here."

He strides across the room and pulls me against him. Usually, I love his spontaneity. But, right now, it feels ill-timed. I wrench my lips away.

"Wait. I'm *trying* to tell you about the exhibition. I've got so many ideas ..."

"And that's fantastic. But all I can think about right now is kissing you." His eyes are filled with desire. "You look so beautiful when you're animated."

He bows his head and presses his lips to mine once more.

"*Josh!*" I push him away, keeping my arms outstretched so that he can't try again. "What are you doing?"

"*I'm* trying to kiss my girlfriend," he says, and I'm surprised by the petulance in his voice. "What are *you* doing?"

I stare at him. I'm so dumbfounded that I don't even stop when I register that that's the first time he's ever called me his girlfriend.

"I don't want to be kissed right now! I want you to *listen* to me!"

He pouts. "I don't understand. I thought you wanted me to be more romantic."

"I do! But it's not the be-all and end-all, Josh." I can't believe I'm having to explain this to him. "There *are* other things which matter. Like supporting me. Listening when I'm talking about something important. Caring about the things I care about."

He just blinks at me, like he doesn't understand what I'm getting at.

"You just don't *get* it, do you?" I grind out. "I need more than just ..."

I trail off. Because, in that moment, I realise where that sentence is heading. And that I'm right. I *do* need more. Romance is lovely and all, but on its own it's just that—lovely. In a hollow, ephemeral sort of way.

If I'm going to be with someone, it has to be based on more than just sparkle and froth. It has to be solid and meaningful. It has to be someone who gets me and who loves me for all that I am, even if we don't always agree.

And Josh ... he doesn't. Not really. He likes the version of me which he thinks he knows, the one who tried so hard to please him. He likes the *idea* of me, in the same way that I liked the idea of him. But I'm more than just an idea, and if our relationship is going to work we have to be prepared for that.

He can't seem to understand that there's more to me than just who I am when I'm with him. My universe doesn't revolve around him, not any more. It never should have done in the first place.

Look, I get that he finds art boring; that's fair enough. But it matters to me, and *that* should matter to him. I think back to that night at the unveiling, where he dismissed the whole thing as trivial. He's never understood it. But, most importantly of all, he's never *wanted* to.

And that's okay. I look at him and, for the first time, I see him for what he truly is. Gorgeous, yes. Fun to be with, absolutely.

But not right for me.

"More than what?" he demands. He looks hopelessly confused and I feel a pang of pity. Of course he doesn't understand. "I'm doing everything I can to make you happy here, to give you what you wanted. And now you're telling me that it's not *enough*?"

"Maybe that's the problem. You're trying too hard. We both

are." I step away from him. It'll be easier to say this if we're not so close. "Josh, you don't *want* this. Not really. You're just playing the part because you want to make me happy. And I don't doubt that you've convinced yourself that it's what you want too. But it's not real. And it's not fair on either of us to carry on pretending that it is."

He seems to shrink before my eyes. But the expression on his face is one of relief, not disappointment.

"You're right. Of course you are. I so wanted to make this work; that's why I thought I could ... I still really like you, Clara."

"I know." I smile at him affectionately. "And I like you. But sometimes that's just not enough."

We look at one another for a long moment. Then, as if of one mind, we move back towards one another and hug.

"Well, that's that then." He sighs. "What happens now?"

"Now, we go our separate ways." As an afterthought, I add, "And I'll probably see you in a couple of weeks when Casper gets himself into another scrape."

He laughs. "I'll look forward to it."

Just as we're pulling apart, the doors slam open with a crash. Josh and I both jump, spinning around to look at the figure in the doorway.

"Adam!" I gasp. "What are you doing here?"

Chapter 30

"So it's true, then." Adam glares at us both. His chest is rising and falling heavily, as though he's been running. "I didn't believe Ruby when she told me. I didn't think you'd be so stupid."

So much for quiet disappointment. I've never seen him looking so furious. His eyes are sparking with an intensity I've never seen before. A wild intensity. It's oddly incongruous with his tweed jacket and sensible brogues, his bicycle helmet tucked under his arm.

For a second I'm too taken aback to respond. Finally, I open my mouth ... to say what, I'm not sure. Perhaps to refute my asserted levels of stupidity. But he cuts me off anyway.

"After everything that happened. I credited you with more sense."

"Shall I tell him?" Josh murmurs in my ear. He sounds faintly amused by the whole thing.

"And *you*!" Adam stalks towards him. He tries to point, almost dislodging the helmet in the process; he has to pause to hoik it back into position, which diminishes the effect somewhat. "Taking advantage of her. Worming your way back into her affections like this. You should be ashamed."

"He did not *worm* his way back into my affections," I say fiercely. Now that the shock has worn off, it's replaced by sheer outrage, any gratitude for how supportive he's been lately dissipating immediately. Who does he think he is, to come charging in here like some disapproving father in an Italian opera? "We discussed it, and I made an informed decision on my own. I *am* allowed to do that, you know. Why does everyone insist on treating me like I don't know my own mind?"

"Because clearly you don't! He's not right for you, Clara. Why can't you see that?"

Josh raises his eyebrows at me in mock question. At least he's enjoying himself. *I'm* simply livid.

Blood's rushing to my head at such a rate that spots have begun to appear before my eyes. I hold onto Josh's arm, mostly to steady myself. But I'm aware that to Adam it'll look more meaningful than that.

Good, I think viciously. I'm in no hurry to tell him the truth. I want to wipe that superior look off his face.

It's about time someone did.

"Oh, because you're *such* an expert, are you?" I say sarcastically, smacking a hand to my forehead. "Of course, I'd forgotten all about your sensational track record in the love department. How *stupid* of me. Of course I should bow to your greater judgement. After all, I can do so much better than someone who's kind, funny, handsome ..."

"Thanks very much." Josh sounds genuinely touched.

"You're welcome."

Adam's gone beetroot pink. "That is *not* the point. A relationship needs to be built on more than that, and you know it."

Damn, he's unwittingly reciting my own words back at me. But I'm definitely not going to give him the satisfaction of knowing that.

"You're right," I say archly. "I'd forgotten the most important thing. He's *fabulous* in bed."

Josh embarks on a choking fit which sounds suspiciously like laughter. I whack him on the back, not entirely charitably. He's not exactly helping matters, after all.

"Why don't you get along, honey?" I say with faux sweetness. "I'll deal with this."

Luckily, he takes the rather heavy-handed hint.

"I'll see you later, then, shall I?" he says huskily. Then, in one fluid movement, he swoops down and kisses me passionately.

Rather *too* passionately, as it turns out. And for rather too long. He's playing his role with more relish than is necessary. I bite the inside of his lip, not hard enough to hurt him but enough to make my point. He releases me, setting me back on my feet.

"Later, Adam," he says cheerfully, as he strolls past on his way to the door.

Adam doesn't respond. Instead he just stares at me in astonishment. "You're sincere about this, aren't you?"

"And why shouldn't I be?" I fold my arms and tilt my chin, ready for battle. "Like I said, he has many great ... qualities."

Adam goes pink again.

"Oh, don't be such a prude," I snap. "And don't look so shocked either."

"I'm not shocked," he says defensively. "I'm just ... amazed that you're willing to sell yourself so short."

"How dare you?" I explode. "How bloody ... *dare* you tell me how to live my life? How *dare* you tell me what is or isn't right for me?" I step towards him and poke a shaking finger into his chest. "*I* will decide what is or isn't selling myself short. Not you, not Heather, not Ruby. No one but myself. Is that clear?"

"I'm not trying to tell you ..."

Suddenly, I don't want to hear any more.

"Just stay out of my life, all right? Stay away from me. You know nothing—nothing at all."

I storm out without looking back. If I look back, I might not be able to keep it together.

And, right now, nothing matters more than that.

Ruby's waiting for me on the stairs, practically dancing on the spot in her excitement. I try to sweep past her; all I want to do is get out of here. But she's not about to let me go that easily.

"What happened?" she says in a stage whisper, dragging me to one side. "He went tearing in there; I've never seen him so agitated. And then there was the shouting ..."

"You heard that from out here?" I groan, my anger momentarily dissipating in the face of this news. Brilliant. Just what the museum needs right now: more scandal. And, yet again, I'm right at the heart of it.

"It was so romantic." Ruby's eyes are shining. "I never knew he had it in him."

I can only assume she's talking about Josh now; luckily, I'm used to the random leaps her mind makes. I watch the man in question as he pushes his way through the glass doors and out into the sunshine. Despite everything, I feel a small pang of longing. It's such a shame; he really was perfect in so many ways. "Well, you've changed your tune," I say sourly. Obviously, he well and truly worked his magic on her earlier. "You couldn't stand him before."

"Such passion," she's saying dreamily. "And so well hidden, for all of this time ... Apparently still waters really do run deep, after all."

I stare at her. I even reach up and feel her forehead to check she's not feverish. "What on earth is wrong with you today?"

Everyone's acting so bizarrely; it's like some sort of distorted dream. And, besides, I'd hardly describe Josh as still waters. More like a bubbling, sparkling stream. The kind that you can't wait to dip your toes into on a hot summer's day.

Oh, Lord, listen to me. Whatever Ruby's got, it's obviously catching.

"Nothing." She regards me uncertainly. "What's wrong with *you*? I thought you'd be happy."

"Why the hell would I be ...?" I shake my head. "Never mind. I'm getting out of here. If Jeremy asks, can you tell him that I've gone home with a headache? I'll make up the time later in the week."

"Sure," she says slowly.

She looks confused, which, in turn, only makes *me* feel confused. I have a fleeting, disquieting sensation that we might be talking at cross purposes somehow but, for the life of me, I can't work it out.

"Clara!" Adam appears at the top of the stairs, glowering down at me. "You are *not* walking away from me this time. Not until you've let me finish."

Ruby's mouth drops open. "What the ...? But I thought ..."

I barely hear her. My ears are already ringing with fury all over again. Just the sight of him is enough.

"Watch me," I mutter.

I turn and whirl towards the door, slamming my way out into the street.

***

I stomp along the pavement, kicking at the leaves which dare to get in my path. Autumn is well advanced now and they've turned an uninspiring brown, their edges curling in upon themselves.

I've never been so relieved to be on my own. Well, as alone as one can hope to be in a bustling place like Cambridge. But there's an anonymity to walking in a city which feels like solitude. None of these people know me. They rush past, not paying me the slightest attention, lost inside their own heads. I could almost be invisible, which is exactly what I want at the moment.

I was hoping that the fresh air and the walk would calm the storm inside me, but it seems I was wrong. It's only intensifying with every step.

My pulse is pounding. I'm still shaking all over. I try to

calm myself down with some meditative walking. Just putting one foot in front of the other, letting my mind go blank. No thoughts. Nothing but the swish of the leaves beneath my feet, the breeze tickling my face ...

What makes him think he has the right to tell me how to live my life?

... the weak, flickering sunlight ...

Seriously, though, what?

... clear the mind, just focus on the breath ...

Because he's such a bloody know-it-all, that's why.

The answer elbows its way through forcefully. I give up on the meditative state. It was never going to happen.

He's insufferable. He's always been insufferable. I should never have got involved with him. He just makes me so *angry*, with his supercilious air and his unwavering conviction that he's always right, even if he knows absolutely nothing about the situation. He simply presumes that because I've confided a few things to him recently he knows everything there is to know about me. And that in turn gives him the right to interfere. It's enough to make anyone see red.

And then it makes me angry that he *makes* me angry. Because I am so *not* an angry person. I'm usually so measured, so ...

"I'm not trying to tell you how to live your life." His voice emanates from somewhere to my right.

I close my eyes briefly. I'm imagining it. I must be.

Except I'm not, and I know it. I turn my head and there he is. On his bike, cycling along the edge of the road next to me.

"Are you following me?" I demand incredulously.

"You never let me finish," he says stubbornly, as though that's all the reason he needs.

"I don't care. I don't want to hear it. Now go away."

I pick up my pace, although of course it makes no difference. He just pedals faster.

I stalk onwards, looking straight ahead. If I ignore him, maybe he'll give up.

"Tell me, what does Josh think about your new exhibition?" he asks casually.

I grit my teeth. I know exactly what he's doing. "He's very excited."

Well, what else could I say?

"Oh, he is, is he?" Adam muses. "And will he be planning to cause a scene at the opening of that too?"

I snap my head around. "I will *push* you off that bike. I mean it; don't test me."

"I'm only saying what you won't admit to yourself," he insists.

That does it. Whatever self-control I've been holding together finally cracks.

"Do you have any idea how *patronising* you sound?" I cry. "As if your own life is so perfect. You can't even stand up to your own father. You're willing to run away from the greatest opportunity of your career just so that you don't have to have an emotional conversation!"

His eyes darken. "Don't make this personal, Clara."

"Why not? *You* are. Apparently my life's fair game for you to cast judgement upon. Why shouldn't it work both ways?"

His mouth sets in a grim line. "We're going off topic."

"I don't think we are." I've hit a nerve, I can tell. It gives me a rush of vindictive pleasure. Let's see how he likes a taste of his own medicine, shall we? "I think this is very *much* the point. Why shouldn't we talk about you? Why should you always be the one who holds yourself at a distance, judging other people's problems like they're some sort of academic experiment? What makes you so superior?"

"Don't go there," he says warningly. The car in front of him pulls in suddenly, and he swerves around it with a bitten-off curse.

But I'm on a roll.

"Why not? There's so much to talk about. Dysfunctional family, emotional repression, inability to hold down a relationship ..." I stroke my chin, pretending to muse. "You know, you're not half as dull as you make out. The question is, where to start?"

"Don't try and make this about me." Frustration colours his voice in vivid strokes. "Why can you never just accept responsibility for your actions? Why is it always everyone else's fault?"

That's so below the belt that I gasp. "I do take responsibility for my actions!"

"No, you don't," he scoffs. "You ... oh, bollocks."

The traffic light has turned red and he's forced to skid to a halt. I carry on walking, feeling jubilant.

Not for long, though, because soon he's back beside me, albeit panting slightly from the sprint he's just put on.

"You lean on everyone around you," he gulps. "You project

this aura of helplessness which makes them all come running to your aid. And then you have the gall to complain about it when they do!" He breaks off, heaves in a deep breath, then says, "Have you never once thought that perhaps the common denominator is *you*?"

"Stop it!" I choke. If it wouldn't just prove his point, I'd put my hands over my ears to block out his words. We're on my street now; I can see my house. Soon, I'll be able to get away from him. From all of it. "I won't listen to this."

"Maybe it's time you did," he says harshly. "It's time someone made you see sense."

"Maybe I don't *want* to see sense," I cry, feeling faintly hysterical. "Maybe I'm okay with taking a risk. Maybe I'm okay with getting it wrong sometimes. I don't want to be like you, Adam. Contained and narrow-minded, never having the courage to leap. I won't live like that. I'd *rather* get it wrong; I'd rather be scared and embarrassed sometimes. I'd rather get hurt and cry it out. Why can't you stand that?"

"Because I can't bear to *see* you get hurt, all right?" he yells, and it's like the words have been ripped from his soul. "Not when ... Christ, Clara, if you'd just wake up and look ... maybe someone else can make you happy."

I stop dead. I feel like a firework has exploded over my head.

"What are you talking about?" Surely he can't possibly mean ... "*You?*"

"Yes, me! It's always been ... Damn! Casper!"

He slams on the brakes, screeching to a halt with such force that he almost goes flying over the handlebars.

Casper, who's sitting in the middle of the road, looks up briefly to see what all the fuss is about, then carries on washing behind his ears.

"This cat will be the death of me," Adam manages weakly.

Chapter 31

"What did you mean, when you said it's always been you?" I repeat. I need to hear it from him. If he's saying what I *think* he's trying to say ...

"Do you mind if I get out of the road first?" He hauls his bike onto the pavement and unclips his helmet. "And you might want to get your cat, before he causes another accident."

I rush forward and grab Casper, who yowls in protest at being manhandled. Just in time, I think; he looked about ready to lunge at Adam.

"What did you mean?" I demand again, even more insistently.

"Surely you know that." He takes off his helmet and ruffles his hair. He looks weary. "Don't tell me you hadn't noticed at all. I don't think I hid it particularly well, despite my best efforts."

I feel dizzy, like all the energy has rushed to my head. Can this be right? Can he really mean ...?

But yes, of course he can. All I can think about is that kiss on the bridge; the way he looked at me in my kitchen, that day after we fell in the river. It wasn't exactly obvious, despite what he might say, but still ... it was there. Can I really have been so unseeing?

More to the point, can I *really* have been so woefully stubborn? Did I just not *want* to see it?

Because Adam ... he's not the one. He can't be. We're so different. And we argue *all* the time. How can we possibly be suited?

And yet ...

And yet. I look into his eyes and I feel that familiar thrum of electricity between us. It's always been there, hasn't it?

Now I'm thinking about it, the images are flying through my mind unbidden. The way my pulse fluttered when I saw him in a suit. The way my pulse flutters even when he wears that hideous tweed jacket. The way I so wanted to kiss him back that night, even though I've never been able to admit it to myself.

The way I love talking to him, even when he's in a bad mood.

The way that when I'm with him, everything suddenly seems all right.

Me and Adam. I test it out in my mind, turning the words over. Somehow, it works. It doesn't seem at all alien. In fact, despite everything, it sort of sounds ... right. There's no other way to describe it. Perhaps it was never meant to be Josh after all; he was only a distraction. Perhaps it was always meant to come down to this.

Adam's standing there, looking at me with such intensity in his face, and my heart begins to pound. Could this be it, then? The *moment*? The one you hear about and dream about?

The moment when everything just falls into place, and you're swept into his arms and ...

Okay, so I'll admit it's perhaps not quite the way I'd envisaged. I mean, ideally he'd have come whizzing along on his bike (unhindered by traffic, of course) which he would then have proceeded to dash to the ground before striding over for a gloriously romantic kiss. As it stands, we've had a blazing row and he's almost run over my cat. *Again*.

But you know, I find that I don't much care. Not about the Casper thing, of course. I'm very glad he didn't run him over. But about the rest of it. Because if I've realised anything today, it's that all of that flowery romantic stuff is overrated anyway. I'd rather have something real.

And if this is what real looks like, then I'll take it.

"Adam ..." I begin stutteringly. Where do I even start? This has come at me sideways; I'm still a bit dazed. I give a weak laugh. "Sorry, it's just ... This is so *not* what I was expecting ..."

"You don't have to say any more." His voice is brusque.

Taken aback, I look up at him. His face is dark with emotion, his hands clenched tightly at his sides. I feel the first warning pang of alarm; something isn't right.

"I'm well aware that I'm not the romantic hero you're after," he says bitterly. "How stupid of me to think that I might stand a chance against your fairy tale expectations."

"Adam, wait ..." I take a step towards him. I can tell that something's got lost in translation. "That's not ... you didn't let me ..."

But he's not even listening.

"You know what?" he says wildly, jamming his helmet back on his head. "Maybe I've been wrong all this time. Maybe you *don't* deserve better. Maybe you deserve exactly what you've got: someone who'll give you all the hearts and flowers you so desperately crave, and nothing of any substance. Because that's all you've ever really wanted, isn't it?"

I'm still reeling from how quickly this has all spun out of control. Dimly, I know that he's just lashing out, but it doesn't stop a responding spike of anger.

"You don't know what I want."

"Oh, don't I? I think you've made it pretty clear. And you call *me* intractable. You're far more closed-minded and prejudiced than I'll ever be. You made a decision about me the first day you met me, and you've never even tried to revise it, have you?"

Okay, now I'm mad.

"Well, you made a presumption about me too!"

"And I was *right*!" he yells. "You're so wrapped up in your daydreams that you can't even see what's right in front of you." He breaks off, looking away. "God, Clara, when I think of the fool I made of myself over you. The things I did ... I jumped into a river after you! I put up with your demonic cat. I even got Jeremy to give you that damned speech! And all for what?"

There's a beat of silence.

"You got Jeremy to do *what*?" I try to swallow, but my mouth has gone dry. "What are you talking about, Adam?"

His gaze shifts away from me. "It doesn't matter now."

"It does to me." My voice is rapidly rising. Another pantomime for the neighbours, I think dimly. They'll be loving this. "What are you saying? That you ... what? Called in a favour? Used your influence?"

"It was nothing like that," he says calmly, but there's a tenseness about his jaw which is telling. "I simply pointed out what an underused asset you were, that's all."

"That's *all*?" I echo disbelievingly.

I feel like the floor has been ripped out from under me.

All this time ... I thought *I* did this. I thought that my hard work had finally been noticed. But it was never that, was it? It was never even anything to do with me. It was just ... politics.

I've never felt so used and humiliated in my whole life.

And then something else occurs to me.

"What else did you offer him?" I ask in a low voice.

Superstar academic or not, Adam's word alone wouldn't be enough. Jeremy would need more incentive than that.

"What did you barter me for?" I rephrase the question less delicately, not bothering to hide the contempt in my voice.

Adam flushes. "You make it all sound so sordid. It was simply a case of ..."

"*What was it?*" I all but yell.

He winces. "The subject of my next two papers. And, if I make head of department, a first year module focused around the contents of the museum."

"You have no respect for me at *all*, do you?" My voice sounds more hollow than angry. I pull Casper closer. I'd almost forgotten I was holding him, he's been so quiet. That's very unlike him; I get the sense that he's listening intently. "You think I can just be moved around like some pawn on a chessboard and it won't matter. *I* don't matter."

"Clara, that's not true." His tone is like steel. "You're overreacting."

If I wasn't still holding Casper, I think I'd be tempted to hit him at this moment.

"Oh, I'm so sorry. I am embarrassing you? But of course, that's all you'd expect from a hysterical ignoramus like me, isn't it? If I were a lofty intellectual such as yourself, I wouldn't take it to heart."

"I compromised my professional code for you!" he blazes, his facade finally beginning to crack. "By rights, I should never have interfered. But I wanted to *help* you. Does that mean nothing?"

"And you expected me to ... what? Fall into bed with you out of sheer gratitude?" My voice drips with sarcasm.

He stills. "Is that really what you think?"

"I think we'll never understand each other." A wave of frustration engulfs me. "Just look at us; we can't even have a civil conversation without it descending into an argument!" I shake my head. "What are we even *doing*, Adam? Pretending that we could ever be friends? That we could ever be more than that? We'd be a disaster from day one. You're better off without me, truly. And I'm certainly better off without you."

Something flashes in the depths of his eyes. "So now you're telling me what *I* need? Does the hypocrisy not strike you?"

"Don't throw that back at me." To my horror, tears are beginning to build up behind my eyes. "It's not fair."

"Life's not fair, Clara. You're a gullible idiot if you believe that it is."

Suddenly, I'm not feeling tearful any more. An icy fury is building within me.

"I can't believe that I ever thought we could be something!" I fling back. I'm aware I sound childish, maybe even petulant, but right now I don't care. I'm half-tempted to stamp my foot, even. "I could never be with someone like you! You're cold and cynical, and ... and ..."

I falter. He waits patiently.

"Yes?" he prompts at last. His eyes rake intently over my face. "And what, Clara? Just say what you really mean."

"... And Casper *hates* you!" I blurt out.

Casper whips his head around and stares at me in surprise. I put him down and he hops up onto the wall, eyeing Adam malevolently. There's a long, tense silence.

"The cat ... hates me?" Adam manages disbelievingly. "That's your argument?"

"Why not?" I arch a brow. "He's an excellent judge of character. If he hates you, it's not without reason."

Adam glances at Casper, who stares him down.

"All right." Adam folds his arms and fixes me with a challenging look. "I'll play. Tell me one thing he hates about me."

"One thing?" I laugh disparagingly. "I could give you ten." I begin to tick them off on my fingers. "You're rude ..."

"*He's* rude!" Adam interrupts indignantly, pointing at a smug-looking Casper. "He dropped a plant pot on my foot, if you recall."

I ignore him. I'm on a roll now. The words tumble from

my mouth in a torrent, as though they've been waiting for this moment.

"... you're sarcastic, you're self-important, you're stubborn, you're *argumentative* ..."

"These all sound more like things you hate about me, Clara," Adam observes quietly. Suddenly, it seems as though all of the fight has gone out of him. His eyes are cast down at the pavement.

"I don't hate you," I whisper. "Not at all."

Quite the opposite.

He doesn't even appear to be listening, or maybe my words were too quiet for him to hear. He's pulling his bike away from where he's propped it against the picket fence.

"You were right; this was a mistake," he says stiffly. "I should never have said anything." Then he looks at me, and his face is like granite. I can't see any hint of the man I've come to feel so much for. "Don't worry; I won't embarrass us both by mentioning it again. You've made it quite clear where things stand."

He casts a final glance at Casper, who's crouching on the wall. "Bye, Casper," he says simply. "Look after her, won't you?"

And I can only watch as he cycles away into the fading light.

Chapter 32

"I've brought you some tea."

I look up to find that Freddie has materialised in front of me, clutching a chipped mug.

"Why?" I ask suspiciously. "What's the catch?"

"No catch. I just thought you might be cold." He sits on the stone bench next to me with a shiver. "It's November. What are you doing out here?"

He says it with such incredulity that it almost makes me smile.

"People *can* go outside in winter, Freddie. We won't disintegrate."

"Yes, but ... why would you want to?" He hands me the mug, wrapping his arms around himself to ward off the cold. "Is it me and Jess? Is it driving you crazy, having us here?"

"Not at all," I say, aghast. "I love having you. Really."

All right, so that's a bit of a white lie. They are driving me a *little* crazy. But that's not why I'm out here. Not entirely, anyway.

I haven't used this bench at the top of the garden for ages. It's half overgrown with ivy, half obscured by bushes. It's a little pocket of privacy in the goldfish bowl of suburbia. Up here, I can breathe. I can think.

I've had a lot of thinking to do lately.

"Well, I've got news for you on that front," Freddie says, stretching his long legs out in front of him. "We've put an offer in on a house."

"Oh," I stammer. All of a sudden, my pulse is thudding in my veins.

If he says they're going back to Manchester, it's going to take everything I have to pretend to be overjoyed for them. The truth is, I just don't know if I can face losing someone else at the moment.

But it's not about me, is it? I've even been practising my response. Big smile. No bursting into tears. That wouldn't do. Bursting into tears can happen later, in private.

"It's on Millington Street," Freddie says. "It's small, and it needs some work, but I don't mind giving it a go. And Jess thinks the garden ..."

I'm so busy bracing myself that the meaning of his words almost passes me by altogether.

"Wait ... Millington Street?" I stare at him, dumbfounded. "But that's around the corner from here."

"You're quick." Freddie grins. "No flies on you, are there?"

"Shut up." I give him a half-hearted wallop in the arm, for old times' sake. "Are you being serious?" My voice wavers a little on the last word.

"Of course." The grin fades from his face. "Why wouldn't I be? You're family, Clara. We want our baby to grow up near its aunt."

"But what about your friends?"

"They're all still living in a student mentality. They won't get any of this." He sighs. "It's time to accept that our lives have moved on. We're not kids any more. And maybe it's more of an abrupt transition than we were hoping for, but there you go. I can't say I regret it. I just hope I'll do a decent job of the whole being a father thing."

"You'll be great." Now my eyes are filling up with tears. I'm so emotional at the moment; anything seems to set me off. On impulse I put my tea down and fling my arms around him, squeezing him tightly. "I'm so proud of you."

He squirms, trying to disengage himself. "Stop it! We're British, remember? Get a hold of yourself."

I just squeeze him more tightly. "And Mum and Dad would be proud of you too."

He stops struggling. "Do you really think so?"

"Of course I do."

"You don't think ...?" He clears his throat awkwardly. "We're not doing so badly, are we? I mean, they wouldn't be *too* appalled, I hope. If they're looking down on us, that is."

Out of the corner of my eye, I see movement at the window. Jess is standing at the sink, watching us through the glass.

"I hope not." I sigh, releasing him. "I worry about that sometimes. I think it's almost harder this way; at least if they were here we'd know how they felt, instead of always having to wonder. But I've come to the conclusion that we just have to do our best with the lives we've got. I'd like to think that's all they'd really want from us."

Casper slinks through the long grass, dropping a headless

squirrel at my feet. He hops up onto the bench beside us, purring.

"See, Casper agrees. He's very wise."

"He's also a murderous sociopath." Freddie moves his feet away from the decapitated rodent. "Does he *have* to take the heads off every single one?"

"He likes to crunch the skulls," I say cheerfully.

Freddie frowns down at me. "You've been spending too much time alone with him. It's a good thing we're going to be nearby. We wouldn't want you growing strange in your old age."

"Never mind me," I shoot back, laughing. "I'm more worried about the prospect of *you* doing DIY. You're not the most practical of men. Do you remember when you were a teenager, and you put that bottle-opener up on the wall at home?"

Freddie groans. "I'll never forget. It fell down after an hour, taking half of the wall plaster with it. Mum wasn't very impressed, was she?"

"No, she wasn't. Not that Dad was much better. He couldn't even hang a picture straight."

"Alas, we've never been a practical family. Fortunately, Jess can supervise. She's actually vaguely competent wielding a hammer."

The mention of Jess makes my eyes automatically travel towards the window again.

She's still there. I feel the first trickle of misgiving. It wouldn't take her that long to wash up, surely?

"Hang on, why is she *motioning* to you?" I leap up, dislodging Casper from my lap. Unperturbed, he simply picks up his squirrel and trots off with it. "This isn't just a cup of tea; it's a *trap*! She sent you out here, didn't she?"

"We're concerned, that's all." Freddie has the look of a cornered rabbit. To be fair, I have to concede that it probably wasn't his idea. This has feminine interference written all over it. "We just wanted to check ... you know, that you're coping."

He turns to the window and mouths, "*She knows,*" at Jess.

"Of course I'm coping." I give a brittle laugh. Then, suddenly, an awful thought strikes me. "Wait ... you're not staying in Cambridge for me, are you?"

That would be humiliation beyond words. As if I haven't had enough of that already.

"What? Of course not," Freddie says dismissively. "I told you; it's the best thing for the baby."

Thank God for that.

"Good." Warily, I perch back on the edge of the bench. "Because I'm fine. I'm quite capable of looking after myself."

"I'm sure you are. But you have to admit it; you've been moping around ever since you broke up with that vet of yours."

"He is not *my* vet," I retort primly. "And this is nothing to do with him."

At least that much is true.

"Wait, then ..." Freddie looks nonplussed. "Who? The professor?"

I just glare at him.

"It *is* the professor!" He turns to the window.

"*It's the professor!*" he mouths exaggeratedly at Jess. She smacks a hand to her forehead.

"*Of course!*" she mouths back.

"Will you two stop that?" I say furiously. "It doesn't matter anyway, because nothing's going to happen now. I've seen to that."

Even as I say it, my chest feels tight.

I never knew I'd miss Adam so much. It's like an ache which won't go away. I even miss arguing with him, would you believe it?

I'd give anything to be arguing with him right now. I'd even let him win.

Probably.

Maybe. So long as he didn't say anything too incendiary.

"What did you do?" Freddie's eyes are wide.

"I ... I told him that Casper hates him," I choke out, half laughing, half crying. Suddenly, it seems almost funny, in a tragic sort of way.

"Why would you do that?"

"Because he *does* hate him."

"Casper hates all sorts of people," Freddie points out reasonably. "It doesn't mean anything. And he takes to the most unlikely of people too. I'm not sure his judgement counts for a lot."

Actually, I have to concede that there is some truth in that. I mean, he likes Dominic, for some unknown reason. I've never been able to understand it.

He likes Jeremy too. Once I had to drop into the museum on the way back from the vet's. Casper escaped from his basket; eventually, I found him curled up at Jeremy's feet under the desk.

Hmm. I'd forgotten about that incident.

So much for my claim that Casper has excellent judgement. Perhaps I ought to review that.

"It's not just that, though," I gulp. "It's ... well, I might have let him think that I'm still with Josh."

Freddie looks blank. "Who?"

"The *vet*," I grind out. Does he not pay attention to anything?

"Oh." Freddie sits back. "Yeah. Him. I never bothered to learn his name; I knew he wouldn't be around for long."

Sometimes Freddie comes out with the most unexpected things. I just blink at him.

"Really? But he was so ..."

"He was a flash in the pan," Freddie says flatly. I smile inwardly; he can sound just like an old woman sometimes. "I knew you'd grow bored of him eventually. Now, Adam, on the other hand ..."

I start, almost upsetting my half-empty cup of tea. I fling the rest out into the flower border, hoping I don't hit Casper with it. I have a feeling he's in there somewhere.

"You know his name?" I'm amazed. Freddie's never used it before.

"Always have. I just like calling him *the professor*, that's all. Sounds very Bond villainish." He stands, dusting off his jeans. "Look, sis, I wouldn't presume to tell you what to do with your life. But let's face it; you're pretty miserable without him. And if all that's keeping you two apart is a cat and a fictitious relationship, then I don't see why you can't work it out. If you want to, that is."

"You make it sound so easy," I say sadly. "But I can't ... It's complicated."

Somehow, I can't bring myself to tell Freddie about the whole thing with my job. It's still too raw and, honestly, too shaming. When it comes down to it, I'd rather they all thought I was just being capriciously stubborn than reveal the truth.

Because, ultimately, whatever I might have said, the rest of it doesn't matter. Well, it sort of does, but it's not fatal. I'm sure we could get past it. But how can I be with somebody who was willing to manipulate and deceive me?

I can try all I like to tell myself that he thought it wouldn't matter to me how it came about. That so long as I got what I wanted, the end justified the means. But I know that can't be true; I saw the look on his face after he said it. He hadn't wanted me to find out, because he *did* know it mattered. He knew that I needed it to be on my own merit. He knew I would never countenance anything less than that.

Yet he did it anyway. I think that's what really gets me.

And then he tried to hide it. Presumably, he planned to do so indefinitely, if we'd got together. The thought that we might have spent the rest of our lives with that secret between us is too much for me to stomach.

"Can't possibly be as complicated as what we've had to deal with recently." Freddie motions towards the window, where Jess is still standing, looking on anxiously. "Look, I know you, sis. Once you've got your mind set on something, nothing anyone can say will change it. But if there's anything I've had to learn lately, it's that love isn't about getting everything right. It's more about the effort you make to fix it when it goes wrong. Think about that, won't you?"

He saunters off back towards the house and I'm left

wondering when my absent-minded, careless little brother turned into such an enlightened young man. But, before I can come up with an answer, there's a rustle in the undergrowth and Casper rejoins me on the bench. Blessedly, there's no sign of the squirrel, or any body parts which might once have conceivably belonged to it.

"Did you really hate him *that* much?" I sigh, stroking his head.

He just purrs noncommittally.

"Because the thing is—" my voice trembles "—I just ... even after everything ... I so wished you could have been wrong. A part of me still does."

That gets his attention. His eyes snap open in affront.

"What? You're not always right, you know!" I retort. "You thought Josh was wonderful. And look how that turned out."

He turns his head away and sticks his nose in the air. I know that look; it means, '*I have no idea what you mean. You must have imagined it.*'

"All right, deny it all you like. I know the truth."

He turns his back on me with a dismissive swish of his tail.

"You're impossible," I huff, crossing one leg over the other. "There's just no talking to you. You're as bad as Adam!" Just saying his name makes my heartstrings twang. How pathetic is that? "Actually, you two have quite a lot in common, come to think of it. Maybe that was always the main issue between you; you're *far* too alike."

He bristles indignantly at the suggestion.

Why do I invite these impossible males into my life? I bury my face in my hands.

"Why can't I seem to stop missing him, Casper?"

The next thing I know, hot tears are squeezing out of the gaps between my fingers and dripping into my lap.

I feel the pressure of paws pressing on my leg and then Casper's reaching up, nudging my hands away. I look into his bright green gaze and I feel like he's trying to tell me something.

If only I spoke cat.

"Your fur's getting damp," I sniff, but he just snuggles closer. His whiskers tickle my chin, making me laugh despite myself.

"At least I'll always have you," I murmur, resting my cheek against the top of his head.

But, for once, that doesn't seem quite enough.

Chapter 33

I do the only thing I can in the situation: I get on with life. I do my regular walkabouts with Jeremy. I help to hang pictures, and I direct people to the Holman Hunt, which now hangs in pride of place in the main hall. I try not to look too hard at the empty window seat where Adam used to sit. Whenever I have to walk through the Roman gallery, I do so quickly, not looking from side to side, trying to ignore the ever-present ache. It's smaller, but it's still there. I'm almost used to it by now.

December looms on the horizon and Christmas decorations start to appear. Pumpkin spice lattes turn into gingerbread lattes. Freddie and Jess have their offer accepted on the house, and official-looking paperwork starts stacking up on the kitchen table. They don't ask me any more about Adam, but I see them sharing worried looks when they think I won't notice. I console myself with the thought that I won't be the centre of attention for long; soon, they'll have someone else to expend their energies on.

I do take Casper back to the vet's, as threatened. I'd expected that it would be strange seeing Josh again, but it isn't. We seem to have made a tacit agreement to go back to where we began, as convivial strangers, and somehow it works. Besides, I don't think he'll be with the practice for very much longer anyway. He's far too restless for a place like Cambridge.

On the whole, everything continues as it always has. Except me.

Oh, I laugh with Ruby and Eve. I drink wine with Heather. I silently mock Jeremy's waistcoats, and I mediate Jess and Freddie's arguments over what colour to paint their nursery. I save any number of small furry rodents from Casper's deadly clutches. I decorate the house with swathes of gaudy tinsel, as I do every year. I try to make eggnog, as I do every year; and, *as* happens every year, it turns out to be revolting and ends up down the sink. Outwardly, I'm the same. But, inwardly, something's missing. The sun doesn't feel as warm on my skin. The sight of ice-skaters in the city centre doesn't make my heart sing. It's like the rosy filter which used to enrobe my view of life has been replaced with a greyish substitute.

I'm getting good at finding excuses to be alone. Right now, I'm rearranging the portrait miniatures in their case. They really don't need doing again but, like I said, I'm trying to stay busy. And this is a small museum; there isn't that much to do. The place has never looked so fantastic, though, I think wryly. I should be heartbroken more often.

The thought makes me go still.

"Am I heartbroken?" I ask the fifth Earl of Kemble, who's sitting in the palm of my hand. "No, I don't think so; there wasn't enough time for that."

He sneers at me from within his gold frame.

"Oh, what would you know?" I huff. "You were more in the business of breaking hearts than having your own broken. I doubt you ever really knew what love was."

I reach into my cardigan pocket for the microfibre polishing cloth, and my fingernails scrape against the cold metal of a USB stick. My stomach gives its all-too-familiar lurch. I can't put it off for much longer, I know that.

I can't keep this up. I can't keep cataloguing artefacts and organising loans and acting like nothing's changed.

And I certainly can't keep preparing for an exhibition which should never have been mine in the first place.

I have to face the truth eventually. I don't belong here, not any more.

The thing is, that's easier said than done. This place has felt like home for the past three years. This job gave me focus after I lost my parents. It's hard to just let go of all that.

"Just a bit more time," I whisper to the Earl of Kemble. "Is that horribly cowardly of me?"

The expression on his face says it all.

"Did anyone ever tell you that you're kind of a jerk?" I shove him back into the case crossly.

"Are you having a row with that portrait miniature?"

My head snaps up. Ruby's hovering nearby, looking amused.

"He started it," I say defensively.

"I'm sure he did." She nods. "Look, could you come and help me with something?"

"I'm a bit busy," I lie, turning back to the open display case.

I expect her to make some smart retort; after all, it's obvious to anyone that this is just a displacement activity. But, to my surprise, she just puts her hands together in a prayer-like motion.

"Please?"

With a put-upon sigh, I shut the case. "Fine. What do you need?"

"It's just upstairs."

I sullenly trail through the museum after her. I'm so lost in my own thoughts that I hardly notice where she's leading me until we stop in front of a familiar door.

A *very* familiar door.

I frown at her. "This is my own office, Ruby."

She doesn't so much as flicker.

"I know." She inclines her head towards the closed door. "In you go."

"Wait." I dig my heels in, both metaphorically and literally. Unfortunately, the threadbare carpet doesn't hold much purchase, so literally's not going to do me much good. Metaphorically it is, then. "What's going on? I'm not going in there until you tell me."

For once in my life, I am not in the mood for a surprise. Even a nice one.

Unless it involves cake. Then, maybe I could make an exception.

"God, you're hard work these days." She reaches behind me and pushes open the door before nudging me in the small of the back. Rather more firmly than necessary, in my opinion. "The sooner we get this sorted out, the better."

My office is looking even more cramped than usual, but

that's probably something to do with the group of people crowded around my desk.

"Ah. You got her." Heather hops to her feet. "Good job. Did she come quietly?"

"Not particularly, no." Ruby casts a reproving glance at me.

"What is going *on* here?" I demand. "Why are you all in my office?"

"It's an ambush," Ruby says gleefully, clasping her hands together.

"An *intervention*, dear," Eve corrects. Or, rather, her voice does, drifting from somewhere at the back of the room. She must be sitting in my desk chair.

"An inter—I don't need an intervention!" I'm aghast. Interventions are for addicts, or people on the verge of self-destruction. I'm just nursing a bruised heart, that's all. "You really didn't all need to come. I would rather have had the cake, to be honest."

Ruby eyes me strangely. "What cake?"

"Never mind." I wave the question away, exasperated. "It doesn't matter. But what's *he* doing here, of all people?"

Jeremy, who's lurking in the corner, looking like he'd rather be anywhere else, opens his mouth, but Heather cuts across him.

"He wanted to be here ... didn't you?" she adds with a laser-like glare in his direction.

He coughs dejectedly. "Yes, naturally. Employee wellbeing is paramount to the efficient running of an organisation."

He sounds like he's read that off the back of a leaflet.

"It's not an intervention, Clara," Heather says softly. "Not as such. But we all feel ... well, that you haven't been yourself lately. We want to help."

This is awful. Somehow, their loving concern is worse than anything. I feel hot shame heating my skin.

"I'm fine," I insist, trying to keep my voice level. "I just ... actually, you know what, it's a good thing you're here after all, Jeremy. There's something I've been meaning to give you."

He looks startled to have been called upon, like a pupil who's been dozing at the back of the class. He mops his brow with a pink spotted handkerchief. It's oversized, like something a clown would have.

"Er ... yes?"

I fumble in my pocket for the USB stick, cursing my shaking fingers. But now's as good a time as any. I've let a sense of misplaced gratitude and duty hold me back for long enough.

It's time to get on with my life. Properly this time. No more excuses.

A new chapter. How terrifying. But also ... how exciting. A leap into the unknown. I have a feeling I'll land on my feet, wherever I might end up.

"Here." I stride across the room in three steps and hold out the USB stick. "You should have this. It's everything I've prepared so far for the summer exhibition. It should help whoever takes over."

He looks at it blankly. The only sound in the room is Ruby's foot tapping nervously against the floor.

"I don't deserve this opportunity," I continue, amazed at how calm my voice sounds. "It wasn't given to me fairly. I can't be a part of it."

Heather's the first one to speak. "What are you talking about? Of course you got it fairly; we all know that. Jeremy?" she prompts.

He just twists his handkerchief round and round in his hands, looking miserable. I'm almost inclined to feel sorry for him.

"Afraid not," I say with forced lightness. "It was all just part of a business deal. Adam arranged it with him."

Three women round on Jeremy. He recedes further into the shadowy corner, as though hoping he might be able to disappear altogether.

"*Tell* me this isn't right," Ruby presses. "It can't be."

"It happens all the time," Jeremy whines. He looks at me beseechingly. "It's not something to take personally, my dear."

"Well, I do take it personally," I say simply. "And I don't care if it happens all the time. I won't be used like that." I breathe in slowly. Here goes. "Which is why I'll be resigning, not only from organising the exhibition but from my role altogether."

Eve gasps, which is so theatrical I almost want to laugh. The whole *thing* is so theatrical; I kind of wish I had a resignation letter to fling in Jeremy's face.

"Wait!" Jeremy's face has gone puce. "But I *need* you! You can't ..."

"Why not?" I counter flatly. "I'm sure you can replace me easily enough. It's not like you ever let me do anything really important." As he stares down at the USB stick in his hand with a hopeless expression, my tone softens a little. "I've also made a hard copy of everything on that. It's in my office."

That was a last act of charity; I know what he's like with technology.

I know it would serve him right if I left him in the lurch. But at the same time my sense of fairness prevails. After all, I've known what he's like for years; a part of me always knew I was never going to get the opportunities I'd so hoped for. If I stayed for too long, then it's on me. How ironic that I threw myself recklessly into relationships yet allowed myself to be so reticent and fearful when it came to my career. If only it could have been the other way around.

With an inward sigh, I turn back to the others. "Now, if that's all, can I go? I've got to pack up my office."

It's only then that I notice that Heather's looking pretty puce herself. "You said that Adam was a part of this?" she manages shakily.

"Yes, why?"

"Oh, dear," Eve says weakly. She raises a ring-laden hand to her forehead as though she's in some old-fashioned farce. "Oh, dear."

"What *now*?" I say hotly. What else could there possibly be? Is a dramatic resignation not enough for one day?

"Clara, I've told him," Heather blurts out.

Everything suddenly seems to go very quiet. Even Ruby's foot-tapping ceases.

"Told who what?" I say neutrally. But I don't feel very neutral inside. I feel like a tidal wave has swept through me.

Because I have a feeling that I know exactly who she means.

She swallows. "I've told Adam that you're not really back together with Josh. I told him that it was all a lie."

"*We've* told him, dear," Eve amends supportively. She seems to have got over her swoon remarkably quickly. "We thought it was best."

"You had no right to do that," I say in a low voice. I don't know if it's anger or shock, or perhaps a mixture of both, but my whole body seems to have gone rigid. "No right at all."

"You were never going to do it," Ruby says mulishly. "So we had to."

"It was all such a stupid misunderstanding between you," Heather says, almost pleadingly. "But we didn't know about any of this. You didn't tell me," she adds, and there's more than a hint of accusation in her voice. "Why the hell didn't you *tell* me?"

"Because it's my life!" I cry. The walls are so thin, I don't doubt that the whole corridor can probably hear. With an effort, I calm myself. "And because no one wants to admit that the person they've fallen for could deceive them like that. Okay? It just hurt too much. It still does."

"But why would he have done that?" Eve frets. "He seems such an upstanding young man. It doesn't make sense. Unless ..."

There's an expectant pause.

Then Ruby's face lights up. "Of course! It's the only explanation."

Slowly, comprehension dawns in Heather's eyes. She claps her hands together in satisfaction. "How couldn't we have seen this? It's so *obvious*, really!"

Utterly lost now, I look at Jeremy, but he just shrugs.

"I have no idea what you're all getting at," I say wearily.

Suddenly, I've had enough. I don't even care any more; all I want to do is lie down in a darkened room.

"He *loves* you!" Ruby crows, bouncing up and down on the spot.

"Ruby!" Eve admonishes her. "Remember what we spoke about. One has to lead into these things gently."

"He doesn't love me," I say automatically. But, even as I say it, an odd warm feeling begins to flood my body, suffusing each and every cell.

"Of course he does." Eve sounds uncharacteristically impatient. "Why else would he have done such a thing? Clearly your happiness matters more to him than anything else. That's love, dear. Plain and simple."

If only. I choke back a laugh. Nothing about this has been simple.

"*And* he did it after he knew you were with Josh," Heather reminds me, looking thoroughly pleased with the hypothesis. "He wasn't expecting you to find out. There was no ulterior motive behind it. He just did it because ... Well, because he loved you."

"Isn't that *romantic*?" Ruby sighs, gazing rapturously out of the window.

Everyone else sighs too. Except Jeremy, who looks nonplussed. And a little revolted.

And me. I'm just standing there, staring straight ahead. Because something in those words pricks at me. These are the very people who told me to be more careful, who told me that being a hopeless romantic would only set me up for failure. And now they're ... what? Urging me to go running across town like some lovesick heroine in a budget film? Towards a man who, when I last saw him, told me that his feelings were a mistake? That we should forget he'd said anything at all?

Haven't I learned better by now than to throw my foolish heart into the ring only to watch it get trampled all over? I just can't do it, not again. Not with Adam. That would be more than I could take. If he rejected me ... Well, at least this way I'll never have to face that possibility.

"Just because he might have feelings for me doesn't mean I have to do anything about it," I say stubbornly. "I don't *need* a man in my life, you know."

"No, you don't," Heather says softly, obviously not buying my false bravado for a moment. "But you *do* need him."

Before I can reply, my phone begins to buzz in my pocket. I finally locate it, just catching it before it rings out. The name on the screen makes my heart sink: *Fire department*.

"Miss Swift?" Trueman's grim tone comes barrelling down the line.

I don't waste time with any preamble. "What's Casper done now?"

"Well, that's the thing." I can practically hear Trueman scratching his head quizzically. "It isn't ... Look, you'd better come and see for yourself."

Apparently, the day's drama isn't over yet. I pocket my phone, already half-turning towards the door. Where Casper's involved, I don't need telling twice. God only knows what he's got himself into this time.

"I have to go," I announce to the room at large. "Sorry. Cat issues."

"Of course—go." Heather makes a shooing motion with her hands. "We're finished here."

Jeremy holds up a tremulous hand. "In that case, could *I* be excused? It's only ... there's a—"

Three heads swivel around and pinion him with a glare. He swallows audibly.

"Not a chance," Ruby says menacingly. "*You* still have a lot of explaining to do."

Chapter 34

The scene which greets me outside my house is nothing short of pandemonium.

A fire engine, blue lights flashing, is blocking half of the road. They've had to stop the traffic and a queue of cars is backing up, horns blaring, heads craning out of windows to see what's going on. Firefighters in high visibility jackets are swarming across my front lawn and a long ladder is propped against the side of the house, reaching all the way up to the roof. The sight of that makes panic gnaw at my stomach but, to my immense relief, I can't see anyone up there.

My relief is short-lived, though, as I round the side of the fire engine to see that an ambulance is parked up behind it. The back doors are wide open and a dark-haired figure sits on the step, wrapped in a red thermal blanket.

"Oh, my God!" I rush forwards, my heart in my mouth. "Are you okay?"

Adam raises an eyebrow, then winces as the paramedic dabs at a cut on his forehead.

"Keep still," she tuts.

He ignores her, his attention fixed intently upon me. His

blue eyes are dark, whether with pain or some other emotion, I can't tell.

"Are you talking to me or the cat?" he asks in a neutral-sounding voice.

My mouth all but drops open. How can he even *ask* me that?

"You, of course! *He's* fine." I wave a hand towards Casper, who's sitting on the pavement, washing behind his ears as though nothing unusual has occurred. "What happened to you? Are you hurt?"

"Just a scratch," the paramedic says stridently, applying a strip of bandage over the cut with practised movements. "He'll live. Although perhaps next time he'll think twice about climbing up onto a roof." She eyes him dubiously. "Didn't you say that you're a professor?"

Adam presses his mouth into a thin line.

"Not exactly very bright, was it?" she continues mildly. "All the degrees in the world apparently can't teach common sense." She stands back, admiring her handiwork. "There. You'll probably have one hell of a headache later, but just count yourself lucky that it wasn't worse. I'll leave him to your care now," she adds to me, as an aside. "Good luck. He's not the easiest of patients. Although I expect you already know that."

Heat rises to my face at the insinuation. "Oh, no. It's nothing like that. We're just friends."

Actually, I wouldn't even call us that at the moment, but I'm not about to enter into the complicated state of our relationship with her.

"Whatever." She smiles, clearly not believing me for a

moment. "It's none of my business. Just make sure he gets plenty of rest. He's going to be bruised and sore for a few days."

"All right," I begin, when she's gone. I put my hands on my hips, glaring down at him. "What's all this about climbing on the roof? Are you *crazy*?"

"Crazy or stupid." Trueman materialises beside me, helmet in hand. "I'm still trying to decide. He was after that damned cat of yours, you know."

"I was trying to rescue him," Adam says stonily.

Casper stops washing for a moment to send him a derogatory stare.

"Some rescue attempt," Trueman chortles. "The cat came down of its own accord, and we ended up having to rescue this one instead. He'd slid down the roof; luckily, he'd managed to grab onto the chimney or it would have been a different story. Apparently he doesn't even like heights! Took three of us to persuade him to attempt the ladder. I thought we were going to have to winch him down at one point."

"I'm glad you find all of this so amusing," Adam grinds out.

"Oh, yes," Trueman agrees jovially, the sarcasm apparently going straight over his head. "We enjoy stories like this at the station. Livens up the boring call-outs, it does. And the Christmas party too. There's even a competition between the fire departments—"

Adam looks like he's about to explode.

"Er ... is that someone trying to get into the fire engine?" I say quickly, pretending to peer into the middle distance.

Trueman snaps to attention like an overly officious Doberman.

"What? Not this again. Bloody kids, I tell you ... When I get my hands on them ..."

He stalks off, muttering a series of threats which seem to involve everything from strangling to boiling in oil.

Finally, I'm alone with Adam. I think. I purposely wait a couple of seconds to make sure that no one else is going to appear before whirling upon him.

"What are you really doing here? And don't tell me that you were just passing, because I won't believe you."

"I wasn't. I came to see you." His gaze meets mine, unwavering. "I've hated these past couple of weeks, Clara. Knowing that I couldn't talk to you. It just felt so ... wrong."

He looks so sincere that it nearly takes my breath away.

He's right; it *has* felt wrong. Like something's missing. Something I never even knew was important until it was too late.

I want to shake myself. I have to be strong; I won't be swayed by a few words, however unexpectedly sweet they might be. I'm different these days, not so easily won. I fold my arms, tilt my chin.

"If you're here because of what Heather told you, then you've wasted your time. It doesn't make any difference."

He just shakes his head. "It's nothing to do with that." There's a pause, as though he's gearing up to something. "I've spoken to my father. I thought you'd be interested to know."

I blink three times in quick succession, totally discombobulated by this unanticipated development.

"Oh."

"You were right; I had no business casting judgement upon everyone else when I can't even sort out my own problems." He looks away, towards the house, where the firefighters are busy dismantling the ladder. "I told him that unless we could find a way to be civil, then we should both drop out of the race. That I wouldn't allow what's left of our relationship to be destroyed over this."

At last, I find my voice. It sounds scratchy, like it doesn't belong to me. "And what did he say?"

"Well, at first he blustered quite a bit. But eventually he calmed down and we had a good talk. Maybe the first proper one we've ever had," he adds ruefully. "I think he finally understood that he could lose me for good, if things didn't change. That had never occurred to him before." He pulls the blanket tighter round his shoulders and in that moment he looks very young. I can almost see what he might have been like as a boy.

"I would never have done it if it weren't for you," he says softly, glancing up at me. His eyes are a deep, fathomless blue. "In fact, there are lots of things I would never have done if it weren't for you."

I swallow at the intensity in his gaze. I'm not ready to go there yet.

"Gone into a crystal shop, for example?" I suggest breezily.

"A *fossil* shop," he corrects, although the corners of his lips are turning up. My heart thuds against my ribcage at the sight, and I curse myself for being so foolish.

"Jumping into a river?" I supply, starting to smile myself at the memory.

"And then having to dress like a teenager in borrowed clothes." He pulls a face, as though that was the worst part of it by a mile.

"Crashing your bike?"

"Twice." He sends me an arch look. "And, let's not forget, climbing onto a roof after that demonic excuse for a cat."

We both look at Casper, who's moved on to washing his back, twisted into a pretzel-like shape.

"You could have been killed." I feel the blood draining from my face as the reality of it hits me. Here we are, joking, when it could all have been ... Actually, I don't want to think about what could have happened. It'll probably give me a nervous attack. "What were you *thinking*?"

"I have no idea," he says. Then a furrow appears between his brows. "Actually, that's not true. I know exactly what I was thinking. I was thinking of how much the infernal beast means to you. I couldn't bear the thought of how upset you'd be if anything happened to him."

Something flutters in my chest at that, but I wilfully ignore it. "So you thought it was worth the risk of breaking your own neck, did you?"

He looks at me levelly. "Apparently I did."

I stare at him for a full five seconds. Then ...

"That's the *stupidest* thing I've ever heard," I burst out. "The most idiotic, illogical ..."

"Incongruous, if you're striving for an alliterative trio?" he provides drily.

"*Agh!*" I throw my hands up in the air, unable to articulate anything more sophisticated.

"I'm afraid I haven't been at my most logical lately." His voice is matter-of-fact, as though he's reciting something from a particularly dry reference book. "You see, it's new to me, this feeling. All I can think about is making you happy; I don't know when or how but, somewhere along the way, it's become the most important thing to me. And that's not logical; believe me, I've tried everything in my power to reason it out. But I can't." He runs a hand through his already disarrayed hair. "I'm sorry about the way I handled things. I was just trying to fix them the way I would with any problem, with cold rationality. It was well-meant, I promise you. Badly handled, but well-meant. I never meant to make you feel manipulated." He scowls, looking annoyed with himself. "I'm no good at this. What I'm trying to say ... Well, you already know. But I don't expect anything from you, Clara. If you still feel the same as you did before ... I can accept that."

Suddenly, my legs seem reluctant to support me, and I sit down next to him.

Was that a declaration of love?

I mean, it *was* from Professor Adam Warwick, so it wasn't in your typical format. It was awkward, and oddly formal, and somehow he managed to make it sound as though the whole thing's a major inconvenience, not to mention one that's entirely *my* fault.

And you know what?

I wouldn't have it any other way.

"What are you thinking?" He brushes a lock of hair away from my face. The skin on my cheek tingles, even though he hasn't actually touched it.

For a moment I don't respond. After all, how do you put all of that into words?

"I can be more romantic about it, if you like." He pushes the blanket off his shoulders and slips down off the step and onto one knee. "Is this better?"

"No!" Horrified, I grab his arms and try to pull him up, but he doesn't budge. He reaches across and plucks a daisy from the grass verge, proffering it to me with a self-deprecating smile.

"I'm sorry it's not roses. And I'm sorry that I'll never be any good at poetry. I'll probably forget to tell you that you look nice, and I'm a terrible dancer. I hate the fact that your house is pink, and I'll probably never understand the appeal of a beetroot latte. But I promise that I will do my best, in my own stilted way, to show you that I love you. Every single day. Although you might have to give me a nudge every now and then," he adds as an afterthought. "Especially if I'm engrossed in a new academic paper. I can get quite single-minded then."

Something's blossoming in the middle of my chest, expanding so fast I can barely breathe. But it's a good feeling. A *wonderful* feeling, like everything's finally just as it should be.

"I don't care that it's not roses," I whisper. "They're overrated anyway."

His face breaks out into a gloriously wide smile. He tucks the daisy behind my ear and stands, pulling me to my feet alongside him.

"Wait." For the first time, I notice that there's something missing. "What happened to your jacket?"

He looks pained. "It got caught between the roof tiles. They had to cut me out of it."

"Oh, *no*." I try my best to feign disappointment.

"There's no need to look quite so pleased about it," he grumbles.

I fight back the urge to laugh.

"I'll buy you another one," I promise solemnly. "Or, better still, I'll have one made exactly the same. You'll never know the difference."

Just then, a belligerent miaow emerges from the floor by our feet, and we both look down. Casper's peering up at us with an interrogative expression.

"Of course, there is another thing I didn't mention," Adam says quietly. "I'm afraid I'll never win the approval of your cat." He looks back at me, and his face is heartbreakingly serious. "Will you still have me?"

Find someone who can actually win round that cat of yours … Suddenly, I'm right back in the café, having lunch with Heather. I can hear her words all over again, as clear as a bell. Except this time I finally understand what they meant.

It was never actually about Casper's opinion at all. Sure, he might have liked Josh, but so what? Josh never had to do a single thing to earn that adoration, whereas Adam … I think back to how he bought him the mouse as a peace offering, how he held out his hand that night after the fiasco at the museum. And now … I risk a glance up at the roof and try not to shudder. It's going to take me a while to get over that.

Adam kept trying. And he did it all … for *me*.

He might have got a lot of things hopelessly wrong, but

he's still here, isn't he? Still *trying* to make it right. My heart swells at the thought.

And so, in answer to his question, I turn away, bending down to pick up Casper, holding him out at arm's length.

"You know how much I love you, don't you?"

Two green orbs stare back at me.

"But this time," I conclude gently, "I definitely know best."

He blinks. Just once, but I take it as a capitulation. After all, cats *never* blink. Well, almost never. I pull him against my chest in a hug and he nestles into me briefly before I deposit him back on the floor.

Adam's been standing there, silently watching.

"What does he say?" he asks. I can tell he's trying to sound casual, but I can see the trepidation in his eyes.

"He says that I should kiss you."

Then I stretch up on my tiptoes and do just that.

Chapter 35

It takes another half an hour for the firefighters to pack up. I stand at the window, watching the engine pull away from the kerb and head off down the street, its blue lights slicing through the gathering dusk.

"Have they gone?"

Adam surveys me from across the room. The paramedic was right; he's a terrible patient. He refused to go to bed; eventually, although under considerable protest, I've managed to install him on the sofa with a bag of frozen peas, a cup of tea and a packet of paracetamol. There are dark smudges under his eyes, and I'm pretty sure that he's in more pain than he's letting on, but I know better than to push it.

"Yes." I let the curtains fall back across the window, obscuring the outside world. Now, at last, it's just us.

Thank God for that.

"Good. Then come here." He holds out an arm and I go to him, curling against his side. He grimaces and I immediately pull back.

"I could kill Casper for making you go up on that roof," I fume.

"You weren't nearly so concerned about me when he knocked me off my bike that day," Adam points out with a hint of teasing in his voice. "You ran straight to him. And there I was, stuck in a thorn bush ..."

I roll my eyes. It was *not* a thorn bush, as well he knows. And he accuses me of over-dramatising.

"Well, a lot's changed since then. Then, you were just a bad-tempered, rude stranger."

"And how about now?" He's smiling, but his eyes glow with a deeper meaning.

I pause, pretending to consider.

"Well, you're still bad-tempered and rude, that's for certain."

"I fear I always will be." He presses the peas against his temple. "Do you think you can accept that?"

"I fear I'll always be headstrong and hopelessly unreasonable," I say softly. "Do you think *you* can accept that?"

"Gladly. I think headstrong and unreasonable is just what I need." He leans towards me. I reciprocate, winding my arms around his neck, but he looks so pained that I hesitate.

"Sorry. Does that hurt?"

"Everything hurts," he says wryly. "But I'm not about to let that stop me from kissing you."

But, before our lips can touch, the front door bursts open and footsteps sound in the hall.

"Was that fire engine coming from here?" Freddie skids into the room. He appears half worried, half thrilled at the prospect. His eyes widen when he sees Adam. "Whoa, what happened to you? You look *awful*."

"Good to see you too, Freddie."

Jess sails into the room, her hands cradling her growing bump. "I thought I heard ... Oh ..." She trails off as she sees us together.

"Jess," I say calmly, trying not to think too hard about the absurdity of the situation. "This is Adam."

"Ad ... Oh, *Adam!*" Her face lights up with such visible rapture that I want to crawl into the back of the sofa and never come out again. "Of course. How lovely to meet you at last."

Adam just looks amused. "My reputation precedes me, then."

"Oh, yes." She flaps a hand in front of her face as tears spring to her eyes. "Sorry. Pregnancy hormones. I'm just so happy that you and Clara ... well ..."

Freddie steers her into the armchair with a comforting pat on the shoulder.

I can't even look at Adam. My face feels like it's about to go up in flames. *Why* do my family have to be so ridiculous? Why can't they be normal, just this once?

Freddie plonks himself on the arm of the chair, looking at us expectantly.

"So what *was* that fire engine doing here? Was it Casper again?"

"Actually, it was me," Adam supplies blandly.

Freddie and Jess stare at him.

"He climbed onto the roof," I add, feeling like more explanation is required.

"To save *your* cat," he reminds me testily.

"Who didn't need saving anyway."

"Well, how was I to know that?"

"You know, when you put it like that, there *was* something quite chivalrous about it all," I say thoughtfully. I smile sweetly at him. "Perhaps there's more of the romantic hero in you than you let on."

He sends me a droll look. "Curiously enough, that wasn't what I was thinking of as I dangled perilously from your roof."

The cat flap rattles and Casper patters into the room. He looks around at us each in turn before hopping up onto the sofa, where, to my profound amazement, he settles onto Adam's lap, curling into a tight ball of orange fur.

"Oh, look, he *likes* you!" Jess beams. "That's a good sign. He usually hates men, you know ..." She breaks off with a frown. "What's wrong with all of you? Why are you looking like that?"

"Oh, he knows all right," Freddie manages faintly.

"It must be a trick," Adam mutters. He's gone rigid, as though he daren't move. "He's going to needle me any moment."

But Casper just purrs innocently.

"Maybe he's changed his mind about you," I suggest half-heartedly.

Adam and Freddie look at me in palpable disbelief.

And then another thought occurs to me. It's so absurd that I almost don't want to voice it. In the end, I lean in closer to Adam so that only he can hear.

"Do you think ...?" I'm blushing even as I say it. "I mean, is there a chance that he might have done all of this on purpose? To bring us together?"

The look he gives is a familiar one. Exasperation mixed with incredulity, except this time there's something else there too. *Love*, I realise with sudden, sparkling clarity. That's what love looks like, reflected in another person's eyes.

"He's just a cat, Clara."

"Of course he is," I agree quickly. "You're totally right."

And yet ... as Casper opens one eye and looks at me, I can't help but wonder all the same.

The End

Acknowledgements

No book is an island, and whilst I may have been the one to put the words on the page, there are plenty of other people who helped to get this story out of my head and into your hands. First of all, thanks have to go to my wonderful editor Charlotte, both for seeing the potential in my writing and asking me to write a rom com in the first place, and for the title, which I can't take credit for. Also to all of the team at One More Chapter who've made this book what it is; I've loved working with all of you.

Thank you to all at the RNA Belmont Belles; your enthusiasm and support for my work has been truly heartwarming. Thank you to my husband, Greg, for being a steady, if bemused, presence against the ups and downs of writing life. Thank goodness you passed the feline approval test on our very first date, or we might not be here now! Thank you to my family, for their endless patience in listening to me wrangle my way through various ridiculous scenarios, and to our cats past and present, who have provided essential inspiration for this book.

Special mention—and the final word—has to go to my

Mum; fellow writer, ultimate cheerleader and best friend. I wouldn't be doing this if it weren't for you. Here's to many more years writing together.